Finn wanted to tell her that she wasn't plain at all, in his opinion.

She had beautiful eyes and a mouth that begged to be kissed. Not to mention that she had a body made for sin.

'Surely you could do better than Fergus?'

There was a stubborn glint in her eye that made him wonder if Miss Bradshaw might actually have a spine after all—until she spoke and spoiled it.

'I am content with Fergus.'

'Oh, *content*, are you? I am glad someone is. Meanwhile, it is me who is now stuck with you! How typical of my brother to leave me with his problems while he swans off to have fun.'

She recoiled as if she had been slapped and Finn felt terrible. 'I did not mean to refer to you as a problem, Miss Bradshaw, I merely meant that—'

She held up her hand to stop him.

'You are quite right, Mr Matlock. Perhaps you would be good enough to arrange for the luggage to be transferred to Stanford House immediate inconvenienced f

Author Note

Who doesn't love a Cinderella story? Ever since I was a little girl I have enjoyed every variation of the tale, in books or film. However, as I get older I cannot help but wonder about the way poor Cinderella really felt, being treated the way she had by her wicked stepmother and ugly sisters. Because if she were a real person that abuse would leave emotional scars, surely?

And as for Prince Charming—he's always such a one-dimensional character. He comes to her rescue and falls in love with her. Yes, he goes on a quest to find her, but we learn so little about the real man she falls in love with and I find it difficult to feel any empathy for the guy.

This is *my* version of the story. Heiress Evie Bradshaw is my Cinderella. A woman who has been ground down by life, who lacks confidence and, to all intents and purposes, is a doormat to be trampled over. But Evie is desperate to reinvent herself and start her life afresh.

Her Prince Charming is definitely *not* charming. He is rude and embittered and has no intention of coming to anyone's rescue. He wants to be left all alone to wallow in his personal pit of calm, ordered despair. Unfortunately the arrival of clumsy, vexing, enticing Miss Bradshaw makes that a very difficult thing to accomplish.

It was great fun following them on their path to happily-ever-after…

MISS BRADSHAW'S BOUGHT BETROTHAL

Virginia Heath

HarperCollins
PUBLISHERS
— Since 1817 —

Published in Great Britain 2017
by Mills & Boon, an imprint of HarperCollins*Publishers*
1 London Bridge Street, London, SE1 9GF

© 2017 Susan Merritt

ISBN: 978-0-263-92559-3

Our policy is to use papers that are natural, renewable and recyclable products and made from wood grown in sustainable forests. The logging and manufacturing processes conform to the legal environmental regulations of the country of origin.

Printed and bound in Spain
by CPI, Barcelona

When **Virginia Heath** was a little girl it took her ages to fall asleep, so she made up stories in her head to help pass the time while she was staring at the ceiling. As she got older the stories became more complicated—sometimes taking weeks to get to their happy ending. One day she decided to embrace her insomnia and start writing them down. Virginia lives in Essex with her wonderful husband and two teenagers. It still takes her for ever to fall asleep…

Books by Virginia Heath

Mills & Boon Historical Romance

That Despicable Rogue
Her Enemy at the Altar
The Discerning Gentleman's Guide
Miss Bradshaw's Bought Betrothal

Visit the Author Profile page at millsandboon.co.uk.

For my husband and best friend Greg.
You know why…

Chapter One

May 1816

There was no escaping the fact that the Marquis of Stanford was drunk. Although inebriation was a state that he was known for, even during daylight hours, the assembled guests were still surprised that he had chosen to be in that state today. While the older generation muttered that it was poor form and gazed at his new fiancée with outright pity, absolutely everyone knew that the only reason the handsome, if slightly dissipated, Marquis was marrying Evie Bradshaw in the first place was because he desperately needed her money.

Some of the younger guests, including Evie's two stepsisters, found the spectacle hugely entertaining. It was hardly surprising, they had muttered maliciously behind their fans, because

Evie was such a Plain Jane after all and so very dull. The poor man would need all of the Dutch courage he could consume just to kiss her and that was if he even saw her in the first place because she did have a tendency to fade into the background and become invisible.

What none of the roomful of guests knew, including her spiteful stepfamily, was that Evie was absolutely delighted that Fergus Matlock, third Marquis of Stanford, had turned up to their unexpected and impromptu engagement party completely foxed. For the sake of appearances, of course, she pretended to be crestfallen and embarrassed by her fiancé's slurring and swaying. And best of all, she had not even asked him to arrive drunk, which was, for want of a better word, perfect. But inside her less than impressive, slightly plump exterior, Evie was dancing. And turning cartwheels. And positively whooping with joy.

Her spur-of-the-moment plan to escape her tedious, invisible life was working. In a few hours, she would finally leave Mayfair, ostensibly to ready the dissolute Marquis's house for a wedding, but in reality she would buy her own house instead. Independent. Uncriticised and guilt-free. The hands on the ornate mantel clock could not turn quick enough.

The root of her current misery, her cold fortune-grabbing stepmother, marched towards her, disapproving lips more pursed than usual. Grabbing her by the arm she dragged her back into the alcove. 'Evelyn, it is time that you put a stop to this sorry excuse for an engagement at once. Everybody would understand and your father, God rest him, would never condone it. Look at the state of that man—he is a disgrace. I simply cannot, in all good conscience, allow you to marry *him*.'

'Fergus is probably suffering from wedding nerves. He is only a little bit drunk.' No, he wasn't. He was positively steaming. 'He will not be like that for the wedding. He has promised.' Not that there would be a wedding. This was a business transaction. Pure and simple. The five thousand pounds it had cost her was nothing compared to the price of her freedom.

Hyacinth Bradshaw's lips almost inverted in protest as she looked down her nose at Evie. The woman hated being thwarted, especially by her disappointing stepdaughter, and would normally deal with her quiet acts of defiance with cold, vocal disdain. Unfortunately, Evie's surprise engagement had pulled the rug from underneath her stepmother's feet. Hyacinth was now painfully aware of her precarious financial situation, so she had stopped shy of her usual vindictiveness in an attempt to appear like a concerned mother who only wanted what was best for her daughter. It was a façade that really did not suit her. Ten years ago, Evie might have fallen for it—would have desperately wanted to fall for it—but too much water had gone under that particular bridge in the intervening years.

'Your father, God rest his soul, would not wish for you to marry such a libertine. Surely you know that Stanford is only marrying you to get his hands on your money?' The same money that Hyacinth was determined *not* to lose. Money that her father's second wife firmly believed should be rightfully hers. The money she freely spent like water whilst constantly berating her stepdaughter for everything from her appearance to her dull conversation.

'Fergus is very fond of me.'

'Nonsense! You have always been such a silly girl, Evelyn. Why on earth would a handsome marquis…?' Realising her mistake, Hyacinth bit back her usually cutting criticisms of her stepdaughter's many shortcomings. The expression on her face made it plain how distasteful she found it. For several seconds her cheek muscles quivered before she forced an approximation of a smile that didn't quite work. 'Why on earth would a handsome marquis, who clearly enjoys the hedonistic delights of the gaming hells and brothels, want to marry *anyone* unless he was seriously in debt? I am sure that if you cast your net wider you will find a more suitable man to marry, given time. This has all been so very hurried. Perhaps I could help you find him? That is what your father would wish for if he could.'

Although up until this moment, Hyacinth had been most scathing about the chances of Evie finding anyone who was desperate enough to be prepared to marry her. She was too fat. Too plain. Too dull and far too old now for *anyone* to wish to be saddled with her. Evelyn should be content with the life she had and she would always have a home with Hyacinth. Of course, what she would have said to Evie, if she were being completely honest, was—you cannot leave because somebody has to pay the bills. 'Besides, this is most improper, Evie. I do not like this silly idea you have to move to his estate before you are properly wed.'

'It is hardly improper. Great-Aunt Winifred is coming with me, so I will be correctly chaperoned, and there is a great deal of work to do on poor Fergus's estate to get it to a state in which it will be presentable for the wedding. He will be staying at the inn for the sake of propriety, so you have nothing to be worried about. Besides, he will probably have to return to London almost immediately so Aunt Winnie and I will be alone. In a month, or two, I am...'

'Winifred is not a suitable chaperon!'

A little devil within her decided to have another poke to see if it could get a rise out of Hyacinth. 'I have asked repeatedly if you and my sisters would accompany me—it would be *so* nice if you would. If Papa had still been alive, he would have insisted that we all travel together as a family.' As if they had ever been a family.

Her stepmother snorted and fidgeted uncomfortably. 'I cannot drag the girls away from London now. Not while so much is still going on. Rose is fresh from her first Season and several eligible gentlemen are actively courting Iris. To take them away from all of the entertainments in town would be nothing short of cruel. We will come up for the wedding, of course, or when the *ton* retire to their country estates for the summer, although it is my sincerest wish that you will come to your senses first and call it off. You are simply being selfish leaving like this, with only three days' notice, too! I have never known such a hasty engagement. Your dear father must be spinning in his grave.'

As Evie was a coward who never, ever argued back in case she did send her father spinning in his grave, she changed the subject. 'This is a lovely party, Mother.' The room was filled with Hyacinth's cronies. Aside from Great-Aunt Winnie, Evie did not call a single person present her friend. All of her childhood friends were now married and had abandoned London years ago. Not that there had been many of them after her mother fell ill and Evie had been dragged from her own life to nurse her, then soon after had to become a nursemaid to her father as well. Clearly fate had always intended she be left gathering dust on the shelf.

'It was the best I could manage on such short notice and on such a *tight* budget.' Hyacinth loathed the very idea of a fixed budget. Up until Evie's father had died, she had spent with impunity and found Evie's control of the purse-strings galling. 'I fail to understand why you would wish to penny-pinch for your own engagement party.'

'I have hardly penny-pinched, Mother. There is plenty of everything and our guests do not appear deprived.' And Evie could not quite bring herself to waste good money on this mockery; not when she had so many plans for her inheritance.

'On the subject of finances,' Hyacinth said

too casually, 'I am a trifle confused as to how all this is going to work, Evelyn. Running this house is expensive.'

How many times in the last few days had they had a version of this conversation? Living entirely rent free in what was now Evie's house in Mayfair was never going to be good enough for her stepfamily. Her father had insisted that Hyacinth should keep everything that she had been bequeathed by her first husband and had left her several thousand pounds a year, so she was hardly on the cusp of entering the poorhouse. As far as Evie could recall, she had never seen the woman spend a farthing of her personal hoard. She much preferred to leech off Evie. 'I shall continue to pay for the staff in my absence, so I doubt that you will have to dip into your own—'

'It is not for myself that I am worried. My dear girls, your *dear* sisters, have grown up accustomed to a particular standard of living which has led them to expect a certain kind of future. I only hope that I can maintain it on my *frugal* allowance, I would hate to see their chances of making a suitable match quashed because we cannot afford to attend all of the right entertainments.'

Hyacinth's definition of frugal left a lot to be desired. 'Surely I am allowed to have a future, too?' Evie even managed to look winsome as she said this, but perhaps the wistful sigh was laying it on a bit thick. Her stepmother's lips pursed again and it took her a moment to choke out a reply.

'Of course, my dear. You know that I wish you *every* happiness.' Just in case Evie changed her mind and threw them all out of *her* Mayfair town house. 'But I am neglecting our guests.'

Hyacinth wandered off, leaving Evie alone hiding in the alcove and watching the festivities from a distance, as usual. Theirs was, at best, a very distant relationship. Even though they had lived in the same house for ten years, any conversation between them longer than five minutes was intolerable for Hyacinth. Her stepdaughter was merely a means to an end. If she had not had substantial 'means', Evie was in no doubt Hyacinth would have happily severed all contact between them as soon as her second husband was in the ground.

'Their' guests were either friends of Hyacinth's or people Hyacinth was keen to befriend. Her stepmother was determined to climb her way into the upper echelons of society by whatever means she deemed necessary. Unfortunately, the upper echelons were less keen on welcoming the social-climbing widow of a merchant into their ranks, but Hyacinth still persisted. Tirelessly.

Evie had no interest in the higher echelons, or the lower ones for that matter. To them, as she was to practically everyone, she was invisible. As a result, she had not bothered ordering a new gown for her final appearance in London society. What was the point? Hyacinth's seamstress despaired of her drab and plump stepdaughter.

Evie couldn't blame her. Her unfashionably generous figure was a difficult canvas. In fine fabrics, it resembled a bag stuffed full of onions and heavy wool just made her wideness wider. As much as Evie hated to agree with Hyacinth about anything, she did agree with her stepmother's often lamented assessment of her unfortunate appearance and the fact that one could not make a silk purse out of a sow's ear, no matter how much money one paid the modiste.

Seeing her standing alone in the corner of the room, her awful fiancé raised his glass in the air in a silent toast, but made no move to come towards her. She waved politely for the sake of the charade and did her best to ignore the rising bile in her throat.

It was difficult to find anything to like about Fergus. He was a selfish wastrel with excessive spending habits. He was also entirely untrustworthy—character traits which had made him the perfect choice. He desperately needed some money and she desperately wanted to be free of Hyacinth, but lacked the courage to tell her. As soon as she had realised that he had a small estate in the north, a good week's drive away from London and in a part of the country Hyacinth would never visit, she tentatively offered him a bargain. On the verge of bankruptcy and with debt collectors hammering on his door, the Marquis of Stanford was delighted to accept.

The house, a place to live whilst she bought one of her own, far, far away from all the awful memories of Mayfair, was the most important part of their bargain. A house. On her own. To do whatever she wanted. No longer the nursemaid, pitied old maid or the source of the funds. Or the dutiful daughter who had promised her father to treat his second wife as she had her own mother. This house was a painful reminder of that vow which Hyacinth took every opportunity to remind her of. The north was a place where she hoped she could reinvent herself, be happy and finally climb out of her chrysalis.

She did not expect to emerge like a butterfly—butterflies were far too lovely an insect for Evie to aspire to—but she was quietly confident that she could perhaps be a moth. In the dark, when nobody saw them, moths still flew. In the north, without all of the responsibilities and reminders of London, there were hundreds of things that she was desperate to do. Yes, indeed, Evie had great plans for the future. And they very definitely did not include the Marquis of Stanford. Fergus could pickle his organs back in London after she was safely ensconced in the north, with her blessing. Quite frankly, she did not care if she never saw the dreadful man again.

Thus she would finally leave this house that held so many bad memories and would start a new chapter in her life. It was time to say goodbye to Miss Evelyn Bradshaw, eternal spinster, wallflower, over-generous benefactor and doormat. Evie had no idea what her future held, but one thing she was entirely certain of. When she drove out of Mayfair later, she was never, ever coming back.

The journey north had been interminable. Never a good traveller, Evie had spent the duration of the five-day trip either ill or on the cusp of being ill. Fortunately, Aunt Winnie, who had always been a force to be reckoned with, had insisted that the journey be broken up with restorative overnight stays at strategically placed coaching inns so that they could regain some of their equilibrium. She and Aunt Winnie retired to their room every evening after supper and Fergus enjoyed the taprooms until the small hours. Judging by the sorry state of him most mornings, Evie wished she had had the foresight to supply him with his own coach.

It had been dark by the time they finally arrived at Fergus's Yorkshire estate and although she was wilting with exhaustion, Evie had been pleasantly surprised by the place. She had expected neglect and dilapidation, but the Palladian manor house was anything but. They were immediately greeted by an ancient butler who appeared totally astounded to see them. Fergus swiftly ushered Evie and her aunt into a well-appointed drawing room while he spoke to the butler and housekeeper alone. Soon a fortifying tray of tea was brought to them which they sipped while their rooms were prepared and luggage carried in. Too tired to explore the house or to socialise, Evie had retired as soon as she was able and her vile fake fiancé and carriage left to settle in the local inn.

Several hours later, Evie found herself wide awake and staring at the strange ceiling more than a little overwhelmed. She had done it! Quiet, plain, invisible Evelyn had done the unthinkable and escaped. Two hundred miles of relentless road now separated her from her awful stepfamily and the life she had once led. It was like having the weight of the world lifted off her shoulders and everything she had dreamed of, so despite the lateness of the hour and the unfamiliarity of her surroundings, Evie felt giddy with success. Sleep would be impossible now, yet it was still far too early, or late depending on your point of view, to wake the servants. There was nothing to stop her exploring the house, though. If this place was to be her temporary home, she might as well find out where everything was.

Finn wearily finished brushing down his horse and then led it into the stall. He was not angry that there had been nobody waiting in the stables to greet him because nobody had expected him tonight. As far as the staff were concerned, he was supposed to be staying overnight in York and travelling back tomorrow. It had been a last-minute decision to travel home this evening. The noise in the inn and the overfamiliarity of the crowded occupants had become cloying and he had needed to escape. Almost two aching hours later and he still did not regret that decision. It might well be two in the morning, but at least he could sleep in his own bed, as far away from people as was humanly possible.

Outside the kitchen door, he pulled off his boots. Stowers, his butler, was too old to be getting out of bed in the small hours and Finn knew that if he got the first whiff he had returned early, the faithful old retainer would insist on attending to him. As he had expected, the house was shrouded in darkness and not a single lamp was lit to ease his way, but he did not bother lighting one. He knew the layout of the place so well he could probably traverse it without incident in his sleep. At the foot of the stairs, something caught his eye and he peered down the hallway. A weak strip of light bled out from under the closed door to the small library. Odd. Perhaps the servants had forgotten to extinguish the light.

The door swung open silently on its well-oiled hinges and the sight beyond rendered him temporarily speechless. A strange woman stood in front of the roaring fireplace, staring into the flames and smiling. Whilst that was shocking in itself, the glow from the fire rendered her billowing nightgown almost translucent and awarded him the wholly unexpected, but not wholly unwelcome, view of her voluptuous figure beneath. It was almost a perfect hourglass. A deliciously rounded bottom, a nipped-in waist and, if he was not mistaken from this odd angle, a magnificent bosom. The sort of figure that would earn her a small fortune as a tavern wench. To torture him further, she bent down to throw more wood on to the flames and the thin fabric moulded to her behind like a second skin, highlighting the way those hips flared and then tapered as his eyes travelled down a shapely pair of legs. After two hours on the road, this unexpected stranger was indeed a sight for sore eyes. Aesthetics aside, she still had no place being where she was.

'Who are you?'

Chapter Two

Her head whipped around and with it a thick, dark plait swung off her shoulder and fell almost to her bottom. One hand automatically went to her heart in shock, drawing his gaze to the magnificent bosom that was indeed there, then her expression changed to annoyance.

'Oh, Fergus! You gave me a fright.'

'Fergus?' If his brother was here, then his first assumption was correct. She was a tavern wench. 'I am not Fergus.'

The woman had a heart-shaped face which was not classically beautiful, but certainly striking. Her mouth was a little too large for classical proportions, her nose a little too strong, but her eyes? Her eyes were quite lovely. Then they narrowed.

'Are you drunk, Fergus?'

'I am not Fergus.'

'Of course you are and this silly game is not at all funny.'

As Evie said those words she began to feel uncomfortable. The more she looked at the man staring at her in the doorway, the more convinced she became that he might, indeed, not be Fergus.

Although he was the spitting image of Fergus.

Except his features were not as soft. The dark hair similar, but the style different. Fergus's locks were always ruthlessly pomaded to maintain the fashionable *à la* Brutus style that was favoured by the majority of the *ton*. There was no evidence of pomade in this man's hair and, now that she thought about it, it was longer. It flopped over one eye quite rakishly and had a windswept quality that Fergus would never allow. Dark stubble covered his chin. Another thing that Fergus would never be seen dead with. Even in the worst state of inebriation Fergus still managed to shave. The clothes were all wrong as well. Her fiancé was a bit of a dandy and had a tendency to wear lace and intricately folded knots at his collar. This man's clothing was more austere with a distinct absence of any froth. And his eyes were slightly darker, his body slightly larger, his posture more commanding. But his gaze was equally as cold. Filling the doorway in his billowing greatcoat, he looked positively menacing.

'If you are not Fergus, who are you?' Her voice was pathetically small and uncertain once again.

'I am his brother. His twin brother. Finnegan.'

Fergus had mentioned in passing he had a married brother, but he had neglected to tell her that he was one of twins. He had also apparently neglected to tell his brother about their visit, hence his unexpected appearance in the middle of the night. 'Although this is quite unorthodox, Lord Finnegan, I am delighted to make your acquaintance. I am Miss Evelyn Bradshaw, Fergus's fiancée.'

His eyebrows lifted and his eyes insolently swept slowly from her face down her body. They lingered on her chest blatantly for a second before they travelled back up to her eyes again. 'You are not his type.'

As far as Evie was aware, she was not anyone's type, but that was by the by. She was not going to get into that sort of discussion with a stranger. 'I can assure that we are engaged to be married, Lord Finnegan. And as such, for the duration of my stay here and for the sake of propriety, Fergus has taken residence in the local inn.'

His features remained deadpan, but his arms folded across his chest. 'Has he?'

Evie smiled in a vain attempt to soften the blow she was about to deliver. She did find it very difficult to be assertive, but in this instance she had to do it. 'I hate to inconvenience you after your late journey, but for the sake of propriety I must insist that you also take yourself directly to the inn as well. My great-aunt and I will be staying here in Stanford House.'

Nerves made her voice wobble and she had the overwhelming urge to curl up into a ball, but, remembering that she was resolved never to be Invisible Evelyn again, she pulled her shoulders back proudly and forced herself to meet his gaze. Several awkward seconds ticked by.

'He didn't tell you, did he?'

'Tell me what?' Fergus's double now appeared to be amused and shook his dark head as he stared up at the ceiling, as if he were seeking strength from the lord.

'This is not Stanford House. This is Matlock House.' He folded his arms over his impressively broad chest. 'My house.'

Lost for words, Evie gaped back at him. When she found her voice it came out in a squeak. 'I have been led to believe that this is my fiancé's house! He brought me here this very evening and made no mention of the fact that this was your house.'

'Yes. Well, in my experience, Fergus's relationship with the truth has always been rather tenuous. He probably brought you here because Stanford House in is no fit state to be inhabited. No doubt he will have constructed a perfectly reasonable-sounding explanation when I confront him about it in the morning. However, right now I am going to bed.'

He turned and, to her utter chagrin, headed directly for the stairs, clutching his boots. 'You cannot mean to stay here!' Now the squeak was so high pitched that she sounded like a mouse.

Evie watched him drop the boots loudly and spin slowly to face her as he walked back into the library, his expression part confusion, part outrage. 'This is *my* house, madam.'

'But for propriety's sake you cannot stay under the same roof as me!'

His hands came up to rest on his hips this time and his dark head tilted to one side insolently. The combative stance made him seem bigger. 'Why ever not?'

Unsure of how to explain why his presence was outrageous, she managed to stutter something incoherent while he glared at her as if she was mad. In the end the best she could manage was one word.

'Because!'

'Because what? Are you afraid that at some point during the night my manly urges might get the better of me? Do you fear that I might hammer down your door and ravish you, Miss Bradshaw?' Evie nodded weakly, painfully aware of the ferocious blush that had now swamped her face and chest. To her complete mortification he laughed bitterly at the implication. 'If I was a man prone to being unable to control his urges, madam, I doubt I would wait until later to act on them. Especially since the firelight is doing a wonderful job of turning your nightdress transparent and giving me a perfectly unencumbered view of your naked body beneath.' Automatically, she used her arms to cover herself and her mouth hung slack in shock. He, on the other hand, regarded her with polite indifference.

'I am dead on my feet and I have absolutely no intention of leaving *my* house now or at any time in the future. Goodnight Miss Bradshaw. Don't bother locking your door. Your precious virtue is perfectly safe with me.'

'As he is not your fiancé, is already married and there are plenty of servants here as well as me, I do not think that there is any danger of your stay here being misconstrued as improper. In fact, it rather legitimises you staying here in the first place.' Aunt Winnie nibbled on the tiny triangle of toast that she had procured from the extensive breakfast buffet laid out on the sideboard. Evie stared down at her matching toast mournfully and tried to ignore the tempting aroma of bacon wafting towards her nose.

'That is as maybe, but now I am gravely concerned that Fergus has lied to me. His brother stated that Stanford House was uninhabitable and I have no intention of staying here for the duration.' Although the house was quite lovely, she had hoped that she would be all alone. Being a guest rather put a dampener on things, especially as their unexpected host appeared to be quite rude. Seeking alternative accommodation that quickly was not something that she had planned for, not that she really had a plan.

'We will make the best of it my dear. And think about it this way—if he has been fibbing it gives you another believable reason to call off your engagement when the time comes.'

Aunt Winnie did make a valid point, she supposed. Her sham betrothal to Fergus was only a temporary means to an end. She got her freedom and he got five thousand pounds for the year she anticipated they would need to maintain their charade. The important thing was Fergus had agreed to those terms. In the grand scheme of things, she would have still made the bargain if she had known that his house was uninhabitable—only she would have instructed her attorney to find a suitable cottage for herself and Aunt Winnie immediately before announcing her engagement to Hyacinth. In many ways, if Stanford House was a complete wreck, then it stood to reason that it would take ages before it was in a fit state to hold a wedding. Evie could delay telling Hyacinth the truth for years—pathetic coward that she was.

You see, Stepmother, I loathe my life with you almost as much as I loathe you. You are a mean, money-grabbing bully and I am tired of being your victim and of being Invisible Evelyn. Pitied, shapeless, plain and dull Invisible Evelyn. I feel as though I am dying inside.

No matter how many times Evie had thought a version of those words they had never seemed quite right so she had bitten them back. Hyacinth was her father's second wife. He had loved her, perhaps, and he had made Evie promise to be a good daughter to her. Unfortunately, if he had made a similar request to Hyacinth, her stepmother did not feel duty-bound to honour it. This separation would give her the distance she needed to pluck up the courage to say them. Probably by letter. Almost definitely by letter. One day...

Out in the hallway, she heard the distinctive sound of a male voice and steeled herself to greet her fake fiancé's rude twin brother. Under the circumstances, she had no choice but to rely on his hospitality until she had sorted out the mess, if the gentleman in question was prepared to extend his hospitality that was. Last night he appeared to be as enamoured of Fergus as she was, which was a worry and made her new situation precarious.

He strode into the room looking just as dark and foreboding as he had last night and regarded his uninvited guests with an air of disgusted resignation. 'Good morning, ladies. Miss Bradshaw.' His eyes flicked from her face to her plain green frock and then back again shamelessly, making no attempt to disguise his disappointment with what he saw. Evie felt the blush creep up her neck and suffuse her face as she recalled his ridiculous claim to have seen through her nightgown and wondered if his disappointment was merely because she was intruding on his privacy or because he really did know what lay beneath the yards and yards of silk. He inclined his head towards Aunt Winnie and took her proffered hand. 'I am Finnegan Matlock, Fergus's brother. I have not yet had the pleasure of your acquaintance.'

'This is my Great-Aunt Winifred. She has accompanied me as my chaperon.' Even as she said it Evie could see the disbelief in his dark eyes. He was probably wondering what use an eighty-nine-year-old woman with a walking stick was as a chaperon, but then again, as Evie was highly unlikely to ever need the true services of a chaperon to protect her virtue, she tried not to be offended. Aunt Winnie was her only living blood relative and, despite the innate difficulties of transporting an octogenarian with rheumatism across the entire length of the country, Evie could have hardly left the poor woman alone with Hyacinth. Even though Winnie always gave as good as she got.

'Welcome to Matlock House, madam.'

'You are better looking than your brother, sir.'

One eyebrow quirked with what she assumed was amusement at Aunt Winnie's forthrightness, although he did not smile. 'As we are identical twins, madam, I find that highly unlikely.'

Aunt Winnie would not be swayed. 'Yes, yes. I see the similarities well enough, young man. I am old, not blind. But there are distinct differences. I have always thought your brother looks untrustworthy. His eyes dart around too much when he talks. Yours are steady. And you wear your breeches better. Do you like to ride, Lord Finnegan?'

Evie's level of mortification ratcheted up a notch and she gave Fergus's brother an apologetic smile. 'Aunt Winifred is very outspoken.' Her plain face was very probably glowing scarlet and that was a colour that had never suited her. Typically, like most people, he ignored her.

'Yes, I do ride. Aunt Winifred—would you care to take a gallop over the fields with me?' Although his face remained impassive his eyes appeared to be smiling. He definitely had better eyes than Fergus. Clearer. Not bloodshot. A little intriguing. The old lady giggled and swatted him with her hand.

'And you are more charming than your brother. Talking of which, where is Fergus?'

'As it is still morning and I dare say he has enjoyed his evening at the inn, unless he has changed his ways in the three years since I last saw him, I assume that he is still asleep. He never was one for daylight.'

Three years? That seemed an excessively long time for any siblings to have not visited one another, let alone twins. 'I take it that you and Fergus are not close, Lord Finnegan?'

He answered with his back to her, more intent on loading his plate with the delicious steaming bacon than being polite to Evie. 'To be honest, Miss Bradshaw, we are virtual strangers. Even as children we had vastly different characters. The only thing we have in common is the same face and the fact that we once shared the same womb.' He balanced a piece of toast on top of his mountainous breakfast and carried it back towards the table. 'Our parents often commented that we were as different as chalk and cheese.'

Which probably accounted for the fact that Fergus had never mentioned that he was one of twins. Finn ate his breakfast heartily, but suddenly paused his fork halfway to his mouth as he noticed Evie's slice of toast. 'Are you not eating?'

The familiar lie spilled out. 'I am not particularly hungry.' In fact, she was starving. She spent a great deal of her life starving in a pathetic attempt to become slimmer and thereby miraculously more attractive. Her excessive weight was one of the many things Hyacinth was merciless about. Unfortunately, even if Evie did manage to reduce her figure by a few inches, the moment she succumbed to temptation and ate a cake she was right back where she started. And she so loved cake.

'Then why you are staring at my bacon so intently? You do not look like a woman who could survive on one piece of toast.'

Horrified and mortified in equal measure, Evie stared back at her toast and tried to think of a pithy retort. As usual, none came so she sat silently and wished she really was invisible as she squirmed under the intensity of his gaze.

'Tell me how you came to be engaged to my feckless brother.'

Evie focused every bit of her attention on the rapidly cooling and unappealing piece of toast and trotted out her practised line. 'We collided at various functions last year, found that we rubbed along well enough and, after a few months, he proposed.' The story was purposefully short and dull because that was easier. Besides, everyone expected Evie to be dull so few asked for further clarification. Lord Finnegan tilted his head to one side and simply stared.

'Are you sure?'

Nobody had ever queried the tale before and it flustered her. 'Well, of course I am sure. Do you think that I would make something like that up?' Already her palms were moist and her heart was racing guiltily. No doubt her neck was already blooming in unbecoming pink blotches. She never had been a particularly convincing liar.

'To be perfectly frank, Miss Bradshaw, I have no idea. You completely bewilder me. You are definitely not Fergus's usual type and the brother I know is about as likely to settle down into marriage of any sort as I am to suddenly sprout wings and soar majestically through the clouds.'

'You, yourself, said that you had not seen your brother in three years. People can change a great deal in three years.'

He snorted his disbelief. 'The sort of change you are suggesting would take a miracle to achieve. Fergus likes to drink, gamble and whore. You do not strike me as a woman who fits any of those criteria. That leads me to believe that there is only one reason why he is marrying you and that reason has to be money. Are you obscenely rich, Miss Bradshaw?'

Her mouth hung slack. Had he just used the word whore in front of a lady? And more importantly, he had just insulted her in the most horrendous manner. Nobody had ever spoken to her quite like that, apart from Hyacinth. Evie's gaze flicked to the fork lying on the table to her left and for a moment she considered picking it up and using it as a weapon. Perhaps Lord

Finnegan's manners would improve if he suddenly found himself with a piece of cutlery embedded in his hand. Or his forehead.

'That is none of your business, sir!'

'So you are obscenely rich.' He calmly popped another piece of bacon into his mouth and chewed thoughtfully. 'You must be scraping the bottom of the matrimonial barrel to have agreed to marry him.'

The man was insufferable. Fortunately, Aunt Winnie was never short for words.

'You are a very rude man, Lord Finnegan.'

'I agree.' Was that really the best set-down she could manage? Evie had promised herself that she was not going to be a doormat any more and as this man was unspeakably rude, it could hardly hurt to practise the new Evie on him. 'And I do not need to sit here and listen to your insults.' At least that sounded more assertive although saying it aloud had now terrified her.

He shrugged and munched more bacon. 'You are quite right, Miss Bradshaw. Should you wish to leave this house immediately, I would completely understand.'

Her lush mouth hung slack again and Finn felt a stab of guilt for being so obnoxious. It was hardly the poor girl's fault that his brother was a scoundrel and that he was a miserable curmudgeon who would rather be left alone than suffer company of any sort. With a sigh of resignation, he put down his fork.

'I am sorry, Miss Bradshaw, my rudeness was uncalled for. It has been some time since I have entertained guests and I am out of practice.' He offered her his best approximation of a smile by way of an apology, although he doubted that it looked like one. Smiling was not something he had much call to do any longer. Besides, it would feel much better to take out his anger on his brother. And his brother would get both barrels. 'What time will Fergus be returning?'

She worried her bottom lip, drawing his attention to it. She really did have a very diverting mouth. 'I am not altogether sure. We had made no firm plans.'

Well, that was odd. But then again everything about Fergus's engagement struck Finn as odd. The oddest part was his unexpected choice of fiancé. He might not have a great deal to do with his brother, but he knew him inside and out. If Fergus was going to take a bride, and that was a very big *if* indeed when one considered his lifestyle choices, then it would be a lady who was more ornament than actual woman. A stickler for the latest fashions, Fergus would never condone the drab, shapeless dress Miss Bradshaw was wearing. Finn was no expert on ladies' fashion, but from neck to hem that gown was a disaster. Why the woman would want to disguise the shapely figure he had seen was a mystery to him. The yards of unnecessary fabric formed one solid, shapeless block that did nothing for her. Nor did the severe hairstyle. The lovely thick, chestnut hair he had seen shimmering in the firelight was so ruthlessly styled that it had lost all of its lustre. If ever anyone was hiding their light under a bushel, it was Miss Bradshaw.

'Never mind. If he fails to materialise any time soon, I shall take myself to the inn later and speak to him.' There were a great many things that Finn had waited three years to say. None of them was pleasant.

This statement appeared to fluster her. 'As I suspect it might take him several hours to materialise after he lied to me last night, I should like to accompany you, sir.' He was sir now, he noted the censure in her voice, but she stuck out her chin proudly even though her expression suggested she would likely bolt at any moment, given half a chance.

It was on the tip of Finn's tongue to tell her to get used to it. Fergus was a consummate liar. It was one of the few things his twin excelled at. But he stopped himself. If she was not aware of that fact already, she would come to know it soon enough without his help. Instead he nodded and took a swig of his coffee.

'Before we leave, it is only right and proper that I introduce myself to your wife.'

Finn nearly choked. Just the mention of Olivia brought it all crashing back when he preferred to remain numb.

'Where might I find her?'

'Where she always is.' Finn stood and ruthlessly quashed all of the unwelcome emotions that swirled in his gut. 'In the cemetery.'

Chapter Three

By late afternoon, it had become apparent that Fergus had no immediate intention of visiting Evie at all. She was desperate to track him down at the inn and ask him what he thought he was about or what he intended to do about the awkward situation he had placed her in. But after spectacularly putting her foot in it with his brother, she was reluctant to seek the man out so that they could go visit her fiancé together. She had not seen hide nor hair of the other Matlock since breakfast, when he had marched out of the breakfast room with a face like thunder and slammed the door behind him.

No doubt her crass mentioning of his wife had upset him and for that she felt horribly guilty, even though she found the man himself most disagreeable. Evie absolutely hated hurting another's feelings. It went completely against her nature. Her own were hurt so often that she knew very well how awful it felt and would never intentionally do something like that, even to a nasty piece of work like Finnegan Matlock. It was yet another thing she intended to take Fergus to task for when he finally deigned to make an appearance. It was bad enough pretending that your brother's house was yours, but to neglect to tell your fiancée that your *twin* brother was also a recent widower was unforgivable.

'Would you like some more tea, Miss Bradshaw?' a maid asked politely and Evie shook her head.

'No, thank you.' Already she was positively swimming in the stuff. Another cup might well cause it to seep out of her ears. 'Do you know where I can find Lord Finnegan?' Sitting around and waiting for one of the Matlock brothers to come to her was becoming very tiresome. Even Aunt Winnie had given up and taken herself off for an afternoon nap.

'I have no idea, miss. Lord Finnegan went out hours ago. He tends to come and go as he pleases so I could not hazard a guess as to when he will return.' The maid bobbed a curtsy and scurried away, leaving alone Evie to wait some more.

This was ridiculous.

She had come to Yorkshire to escape having her life controlled by others, to climb out of her suffocating chrysalis and breathe, not to allow two obnoxious men to step into Hyacinth's shoes and force her to dance to their tune. If Fergus was too cowardly to face her here, then she would go and track him down herself. She was the new Evie Bradshaw after all, no longer a convenient doormat, and she was intending to be more fearless and independent. Feeling suddenly decisive, she stood and went off in search of the stables. She would avail herself of Lord Finnegan's carriage and take herself to the inn.

But there was no carriage in the stables. Lord Finnegan, she was reliably informed, had no use for one. They would, however, saddle a horse for her should she require one or she could walk the two miles to the village seeing as it was a lovely day. As there was no way Evie was going to climb on to the back of a horse, she set off across the pretty meadow in the direction that had been pointed, ignoring the early summer heat and the inappropriateness of her footwear. Half a mile on and her thin slippers began to rub and Evie found herself becoming quite hot in the long-sleeved dress she had stupidly chosen to wear. Far off in the distance she could just about make out the spire of a church nestled amongst the gently rolling hills, which meant that she probably still had a good thirty minutes of walking ahead of her. Thirty more minutes of perspiration and foot pain.

With a sigh she flopped down into the grass. Perhaps going off to visit Fergus alone was not such a good idea. She would probably lose her nerve the moment she laid eyes on him, anyway, and any reprimand would come out sounding squeaky and pathetic. She should probably just return to the house.

For several minutes Evie just sat there, until a pretty butterfly floated passed. Only then did she remember why she had come here in the first place. Freedom. She had intended to enjoy and embrace life on her own, not sit around waiting for life to come to her. Here she was, sat in a beautiful meadow. The sun was shining and she was all on her own. Instead of feeling miserable she should be revelling in this. Why was she in a hurry to seek out Fergus when he was clearly in no hurry either? Aside from five thousand pounds, she owed Fergus nothing.

And as there was nobody to see her here, why was she suffering? Feeling emboldened, Evie yanked off her silly slippers, then rolled off her stockings. She could put them back on nearer to her destination, but for now she would enjoy the pleasant sensation of the air around her bare legs. It was delightful. So delightful that when she had her own house she would never wear stockings in summer. Or corsets.

Feeling a little naughty and rebellious at such scandalous thoughts, she wiggled her toes and then unbuttoned the high neck of her dress all the way down to her collarbone before rolling up her sleeves as well. It was too hot for buttons and sleeves. For good measure, she took off her big straw bonnet and stuffed her discarded clothing into it, then tied the ribbons to make a carrying handle before she set off again at a much more leisurely pace. Already that all felt so much better and unrestricting. She would embrace the inevitable freckles joyfully. She had long ago accepted spinsterhood, so why should she care if her skin was not fashionable? If she had not been on her way to visit Fergus, she would have also unpinned her hair. Perhaps, when she bought her own house here, she would ensure that it also had a secluded meadow so that she could go completely wild and strip off to just her shift while she cavorted amongst the flowers like that butterfly?

From then on her little walk was like an adventure. Evie stopped to watch the different birds as they went about their business, stared at the shapes made by the clouds and picked some of the prettier meadow flowers, even tucking a vibrant, fat dandelion carelessly behind her ear. When she found her path blocked by a wide stream it did not faze her as it normally would. At most, the crystal-clear water was barely five inches deep and, because she was now at one with nature, Evie decided to wade through it rather than find a way around it. Except, the moment her toes came into contact with the refreshing water, she could not find the motivation to move from that perfect spot.

As a child she remembered paddling in the sea on a trip to Brighton and that memory took her back to happier times when there had just been Evie and her parents. Mama was in fine health, laughing and holding her hand, and Papa was threatening to splash them both. How long ago had that been? Too long, she realised with a jolt. Almost fifteen years since she had enjoyed the joyous pleasure that came from simply splashing in the water.

On a whim, Evie tossed her bonnet basket back on to the bank and then bent down to knot her skirt above her knees. This afternoon, she would splash again. Simply because she could.

Finn was seething as he crested the hill, an emotion that he did not experience often but one that his brother almost always managed to rouse. Why did Fergus always do exactly as he wanted without any thought to the consequences? And how wonderful must it feel to selfishly skip through life without the burden of even a modicum of guilt for the chaos that you left in your wake? Once again Fergus had made a mess and left Finn to clear it up. What he expected him to do with his new fiancée, Finn had no clue. The small, loyal part of him wanted to make excuses for his brother, but his conscience would never allow that. It would be the kindest thing all around if he told her the truth. Yes, it would break her heart in the short term, but in the long term she would be spared the awful reality of being shackled to Fergus for all eternity. Nobody deserved that. The sooner he appraised Miss Bradshaw of the truth, the better. With her gone, life would return to normal and he would have peace and quiet again.

Horatio, his favourite horse, meandered towards the stream. They usually stopped there on their way back from the village so that the old boy could take a drink and a rest, and despite his bad mood, Finn could not quite bring himself to deprive the animal of that tiny pleasure. It was hardly Horatio's fault that Finn's brother was a scoundrel of the first order. Besides, the longer it took him to get back to Matlock House, the longer he could delay having to tell his brother's future bride that the reliably unreliable Fergus had disappeared.

But as they got to the stream, fate decided that the bad news could not be put off any longer. Miss Bradshaw was there. Not that she had seen him yet, which was no surprise since she had her back to him again. Finn would have called to her, but she was having far too much fun kicking water into the air like a child. Despite his foul mood, there was something sweet and arresting in the sight of her so easily content which made him pause and simply watch her. Her ugly dress was hoisted above her knees to keep it out of the water. She had managed to get it soaked regardless, so it clung heavily to her shapely legs as she dragged her feet aimlessly through the water.

Finn quietly slid off of his horse and began to walk towards her. As he got closer it became apparent that Miss Bradshaw was also singing—although her voice and choice of song were surprising. For a woman who squeaked and blushed at everything, that voice was surprisingly strong and earthy as she sung some song about a highwayman who was wooing two women simultaneously. If she had of been a tavern wench as he had first thought, that voice, like her figure, would earn her a small fortune.

She must have heard him because she suddenly stopped and whipped her head around. A cheerful yellow dandelion hung listlessly from her hair and her mouth formed an 'o' of surprise at being caught. Thanks to the open buttons, Finn got to witness the ferocious blush as it spread up her neck and bloomed over her face, and found himself inexplicably charmed by the sight.

'Lord Finnegan!' Her hand came up to her throat and denied him the view of the hint of cleavage he had spotted under the blush, and then as an afterthought, she snatched the lolling flower from her hair and held it limply in her hand. 'I was heading to the inn to see Fergus.'

'Then I shall save you the journey. He's not there.'

Miss Bradshaw bent slightly and wrestled with the wet knot in her skirts and the hint of cleavage came back into view, reminding him that he was a man and that he had not seen that particular part of a female in a while. Finn felt a pang of guilt at the temptation to stare and forced his eyes to focus on the top of her head.

'Perhaps he has headed to Matlock House and you missed him.' The knot was finally worked free and her heavy skirt fell back to her ankles and floated on the top of the water.

'He is gone, Miss Bradshaw. He apparently left first thing this morning.'

She stared back at him in shock. 'Gone where?'

'He left you a letter which I have in my saddle bag. I dare say that might give us some clue as to his destination.' Finn gestured back to his horse with a shrug and then started back along the bank to fetch it. Miss Bradshaw followed, although she chose to still wade parallel through the stream, apparently oblivious to the fact that her petticoats were now absorbing it.

When he handed it to her, she hastily broke the seal and scanned the contents with a look of pure irritation, then refolded it and stuffed it into a hidden pocket in her skirt. 'He says that he has gone further north, but does not state how long for or why he has gone there.'

Which left Finn with an uncomfortable dilemma. Should he tell her what he suspected or pretend that Fergus would return presently? In the end, lying seemed futile. He owed Fergus nothing and the very last thing he wanted was a pair of uninvited houseguests for a prolonged period of time. 'Did you give him any money, Miss Bradshaw?'

Her eyes widened and he realised that they were quite an unusual shade of brown. The golden flecks in the irises gave them a feline quality. 'I did give him a little.'

'How much did you give him?' Because that dictated how long he would leave the poor girl stranded. Fergus got through money as though it was going out of fashion.

'Oh, dear.' She stared down at the dandelion in her hand and Finn experienced a trickle of unease.

'How much?'

'A thousand pounds.'

'A thousand! Are you mad? Fergus will only gamble it away.'

Her dark eyebrows came together and her plump lips flattened. 'At the time, it seemed like the right thing to do.'

'Well, congratulations, Miss Bradshaw. With a thousand pounds in his pocket, I doubt you will see your beloved for months.'

She took this news remarkably well. 'He will have lost it all in a few weeks, not months. Fergus is not a particularly talented gambler.'

Which begged the obvious question. 'If you knew that, why on earth would you give him the money?'

She turned away from him then and idly

swished her foot from side to side in the water. 'He is my fiancé and it is only money.'

'But it is *your* money, Miss Bradshaw, and you seem to be forgetting the fact that he has dumped you in my house and then abandoned you as if you are of no consequence while he goes off to spend it.' Harsh words, but the truth none the less.

She was quiet for a long time, aside from the incessant swishing of her foot as she stared off into the distance, and then he watched her inhale slowly and straighten her shoulders. 'I suppose this all appears a trifle odd from where you are standing, Lord Finnegan, but it is what it is and I shall make the best of it.'

Did the woman have no pride? 'And that is it? You have been abandoned without so much as a by-your-leave, one thousand pounds poorer, but that is of no matter? I can only believe that my original assessment of you must be correct, because only a woman who is, indeed, scraping the bottom of the matrimonial barrel would accept such shoddy behaviour just to get wed.' She turned to him then and he saw the flash of pain in her eyes at his cruel words.

'I am scraping the bottom of the matrimonial barrel, Lord Finnegan. Of that fact, I am painfully aware. I hold no illusions that your brother holds me in any regard whatsoever because you summed up my situation perfectly. I am a plain spinster who has been left on the shelf but I am, as you so crudely put it, obscenely rich and we both know that Fergus is in dire need of money. Beggars cannot be choosers. It might not be the most romantic of arrangements, but your brother is agreeable to it and I find that it suits me well enough.'

Finn wanted to tell her that she wasn't plain at all, in his opinion. She had beautiful eyes and a mouth that begged to be kissed. Not to mention that she had a body made for sin, but saying that felt disloyal to Olivia. 'Surely you could do better than Fergus?' There was a stubborn glint in her eye that made him wonder if Miss Bradshaw might actually have a spine after all, until she spoke and spoiled it.

'I am content with Fergus.'

'Oh, content, are you? I am glad someone is. Meanwhile, it is me that is now stuck with you! How typical of my brother to leave me with his problems while he swans off to have fun.'

She recoiled as if she had been slapped and Finn felt terrible. 'I did not mean to refer to you as a problem, Miss Bradshaw, I merely meant that—' She held up her hand to stop him.

'You are quite right, Lord Finnegan. He has

shamelessly foisted my aunt and I upon you and for that I am sorry. Perhaps you would be good enough to arrange for our luggage to be transferred to Stanford House immediately so that you are not inconvenienced further?' She stood proudly, her elegant hands clasped in front of her, the whimsical dandelion now dropped into the water and despondently floating away much like all broken dreams did eventually.

It was the matter-of-fact stoicism that undid him, almost as if she was quite used to being considered an unwelcome burden and treated with a lack of respect, and for some reason that bothered him. 'There is no need. Stanford House is a wreck and there are no servants there to attend you. You can stay at my house while I make the necessary arrangements to return you to London while you wait.'

The flash of temper was so sudden and unexpected that it shocked him. 'I will not be returning to London!' By the stunned look on her face it had also shocked her. She sucked in a deep breath, blinked twice and then continued. 'I am resolved to live in Yorkshire from now on, sir, and nothing with dissuade me.'

'Fergus could be gone for months! And I am to be inconvenienced in the process? Until yesterday I had no idea you even existed and now

I am expected to be responsible for you and your aged aunt, while Fergus goes off and enjoys himself at cards. Or whoring as he usually does?' He watched her face pale, but ploughed on. It was better that she knew what she would be getting into with his twin before the wedding. At least then Finn's conscience would be clear. 'I owe my brother nothing, Miss Bradshaw, and my charity only extends so far.' And more importantly Finn wanted to be left all alone. Away from people and their lives and hopes and dreams. The last thing he needed was this voluptuous creature, who sang bawdy songs and paddled in streams, and reminded him that he was a man.

'As I have already stated, Lord Finnegan, I have no desire to inconvenience you any further and would prefer to remove myself to Stanford House presently.'

'I keep telling you that house in uninhabitable—' That delicate hand cut him off again.

'Stanford House will do well enough until Fergus returns—and he will return. So do not trouble yourself on my behalf. I have no need of your charity, sir. I am an independent woman, Lord Finnegan, with independent means. A *vast* amount of independent means! I shall hire my own servants and make the house *habitable*.

And because I have no desire to be considered as one of your problems, we will leave tomorrow and gladly so.' She thrust her chin out and glared down her nose at him imperiously with outrage shimmering in her eyes. And managed to look quite splendid as she did it. 'Good afternoon to you, Lord Finnegan, I shall not inconvenience you any further.'

With that she turned and stubbornly waded up the bank towards her discarded bonnet and shoes. She picked them up and began to march barefoot back across the meadow without giving him a backwards glance, the sodden heavy skirts slapping against her legs loudly. He could tell, by her posture, that she was indignantly proud of herself. The beginnings of a smile nudged at the corners of his mouth.

Underneath all of that awkward exterior, Miss Bradshaw had some gumption. It was obvious that she was not usually a person who took someone to task. Throughout the whole exchange her voice shook nervously and her neck bloomed with angry red blotches, but she persevered. Once she got started, there had been no stopping her. Most people just tolerated his brusqueness nowadays.

Poor Finn Matlock. All bitter and twisted. Even his wife could not stand to live with him.

It was quite refreshing to have been called on it for once. He actually admired her determination to stay at Stanford House just to spite him, although Finn doubted she would be quite so determined once she saw the place.

He swung himself back on to Horatio and nudged the beast to wander slowly in Miss Bradshaw's irate footsteps, while he watched her delectable, wet, rounded bottom sway as she stomped purposefully ahead a few yards away, resolutely pretending that he no longer existed at all. He doubted she would be quite so enamoured of the idea of marrying his dissolute brother when she saw his home. The only thing that would make Stanford House habitable would be to raze it to the ground and start again. Once she saw it, she would have to back down and return whence she came, and that actually did make him smile. Would she be all indignant and blotchy or would the squeaky, nervous Miss Bradshaw return? Either way, it would be entertaining to watch. For the first time in a very long time, Finn found himself actually looking forward to something.

Chapter Four

Evie had gone to bed feeling very proud of herself and then slept like the dead. The other Matlock, with his cutting words and his brooding, insolent eyes, had brought out a side to her character that she never knew that she possessed. For the first time in her life, she had stood up to someone and it had felt marvellous. He had made it plain that she was unwelcome in his house and she had made it equally as plain that she had no intentions of staying there or of being shipped back to Hyacinth and her malicious daughters. The very last place she would ever want to stay was with another obnoxious and nasty person who underestimated her and undermined her at every opportunity. Not after she had spent ten long years living with Hyacinth, having every ounce of joy and confidence gradually chiselled away until there was nothing left but the doormat she hated.

Of course she was angry at Fergus. The shoddy behaviour of that vile wastrel was beyond the pale—however, it was not wholly unexpected. Not really. Not when one considered his weak character and intrinsically selfish nature—the two character traits that she had needed him to possess in order for her escape plan to work. She had not expected him to stay long in Yorkshire and in all honesty would have been glad to see the back of him had it not been for the fact that he had left her in the lurch as an unexpected and unwelcome guest of his brother.

But she had not anticipated that he would bolt within a few hours of her handing over the first instalment of his payment. Fortunately, she had had the good sense not to give him the entire five thousand pounds in one go—the rest of the money was safely stored in a locked box amongst her small things in her trunk—although he had become quite unreasonable when she had explained this to him. In fact, just before he had left for the inn he had thrown quite a tantrum, but Evie had held firm. Two staggering examples of new-found assertiveness in less than twenty-four hours! Who'd have thought it?

But one thing that she had learned from her stern father, and his many years of business, was that you never paid up front for goods or services you had not yet received. While Fergus might well have delivered her to the north, he still had to uphold the rest of their bargain. That meant, from time to time, he had to play the role of her fiancé for as long as she deemed it necessary.

His curt letter had given her an address where she could reach him in York as well as a reassurance that he would go nowhere near London until Evie was satisfied that he could return without raising too much suspicion about their engagement. He made no apology for disappearing nor for failing to appraise her of the fact that he had left her at the wrong house, but he had been adamant that 'good old Finn' would look after her in his stead until he returned, which just went to show how little Fergus actually knew about anything.

'Good old Finn' could not wait to see the back of her and that feeling was quite mutual. The man was viler than his brother, but for completely different reasons. The fact that Fergus had apparently declined to tell his own brother the truth about their situation had given her pause and stopped her from sharing the contents of the letter. If Fergus did not wish his brother to know about their arrangement, there was probably a very good reason. It was obvious his twin was no fool, nor did he strike her as the type to suffer fools like Evie gladly. She sincerely doubted such an outspoken man would have a great deal of sympathy for her inability to stand up for herself in her own house. Selfishly, Evie had kept quiet because she had feared that she would be cast out on her ear if 'good old Finn' realised that the engagement was a sham and it was obvious he had little time for his wastrel brother.

He had said that he and Fergus were as different as chalk and cheese. Now that she had some experience of both of them that really was a very apt description. Like chalk, Fergus Matlock was weak and slowly eroding away, while Finnegan definitely left a sour taste in the mouth, just like rancid cheese. What gave him the right to say such hurtful things to her anyway?

'You do not look like a woman who could survive on one piece of toast...'

'Scraping the matrimonial barrel...'

'Your precious virtue is perfectly safe with me.'

All she had spent was a few scant minutes in his company and already she wanted to kick him. He made her so nervous. During each of their brief, tense exchanges, her heart had positively hammered against her ribs and her mouth had filled with cotton wool. His twin did not have that effect on her. With Fergus, Evie felt in control. But then she held all of the cards. He was a means to an end and theirs was a business transaction. While Finnegan looked almost exactly like Fergus, she certainly did not react to his presence in the same way. The man was so vexing and disagreeable. And unfortunately, he possessed all of the intelligence that Fergus lacked. She got the distinct impression that those mesmerising dark eyes saw right through her and her veil of lies. Under those circumstances, it was actually a good thing that he wanted her out of his house.

This morning, Evie intended to move into Stanford House whether there were servants there or not. As if living in less than luxury would bother her! She who had slept for more hours than she cared to remember in a chair at an invalid's bedside, doing all of those intensely personal and demeaning tasks that one did in a sickroom in order to spare her parents the indignity of being attended to by a servant. No, indeed, she would happily attend to both her own and Aunt Winnie's needs for as long as it took to find some staff and she would even enjoy it. For too many years Evie had dreamed of escaping the shackles of her old life and, now that she had, she was damned if she was going to let either one of the Matlock twins spoil it for her. Especially not the one who wore his breeches better, or who had floppy dark hair and soulful, insightful, mesmerising, dark eyes.

To that end, she was already up and dressed and it was barely past dawn. The first thing she was going to do was take herself to Stanford House and prepare a couple of bedchambers for herself and Aunt Winnie. Once that was done, later this morning she would oversee the removal of their luggage from Lord Finnegan's fine house and would never darken the man's door again.

Charity!

Hah! He could go to hell.

Feeling empowered and invincible, Evie stomped downstairs in her most sensible gown and walking boots.

'Good morning Miss Bradshaw! Are you looking forward to your move?'

He was leaning against the doorframe of the breakfast room with a steaming cup of coffee in his hand. Smiling. As Evie had never seen him smile, she was not fully prepared for the effect it would have on her. Those dark eyes were dancing with mischief, one of them slightly hidden behind a lock of hair that her fingers wanted to push back, and just like the first time she had seen him his chin bore the evidence of fresh stubble. But that smile did funny things to her insides and made her suddenly twitchy and self-conscious. She felt every inch the fat, frumpy, plain spinster she was up against his artless attractiveness. It was intimidating. However, the new improved Evie Bradshaw would not invert with shyness, no matter how much she wanted to. No, indeed! The foundations of their acquaintance had already been laid and this morning she was invincible.

'It is a good morning, Lord Finnegan. I find myself quite delighted to be leaving.' Her heart practically skipped a beat and her palms grew hot, but she managed to look directly at him as she spoke. Unfortunately, her voice wavered a little on the 'Lord Finnegan' and his clever eyes narrowed almost imperceptibly as he heard it. Almost as if he were looking forward to seeing her falter and he was just waiting, like a predator, to pounce.

'But not before breakfast, I hope. You can hardly ready an uninhabitable house on an empty stomach.' The forced joviality worried her. He was definitely up to something, she was certain. But then the inevitable insults came out and they forced her to put some steel in her spine. 'My cook has ensured that there is plenty of that delicious bacon that you were eyeing so covetously yesterday. I know you don't eat much, but I am sure you can choke down a few bites in the spirit of politeness. And I am quite I sure that you would hate to offend my cook by only partaking of toast when she has organised a breakfast banquet in your honour.'

Evie had hoped to be eating alone. Now he had stepped out of the doorway and was welcoming her into the room with his outstretched arm.

'Stowers, would you be so good as to bring Miss Bradshaw a hot beverage? Is it tea or coffee you prefer?'

The little devil inside her spoke up. 'I prefer chocolate in the mornings, Lord Finnegan. If it is not too much of an *inconvenience*.' Reluctantly she entered the lion's den and sat down primly as far away as it was possible to sit from the master's chair. To her horror, he began filling a plate for her. Eggs, bacon, sausage, more bacon and finally a piece of toast formed a mountain on the plate which he put it before her with great ceremony. Then he did the same for himself and sat next to her rather than at the head of the table. Just to intimidate her further.

'I thought I would accompany you this morning, in the spirit of being a good host.'

Evie's spirits sank. 'There really is no need, Lord Finnegan, I am sure that you have much better things to do with your day.' The smell of bacon was making her mouth water and reminded her that she was ravenous. Demurely, she cut off a tiny piece and popped it into her mouth and tried not to sigh at the sublime savoury taste.

'Oh, I insist, Miss Bradshaw. In fact, I am rather looking forward to it. Do you ride, Miss Bradshaw?'

'I do not, Lord Finnegan, I intend to walk.'

'How splendid. A brisk walk across the parkland will be most invigorating. Perhaps we could take the time to get to know each other a little better? I feel as though we have got off on the wrong foot. In fact, perhaps we should start now?'

In answer, Evie shoved an enormous piece of sausage into her mouth that prevented any further conversation and took for ever chewing it. She had no desire to know Finnegan Matlock any better than she did his dissolute brother. She followed the sausage with a healthy chunk of bacon. After the second forkful, he got the message and concentrated on his own breakfast, but he did it so smugly that she found herself frowning. He probably thought that she would faint dead away at the sight of Fergus's dilapidated house. Frankly, she did not care if it was overrun with vermin and as damp as Scotland in winter. At least she would be on her own, aside from Aunt Winnie, of course, and then she could set about starting again. Tomorrow she would visit the attorney that her own solicitor had recommended and instruct him to begin searching for suitable properties immediately. The sooner she found her own house, the sooner she could end the charade with Fergus and live the sort of life she had always dreamed of. Free. Happy. Not a doormat. What was the point of having a fortune if you never got to enjoy it?

Miss Bradshaw remained stubbornly mute for the duration of the meal, which Finn found surprisingly amusing. Even more amusing was the way she closed her eyes in sheer bliss every time she put a new morsel of food into her mouth when she assumed that he was concentrating on his breakfast. This was a woman who enjoyed her sensual pleasures. Splashing water, joyous singing, hot, crisp bacon…everything she did when she thought nobody was looking, she did with such passion. It made him wonder what she would be like in the full throes of it, until he ruthlessly dismissed the errant thought when the usual guilt began to niggle. He had no right to be thinking such things. Not after Olivia.

Except he had been thinking them. Suddenly he could not stop thinking about them. For two nights now, he had lain awake not thinking about his darling wife, but about the woman who had suddenly invaded his quiet life. It was difficult to get the image of her silhouetted body in that oh-so-proper nightgown out of his head. Or the way the firelight and sunlight had made the copper strands in her thick chestnut hair glow. Or the earthy beauty of her voice as she had sung in the stream. Even in her current shapeless dress, there was something about his brother's fiancée that intrigued him and called beneath the dead exterior he shuffled around in, to the remnants of the man that still, miraculously, lurked beneath the surface.

Once the meal was finished, she did her best to dissuade him from accompanying her. 'There is no need for you to come. I would prefer to go alone.' The pink blotches creeping up her neck bore witness to the effort it took her to be impolite. Instead of making Finn feeling awful, her discomfort spurred him on.

'Oh, I wouldn't dream of it, Miss Bradshaw. For the moment, at least, you are still my guest and I do feel responsible for you.'

'Then perhaps you should ride to Stanford House later. I am certain that you will find the walk with me dull.'

No, he wouldn't. There was nothing dull about her, aside from the dreadful dress. Finn had never seen quite so much fabric in one garment in his life. It must weigh a ton. 'Nonsense. We are to be brother and sister, Miss Bradshaw. I am keen to further our acquaintance, aren't you?' Because he knew that it would vex her, Finn held out his arm. For a few seconds, she simply stared at it as if it were something distasteful, until her innate good manners forced her to take it. But she stared resolutely ahead as they set off towards his childhood home and she made no attempt at making conversation.

It was probably just as well. The moment they set off, Finn became painfully aware of her hips. They seemed to undulate as she walked, in a graceful figure of eight, and with each alternate step they lightly brushed his thigh. After a few yards, it was torture, so he stopped to pretend to check the time just so that he could sever the contact.

Chapter Five

Taking Finnegan Matlock's arm was not to be recommended. The moment she had threaded her own through his, Evie quickly learned two things. Firstly, he had the body of a man who spent a great deal of time outdoors. Not that she had a great wealth of experience of the male form to draw upon, but he certainly did not feel anything like her occasional dance partners or her fiancé, whose arms were quite soft in comparison to his irritating brother's. And secondly, and perhaps more importantly, just the feel of that solid, muscled, male appendage did funny things to her.

Instantly, Evie felt warm, her heart began to flutter in her chest and her fingers desperately wanted to run themselves all over the muscles to trace every intriguing plane and bulge. She was excessively grateful when he checked his pocket watch and then failed to offer out the offending arm again.

'Stanford House is about a mile away,' he said without any trace of his usual sarcasm or surliness. 'Just over that hill.'

The gently rolling landscape of the Dales was spread out before her and Evie could not help smiling at the sight. 'It is beautiful here.'

'I have always thought so. Quite a change from London, I suppose?'

Good grief—were they actually exchanging pleasantries? 'Indeed, Lord Finnegan, the only opportunity to see nature at all is in the parks and they are always so crowded.'

'I cannot imagine that. I find York stifling enough.'

'Have you never been to London?'

'I have never had cause to go there, thank goodness. I am certain that I would dislike it immensely.'

'I loathe London.' Had she just said that out loud? By the way he turned to look at her, his dark head slightly tilted to one side and his expression curious, Evie realised that she had. And to him, of all people.

'Why?'

How to explain something that she had never verbalised before? 'It is crowded and unforgiving.' Perhaps not the best choice of words, but fitting.

'Unforgiving?'

Oh, dear, definitely not the best choice of words. Now she had to explain herself and he would no doubt think her pathetic. 'Even though it is filled with people, the society there is very close-knit. Everybody knows everybody else's business.'

'It is like that in the countryside also.'

'Yes—but...' Evie sighed, becoming increasingly aware of his intense gaze. 'In London, everybody is judged. And once judged, it is impossible to be anything other than what you are perceived to be.' She really should not have said that. Except, that was how she felt. Bottled, labelled and displayed on the shelf. In London, she was Evie the spinster. The plain wallflower with the dull personality. A woman whose ship had not so much sailed, but failed to leave the harbour. A nobody. A nothing. She doubted this splendid-looking man would understand how draining it was to be of no consequence.

'And how are you perceived to be, Miss Bradshaw?'

The question startled her and she blushed ferociously. She could hardly admit to the truth—but then again, she already had, she supposed. 'I am perceived exactly as I am, Lord Finnegan. A plain, plump wallflower who has been so long on the shelf that she is almost a part of it.'

'How old are you, Miss Bradshaw?'

Goodness, the man was rude. Nobody asked a lady's age. 'Almost six and twenty.'

'That is not old. You still have plenty of child-bearing years left.' Another thing that, frankly, should never be discussed, especially as Evie's heart lurched at the mention of the children she would never have. 'And you are neither plain nor plump.'

'You do not need to spare my feelings, Lord Finnegan.'

The corners of his mouth curved up as he stared straight ahead. 'I believe you know enough about me, Miss Bradshaw, to know that I am not a man to spare anyone's feelings. If you want me to be completely honest, I believe that your choice of attire and matronly hairstyle make you *appear* plain and plump. And old, Miss Bradshaw. Far too old.'

'You are a very insulting man, Lord Finnegan.'

'Yet a moment ago you accused me of sparing your feelings?' Evie could not think of a quick enough answer to that so marched on ahead to the crest of the hill. When she got there, and stared down, she stopped dead in her tracks.

Ahead of her was what she assumed was Stanford House. Like Matlock House, it was Palladian in style and perfectly symmetrical. Unlike Matlock House, it appeared to be missing a roof.

'I did tell you that it was uninhabitable.' He came level with her and then jauntily bounded down the hill with a definite smug spring in his step, leaving Evie to trail despondently behind. Insufferable man.

By the time she caught up with him he was a few yards from the shell of a house with his arms folded. It was obvious by the lack of glass in several windows, and the black stains that blotted the pale stone above those gaping holes, that there had been a horrendous fire. A horrendous fire that Fergus had neglected to tell her about during their hasty negotiations. Was nothing about her move to Yorkshire going to go to plan?

'What happened?'

'About three years ago, my dear brother had one of his house parties. I have never really got to the bottom of who did what and when, Fergus never invited me to any of his many entertainments and I would never have gone even if he had. Suffice to say, at some point during the night someone set fire to something. Because it had been a particularly hot summer and because they were all so deep in their cups that nobody had the good sense to throw water on the flames quick enough, the place went up like a firework. You might have noticed that the roof is missing. If you go inside, and I do not recommend that you do, you will also discover that the entire upper floor has collapsed as well. You could always pitch a tent in the grounds.'

'You are enjoying this, aren't you, Lord Finnegan.'

His mouth curved upwards again and he nodded. 'So—it's back to London for you, I suppose.'

The rush of pure, unadulterated fury was so sudden and so visceral, Evie quite forgot herself. Of their own accord, both of her hands shot out and pushed him firmly in the chest, sending him backwards so that he landed unceremoniously on his bottom on the ground. He stared at her in shock.

'I am never going back to London! I do not care if I do have to pitch a tent! I am never, ever going to live with Hyacinth again! I hate that woman. I hate the way she makes me feel. And I hate her stupid, spiteful daughters. And most of all, I hate the way that I am when I am around them!'

Evie covered her mouth with her hands and simply stared at him, shocked at her own lack of control. The anger on his face, changed to bewilderment. 'Who's Hyacinth?'

Evie's voice was shaking and so were her hands. She had just pushed a grown man, a very big, solid, hateful grown man, to the ground and she had no idea whether to be mortified or exulted. 'She is my stepmother.'

His dark head tilted to one side again as he assessed her from his seat upon the ground. 'Why do you hate her so much?'

A painful knot formed at the base of Evie's throat and for a few moments she was certain that she might cry. 'This is really not what I had hoped for when I came to Yorkshire.'

In resignation, she lowered herself to sit on the ground as well, where she took several calming breaths. 'My stepmother married my father for his money. When he died, the only reason she kept me on was because my father had left the bulk of his fortune to me, not her. But she resents me for it and spends every minute of every day reminding me of my shortcomings, making me miserable while she happily spends my money on her life and all I get to do is watch. In London, I am a doormat. An invisible nobody. I came here because I wanted to stop being a doormat. I am running away, you see, Lord Finnegan. I know that you probably think me over-dramatic or lily-livered for not standing up to Hyacinth, but if I stay there I will continue to fade away until there is nothing left of me but an outline. I cannot go back there; no matter how awful things are here.'

Finn did not want to feel sorry for her, but he did. He could see the tears shimmering in her pretty eyes that she would not allow to fall, saw the light of hope in them dull and hated the sight of it. He knew how painful it was to have all hope die. But she had misguidedly put all of her hope in Fergus so she was already doomed to be disappointed. 'I doubt your life will be any better here with my brother, Miss Bradshaw. He will spend your money, too, and probably a darn sight quicker than this Hyacinth woman. And he will never be here. Already he has abandoned you for the gaming tables and I fear that he will always do so.'

'I do know that, Lord Finnegan. It was one of the reasons why I became engaged to him.'

Now Finn was truly baffled. 'You willingly became engaged to a man who will make you miserable and ignore you, just as you claim this Hyacinth woman does?'

'I suppose, to you, that does sound silly, but I have no desire to spend any more time with your brother than he does with me. I came here to live my own life, Lord Finnegan.' She inhaled deeply and closed her eyes, and in doing it was almost as if she was repairing herself. When those eyes opened again there were no more tears there. 'I shall buy a house, Lord Finnegan. A fine house. And I shall live in it. I am not a doormat any longer. The new improved Evie Bradshaw is resilient and determined. This is only a setback—not a defeat. In the meantime, I shall take rooms at the inn.'

She stood up then, smoothed down her skirts and started to walk back towards the hill. Whilst he admired her tenacity, her lofty plan was flawed. 'It could take many weeks, months even, to find a house and complete the sale. Your aunt cannot stay all that time in an inn.'

'My great-aunt is made of stern stuff, Lord Finnegan. We will do well enough whilst we wait. Besides, I would not send her back to Hyacinth. That woman is a nasty bully.'

A nasty bully? The way she said it suggested she had been on the receiving end of such harsh treatment. A new knot of guilt was forming in Finn's gut.

'There is no need to send your aunt back to

Hyacinth Whoever-She-Is.' Good heavens, what was he saying? 'And there is no need for either of you to go to the inn. Under the circumstances…' *Stop, man—before you say something that you know you will regret!* '…and as we are to be brother and sister, I would prefer it if you stayed at Matlock House while you search for a new home.'

Finn stared at the sky and cursed his parents for bringing him up to have good manners.

She stopped walking and turned to face him. 'I do not wish to inconvenience you, Lord Finnegan.' But there was hope sparkling in those golden-flecked eyes again and he did not want to be the one to dash it.

'It is not an inconvenience, madam. Just do not expect me to be a good-humoured host.'

When she rushed at him and wrapped her arms around his neck and kissed his cheek in gratitude, Finn had the overwhelming urge to respond in kind. Except it was not her cheek he wanted to kiss. Instead, he stood stiffly and hoped that the sale would go through more swiftly than any sale had ever gone through before. 'I suppose we should head back.' His voice sounded gruff and she disentangled her lush body from his. Instantly, he had the overwhelming desire to pull her back, but resisted.

They set off up the hill and his brother's fiancée could not stop smiling. And perhaps smiling was contagious because Finn felt the urge to smile back at her. Clearly doing good deeds warmed the heart and his cold, shrivelled heart felt inordinately pleased with itself.

'Now that you are no longer a doormat, what will you do with your days?'

'I intend to do whatever takes my particular fancy rather than Hyacinth's. I am tired of being dragged around town while she makes endless calls on people who are always glad to see the back of us. I hate balls and parties and sitting with the wallflowers. So you see, Lord Finnegan, by contrast this place is paradise. I shall paint outdoors, sing folk songs loudly, wear unsuitable gowns…'

'The one you are wearing is quite unsuitable enough. It does not fit and it is ugly.'

'You are a very rude man, Lord Finnegan.' But she was smiling as she said it.

'Perhaps. Would you prefer me to lie to you with idle flattery? I assumed that the new and empowered Miss Bradshaw would have the gumption to insist on complete honesty.'

'I do not have the right figure for gowns to fit properly.'

'Any decent dressmaker could make you a

gown that fits properly. That abomination is shapeless and far too capacious.'

She stiffened in outrage but the faint blush that stained her cheeks was actually very becoming and certainly something that she should do more often. 'More fabric is flattering to someone with a more generous figure!'

Knowing full well what lay under all of those acres of stiff fabric, Finn was inclined to disagree. 'Is that one of your awful stepmother's pearls of wisdom?'

She paused thoughtfully before answering. 'Yes, it is! And as I am no longer a doormat, I should probably ignore all of her advice going forward. I shall find a new dressmaker as well as a new house.'

'That's the spirit.' Her good mood was infectious. 'Perhaps you should find a new fiancé while you are about it?'

She simply grinned at that and chatted about everything and nothing all of the way home while she idly picked wild flowers that he wanted to weave into her hair.

Chapter Six

⁓⁓⁓⁓⁓

Over the course of the next week, Evie fell into a new routine which she rather enjoyed. Because she was an early riser, most mornings she collided with her surly host over breakfast. Usually he was gruff and forthright, occasionally sarcastic, but he never failed to look at whatever gown she wore with utter disgust. This appraisal was always accompanied with one cutting word, although the choice of word varied. Yesterday it had been *dull*, the day before it had been *foul*. *Hideous*, *matronly* and only one two-word insult—*good grief!*—had also featured in his daily criticism.

Yet those cutting words somehow spurred her to be the better, braver Evie Bradshaw. The no-longer-a-doormat Evie Bradshaw that she wanted to be. Yes, he criticised her appearance much like Hyacinth had, but her stepmother had criticised Evie personally: her face, her figure, her hair; *his* criticism was directed solely at the awful gowns Hyacinth had chosen for her. Gowns that Evie had always hated, but had been conditioned to believe were the best she could expect when she was as unfortunately shaped as she was—Lord Finnegan, in his own curt, unfriendly manner, made her wonder if perhaps Hyacinth might have dressed her like that on purpose, which, strangely, motivated her to undo that damage.

Underneath all of that surliness, he was occasionally uncharacteristically considerate, although he did his best not to show it. If he saw her nibbling on toast he put bacon on her plate; he was kind to Aunt Winnie, even though he pretended to be completely put upon. Aunt Winnie insulted him playfully and he gave as good as he got. But even when he was being sociable he never laughed and even the rare approximations of a smile were few and far between. At all costs he avoided them.

Aside from breakfast, the only time Evie got to see him was in passing because he gave his guests a very wide berth. He never ate dinner with them, preferring to take a tray into his study rather than sit down with them, and he apparently never ventured into the bright and airy drawing room at any time of the day. Whether that was because he really had no desire to have anything more to do with them than was necessary, Evie could not say, but she much preferred those few minutes with him in the breakfast room to the hours she sat in the drawing room with Aunt Winnie.

The housekeeper had explained her master's reluctance to go into that room was because it reminded him too much of his beloved wife. Hardly a surprise when the room was dominated by a large painting of a lovely blonde-haired young woman with a butterfly perched in her open hands.

His wife.

Olivia Grace Matlock.

Perhaps it was the butterfly, when Evie was merely a moth, or perhaps it was the fact that the ethereal beauty of the woman made Evie feel plainer than usual, or perhaps it was the fact that she suspected that this woman still haunted this house and its surly owner—whatever it was, the drawing room was intimidating. And she quite missed his company there.

When their paths did cross, he would engage in brief, usually curt, conversation and then he would take himself off to his study and she would not see him again until the following morning. Though as silly as it was, Evie really looked forward to those mornings. Later in the day, when he was tired, there was an air of sadness about him, almost as if he was already quite done with the day and the effort of being part of it. But in the mornings, he seemed less burdened, much as Evie was feeling decidedly less burdened with each day that passed that she was not in London. Already she had made inroads into the huge task of restarting her life.

The same day that Finn had agreed to allow her to stay had been the very same day that she had made an appointment to visit a dressmaker.

All on her own.

The dressmaker, a lovely woman with a brash northern accent and enormous, coarse hands, had stared at the frock she was wearing in disbelief and asked if the woman who had made it had had the cheek to want paying for such a disgrace to the profession. Then she had gone about draping all the soft and floaty fabrics that Evie had always been told to avoid over her body and dismissing all of Evie's panicked comments to the contrary.

Some of her assertions had made Evie blush, especially her recurring compliment of, *'You have a wonderful pair of bosoms, Miss Bradshaw, you really should show them off.'* But as the dressmaker also made dresses for the vicar's wife, Evie was trying not to panic about how revealing the finished garments would be.

Later today, the first new gowns would finally be ready and, fear of showing too much of those bosoms aside, already Evie was brimming with excitement and looking forward to wearing one of them to breakfast in the morning to gauge Finn's opinion. The change of appearance somehow signalled the start of her new life. A life that she was determined to grab with both hands.

Her new attorney was already hunting for suitable properties and as soon as he forwarded his findings to her, then Evie could start to look at them and decide where she was going to live for the rest of her days. But until then, she would enjoy doing what she had been doing since her arrival in this stunning part of the country. After breakfast, she would spend a few hours chatting and reading to Aunt Winnie. When her aunt went for her afternoon nap, Evie would take a walk over the meadow, paddle for a while in the stream and then go to the village. Going out on her own, whenever and wherever she wanted, was a novelty that she doubted she would ever grow tired of.

It was so wonderful to be out in the sunshine and fresh air rather than being cooped up in some other person's drawing room that Evie had no real interest in and to whom Evie was of even less interest. Hyacinth was a stickler for morning calls. Every day, Evie would be dragged along to one house or another and, as far as she could make out, the sole purpose of her presence on these visits was to make her stepmother appear benevolent. Evie would be largely ignored while Hyacinth ruthlessly promoted her two daughters to whichever unfortunate hostess had not had the good sense to pretend *not* to be at home. The fact that Hyacinth spent a small fortune every month on calling cards was telling in itself, not that Hyacinth would have the good sense to realise why.

Evie wanted to find friends—but not by using Hyacinth's pushy methods. She wanted her friendships to be forged naturally, the way she had made friends in her youth, real friends that would actually want to talk to her, and the daily visits to the village were helping. Already, she was on speaking terms with a few of the local ladies and had been invited to take tea at the vicarage by the charming vicar's wife who was a similar age to Evie. Absolutely everyone had been welcoming and, so far, nobody appeared to find her dull or invisible. If they thought her plain and plump, thankfully they kept it to themselves. If her attorney could find her a suitable property close to this village, Evie would be extremely happy to live hereabouts for ever. The undulating Dales, a beautiful sea of green grass and meadow flowers, which stretched on and on as far as the eye could see, had already wormed their way into her heart more than any other place ever had. They felt like home and Evie felt at home there. A comforting sensation she had not experienced in almost a decade.

'You are still here, then, Miss Bradshaw?' On cue, he strode into the breakfast room, looking as surly as usual.

'Indeed I am, Lord Finnegan. Where else would I be on this fine summer's morning?' She smiled innocently and nibbled her toast, waiting for the morning sparring to begin.

'I live in constant hope that you will take yourself, and that troublesome aunt of yours, back to London where you belong.' He began to pile food on a plate. 'Having you here is a great inconvenience.' As he took himself to his chair, two crisp slices of bacon dropped on to her plate as he walked past. 'I cannot fathom why you would wish to stay here when you have the means to take yourself anywhere in the world.'

'I am waiting for Fergus, as well you know. Shall I pour you some coffee?'

He nodded absently and began to eat, but as soon as Evie stood and walked towards the coffee pot, his fork suspended midway between his plate and his mouth as he allowed his eyes to travel down the length of her body slowly in abject disbelief. After a long pause, during which he shook his head and appeared affronted, he finally passed judgement on her clothing.

'Monstrous.'

'That is a big word first thing in the morning. Is this gown so very offensive?' Evie had worn the pink disaster on purpose. It was the absolute worst dress Hyacinth had ever had made for her, although both Hyacinth and her two spiteful daughters had positively raved about it, and she wanted it to be the very last of her stepmother's concoctions that she ever wore as a matter of principle. Only doormats wore gowns like this one.

'That, madam, is the most horrific I have seen so far. What colour is that exactly? Puce?'

Even stared down at the stiff, unforgiving silk and shrugged. 'I suppose it is.'

'Any colour that has the audacity to be called puce should not be worn. Ever.'

'Much as it pains me, Lord Finnegan, I am inclined to agree. Tomorrow, my new dresses will have arrived and this monstrosity, along with all of the others, will be thrown on to a bonfire.'

His dark eyes were amused, but that amusement never touched his handsome face. 'Then I would ask that you build your bonfire well away from my house and outbuildings, Miss Bradshaw. Only, there is a great deal of fabric in that dress and I fear that burning such a weighty garment might cause the flames to become out of hand. The fire might burn for days and I would so hate my house to resemble my feckless brother's.'

'You are a very impudent man, Lord Finnegan.' But she was smiling as she said it. He stared at her for a few moments before turning all of his concentration back to his food in the way she had learned signalled the end of conversation. However, he could not resist one final salvo to vex her.

'Eat your bacon, Miss Bradshaw. You know that you want to.'

Evie stared at her reflection in abject disbelief. There was a strange young woman staring back at her in a light, fitted gown of pretty patterned muslin and, miracle of miracles, she looked quite presentable. The scooped neckline of the bodice showed more skin than Evie was used to showing, but it elongated her neck and drew attention upwards, rather than downwards, which had to be a good thing. Under the bust, the soft empire cut of the fabric flattered her full figure, emphasising the waist that she did not know that she possessed and floating over her wide hips in a most becoming way.

She definitely appeared less wide, which was pleasing, and, if she said so herself, younger. She even liked the new hairstyle that the pushy dressmaker had insisted on creating before she had allowed Evie to look in the mirror. Her thick hair was arranged in a looser style, which was not only more comfortable because it did not pull tautly at her scalp, but the loose tendrils that framed her face made the usually dull brown strands appear almost vibrant.

The older woman appeared inordinately proud of her creation. 'You look ten years younger, Miss Bradshaw!'

Evie could not disagree. She not only looked younger, she felt younger. Much younger and less ungainly. Almost…almost…pretty. Unexpected tears formed as she continued to stare at herself, turning this way and that in the mirror.

'Thank you.' Her voice was so small it was barely more than a whisper because of the emotion clogging her throat.

'Don't thank me just yet. That is still only the first gown. You have another five of this first batch to try on.'

Yet each of the new dresses were perfect, so perfect that when it came time to leave, Evie could not bring herself to don her old clothes again as she had intended and breezed out of the little shop with a definite spring in her step.

Eager to share her joy with someone, Evie decided to be brave and to call on her new almost-friend the vicar's wife. As her mother always had, she decided to take a small gift to her hostess and stopped in the bakery for a sweet tart before cheerfully walking through the village towards her house. The vicarage lay behind the quaint, Norman church, so Evie had to cross the churchyard. She had barely put one foot into the ancient cemetery when someone caught her eye and halted her progress.

Finn was a few yards away, hat in hand, and staring down at the flowers growing about his booted feet with a faraway look on his face. The gentle summer breeze played with his hair, mussing it delightfully and the sight of him warmed her, even though it shouldn't have. Her initial reaction was to bound over to him, spin in a circle and proudly show off the transformation that he had been instrumental in. Would he think her greatly improved? Or, heaven forbid, even slightly pretty?

Just thinking about his reaction made her feel excited and a little dizzy. If he was complimentary she knew that she would blush and she didn't care. She wanted a compliment from a handsome man. Just this once, she wanted someone to tell her that she looked nice and she wanted to feel attractive. And his good opinion would be valued above all others because she could trust him to be brutally honest. But by the same token, if he disapproved that would crush her. Not when she was feeling more confident about her appearance than she ever had and not when she wanted his approval so very much that it scared her.

Good gracious! She actively wanted his approval? That was a terrifying thought. And a stupid one. Finn had made no secret of the fact that he found her presence annoying—yet here she was, desperate to impress him. And for what? To see if he found her appearance attractive! What nonsense was that? She might well be the new, improved Evie Bradshaw, but that did not mean that she should start getting ideas above herself. Aside from the new dress, she was still hurtling towards thirty, still plump and still plain. She was definitely not the sort of woman that men found attractive. And twirling in front of a man was almost flirting and Evie could never do that. Ever. Especially as she was pretending to be engaged to avoid certain eviction! Clearly she had gone soft in the head.

Evie experienced the urge to hide, but stopped herself. She was not going to be that timid person any longer. It shouldn't matter what he thought, although apparently it suddenly mattered a great deal. If she needed to know what he thought, then what better time was there than now? It hardly meant that she had *those* kinds of feelings for him. So what if she wanted to feel attractive? That certainly did not mean that she wanted Fergus's surly twin to be attracted to her. No, indeed. She merely wanted his honesty and to surprise him for once. There would be no twirling or grinning. She would simply march over there and ask for his honest appraisal.

Steeling herself with a deep breath, Evie went to call to him, but his stance made her hesitate. Only then did she realise that he was not simply standing in the churchyard, he was standing at a grave. Staring *desolately* at a grave so intently that to say that he was lost in his own world would have been an understatement. Even from this distance Evie could see the sorrow etched on his face and the tenseness in his broad shoulders beneath his coat. It was obvious that nothing else existed for him except his grief for the woman sleeping beneath his feet. It was one of the most tragic sights she had ever seen and one that moved her to her core.

Underneath that detached, sour exterior Finn was in pain.

And as much as Evie hated to see anyone in that state, the surge of jealousy she experienced for the dead woman he clearly still adored was as surprising as it was unwelcome. She had not come to Yorkshire to have odd pangs of longing for a man who was little more than a stranger to her and the brother of a means to an end. She had come here to start all over again. Independent, *not* dependent. And even if she was feeling such things, the very last person she should be feeling them for was the twin brother of her pretend fiancé. What a tangled mess that would make of all of her well-made plans.

It was also quite ridiculous to expect him to have even the slightest interest in her new dress now. The poor woman had only just died and he was still in the midst of raw grief, for goodness sake. The very last thing he would want to be confronted with now was his unwelcome house-guest, who was so desperate for a compliment that she would even consider approaching him in a cemetery and twirling around like an idiot.

Feeling inordinately stupid, Evie darted behind a large gravestone to wait for him to leave. In the grand scheme of things, avoidance was definitely a more agreeable option. Except he was in no hurry to leave, leaving her feeling like a voyeur watching this intimate display of such intensely personal grief.

It was heartbreaking to witness. After a few minutes of just staring, he crouched down and lay the flat of his palm against the grass-covered earth and she saw him close his eyes briefly, before that hand closed into a fist of frustration at the cruel irony of fate. Then he finally stood and turned away, all deflated and defeated and not the least bit surly. Evie wanted to go to him, wrap her arms about him and allow him to absorb her strength—but instead she remained rooted to the spot, praying that he would not see her.

He walked purposefully along the path in Evie's direction, which made her cower behind the headstone as she worried about exactly what she would say to explain why she was cowering if he actually caught her there. But in the end, she needn't have worried. He walked straight past her in blissful ignorance of her presence, too absorbed in his own desolation to be aware of anything else on this pleasant summer's morning, let alone the silly, plump spinster who suddenly wanted his approval.

Only when she was completely certain he was not coming back did she venture from her hiding place, not quite as confident as she had been a few minutes before and heartily ashamed of herself and her errant, pathetic vanity. She should just call on her almost-friend at the vicarage and put all further thoughts of the mesmerising Finnegan Matlock, and the pain swirling in his dark eyes, out of her head.

Except Evie's feet were first drawn not to the vicarage, but to that well-tended grave he had been so consumed with.

Olivia Grace Matlock
Beloved wife
All days are nights to see till I see thee

It was such a heartfelt message of despair. She recognised the line from one of Shakespeare's sonnets and empathised with the message. Evie had felt much the same when her mother had died a decade ago. That overwhelming sense of loss and loneliness that engulfed you was all-consuming and draining at first. It sucked everything out of you until the mundane motions of waking up and eating became too much of an effort. Everything, your thoughts, your world, became grey. Of course, life eventually moved on and the raw wound of grief was lessened as time healed it. The world regained some colour. But it never went. Not really. Even with so many intervening years, there were times when she felt the bitter sting of sadness at her dear mama's passing.

Fortunately, those negative memories were now overshadowed by the happy ones, all of the times when there had been laughter rather than tears, a more fitting memorial to the woman who had birthed her. More often than not, when she thought of her mother, it was with fondness now rather than despair. Positive, happy memories. The sort her mother would have wanted her to have. In time, Evie hoped Finn would also find that peace.

Her mood now decidedly less buoyed, Evie eventually knocked on the door of the vicarage while wondering if the impromptu visit would be better abandoned.

Chapter Seven

'Miss Bradshaw! How lovely to see you!' Mrs Cardew, the vicar's wife, opened the door herself and ushered her inside with a welcoming smile. 'Don't you look lovely? I see your new dresses are ready at last. Are you pleased with them?'

Evie could not help smiling at the compliment despite her now-dulled mood. 'They have turned out so much better than I had hoped, Mrs Cardew. Thank you for recommending the dressmaker to me. As a gesture of my thanks, I have brought you something from the bakery.' Evie passed over the wrapped tart, feeling a little self-conscious at being so forward.

'How wonderful. We shall have some with tea and you must call me Charlotte as we are now friends who share cake and talk fashion.'

To her complete surprise, the next half an hour passed much more pleasantly than any visit

Evie had had in years. Charlotte was inquisitive, irreverent and quite without artifice. Without realising it, Evie felt her spirit lift and she began to behave as herself, something that she rarely did in company.

'How long will you be a guest of Finn's?' It was interesting that Charlotte spoke of Fergus's twin so informally. It suggested that she knew him well.

'Only until I can find a suitable place for my aunt and me to live. I do not wish to be a burden to Lord Finnegan. Not when he has been so recently bereaved.'

'Recently bereaved? I believe you have been misinformed, Evie. Finn's wife died three years ago.'

'She did?' This news brought up so many questions about her host and all were disconcerting. 'I saw him in the cemetery on my way here and the grief I witnessed appeared so stark I assumed that he was barely out of mourning.'

Charlotte poured them both more tea and settled back in her chair. 'He visits her grave several times a week, the poor thing. It is quite heartbreaking to witness. Sometimes I think he will never get over Olivia's death.'

Evie remembered the way he had laid his hand flat on the ground as if he would be able to touch his wife, absorb her essence in some way, through the compacted soil. *All days are nights to see till I see thee.*

'He must have loved her very much.' She had never dared hope that anyone would ever feel that way about her. How wonderful must that sort of adoration be? Once again she felt envious of the dead woman and ashamed of herself for thinking such things.

'He was devoted. They were childhood sweethearts. And both so very young when they married.' Charlotte sighed wistfully at the memory. 'Everyone in the village was certain they would blissfully live out their days together—they were such a lovely young couple—but, alas, it was not to be.'

'How did she die?' Because it was obvious that Olivia Grace Matlock, adored wife of her devoted husband, had been very, very young when she left this mortal coil.

'It was a tragedy, to be sure, and one nobody expected. She had an unexplained wasting sickness which caused the creeping paralysis. It was not long after they were wed that she fell ill. It began as an odd numbness in her limbs and extreme fatigue, but those symptoms only persisted and worsened. The physicians had no idea what caused her ailment or how to treat it and we are all still none the wiser as to what it was, but with every passing month she became weaker and weaker till eventually she could not even walk. Finn had to carry her everywhere. Then she began to lose feeling in her arms. In the final month her vision began to fade, too. Olivia had always been so vivacious, you see, and very mischievous. It took those things from her. It was heartbreaking to watch the decline.

'Yet the illness dragged on and on for years and Finn tirelessly cared for her throughout. Sitting with her, reading to her, inviting her friends to come to Matlock House so that she did not feel isolated or left out of village life. He was always so protective of Olivia. He hired a procession of the most brilliant and expensive doctors, and tended to her himself right up until her death.'

Evie knew full well how draining that could be. She had done it twice. She had never resented a moment of caring for her mother. But she carried the guilt of resenting having to do it all over again, and so quickly, for her father. He had brought Hyacinth and misery into her life when Evie had still been grieving her mother and she had not enjoyed a day of complete happiness in Mayfair since. Evie would never regain those ten wasted years of subservience, ten years of ageing and watching life fly by without her, but she was determined that she would not waste ten more.

'Her death, when it finally came was a blessing. She was in constant pain, the poor thing, and wanted it to end. Some days she was better than others, but she was bedridden and miserable. The last time I visited her, there was a calmness about her, almost as if she accepted that death was imminent and had made her peace with it. When I got up to leave, she took my hand and said goodbye. I believe that she said her farewells to every person that she cared for, so when she died peacefully in her sleep a few days later, although we mourned her, none of us was surprised that she was gone. Except Finn. Finn still keenly feels her loss. It is so sad to see. He is much changed since Olivia's passing. Detached. Subdued. Almost as if a part of him died when she did.'

The breakfast room was empty when Finn strode in, but instead of feeling relieved to have some peace he felt an overwhelming sense of disappointment that his unwelcome houseguest was not there. That was one of the main objections he had to Miss Evelyn Bradshaw. The woman amused him, when he had no right feeling amused. As each day passed she became bolder, happier and more confident in herself. It was a bit like watching a newborn foul taking its first wobbly steps into the world. Miss Bradshaw was learning to walk, but soon she would begin to gallop.

Finn found himself attracted to her brave, cheerful spirit and equally repelled by it at the same time. He wanted to be left alone—but increasingly he found that he wanted to seek her company. Every day since her unannounced arrival, he had often caught sight of her from a distance, wandering across his meadow, picking flowers and singing to herself. When she reached the stream, she hitched up her skirts, kicked off her shoes and paddled for ages, enjoying the simple pleasure of just being alive. Not only was it charming to witness, it made him yearn to join her in the hope that some of her enthusiasm for life would rub off on him. To that end he had limited himself to only seeing her at breakfast. It was the one bright part of his grey day and the only shaft of light he would allow himself because…because he owed it to Olivia to remember her and, in the last few months, those bittersweet memories were becoming so much harder to hold on to.

Every day he forced himself to recall those last hours of her life, to remind himself that if he had behaved differently, if he had only been there, then perhaps she might have seen more mornings. But he hadn't. He'd been angry and frustrated. He had walked out of her bedchamber when she had told him that she no longer wanted to be a burden and wished that she were dead. It had become such a familiar conversation and one that frightened him so very much that he had hoped that, if she saw his determination for them to stay together, she would have found some hope in her heart and continued to fight.

'It is not fair on me,' she had said in that matter-of-fact way that she had whenever his temper got the better of him, 'and it is not fair on you.'

Not fair on you.

The very last words he had ever heard from her sweet lips. Had he known that was how their time together would finish, he would not have stalked out of her room and slammed the door. He would not have walked to the stables and ridden for two hours in an attempt to calm down. By the time he came home and saw the bleak expressions on his housekeeper's and butler's weathered faces it was too late. His lovely, delicate, broken wife was gone. Beneath the empty bottle of laudanum was a brief note.

I hope you are happy, my darling.

Seven words that had haunted his days and nights since. Had he made her think that he wasn't? Sometimes the guilt he suffered was so intense he wished he were dead, too—only lately, these last few months, he had had to remind himself of the guilt in order to fully feel it. There had been occasions when he had forgotten it altogether and those occasions were now coming with alarming frequency. Only yesterday, when the afternoon sky had begun its descent in the sky, had it occurred to him that he had not mourned his wife once yet that day or remembered how she had died to ease his burdens.

Of course, he could justify it to himself by explaining that he had been busy. It was the tail end of the lambing season and soon his flocks of sheep would have to be sheared while the dairy heifers were on the very cusp of calving. The crops needed fertilising. At this time of year, the crops always needed fertilising. With no land manager to oversee the farm labourers and co-ordinate their work, Finn needed to be out from dusk till dawn. He preferred it that way. The work gave him a reason to get up in the mornings.

But these were all excuses. In his heart, he knew that. He also knew that his mind had a new tendency to wander to places that it had no right straying into and wanting things that it had no right wanting, not while his wife slept because she had believed that living was not fair on him. So he had gone to Olivia's grave to remind himself of what he had done and how his actions then must have driven her to do such a terrible thing, desperately hoping that the fresh reminder would stop him from wishing that he wasn't so alone.

Clearly it had not worked because he was sat here waiting, delaying filling his plate or pouring his coffee until his brother's fiancée made an appearance and brightened his morning and added a brief flash of colour to his interminable, drab day. Angry at his own selfishness, Finn stood and marched to the sideboard. He had just begun to pour the hot coffee into his cup when heard her come to the door.

'Good morning, Lord Finnegan.'

Finn grunted in response and did not take his eyes off of his task. It was one thing to know that you were inordinately pleased to see your unwanted houseguest, it was another thing altogether to show it.

'I see that you are in your usual surly mood this morning.'

'My surly mood, madam, is because of your continued…' Whatever he was about to say dried up in his throat the moment he turned towards her. Hot coffee poured over his hand and he winced, but managed not to drop the cup in shock.

'My new dresses came.'

Finn could see that. He wished desperately that he couldn't. He had suspected that she had been hiding her light under a bushel, but the bushel had apparently evaporated and she was positively glowing. The soft green fabric moulded to her curvy body like a lover's caress, allowing him to see how her hips flared beneath her waist and how her full bosom jutted proudly above it. Meadow flowers had been embroidered on to the skirt and grew up her legs, which only served to make him think about them. And the hair! It was all so loose that he suspected that the removal of just one strategic hair pin would send it all tumbling to her waist. Finn suddenly wanted to tug out that pin more than he wanted anything. All at once he was hot. Too hot and completely at a loss as to what he should say as she smiled up at him expectantly.

'What do you think?' The smile wavered and slid off of her face while his brain struggled to work correctly.

'Better.'

'Better!' He could see he had offended her by

the way her dark eyebrows drew together over her troubled eyes.

'I meant to say lovely. You look quite lovely, Miss Bradshaw.' Which she did. Lovely and luscious and womanly. Definitely womanly. Finn swallowed nervously and picked up the cup again to give his hands something to do which did not involve plucking a hairpin out of all that wonderful hair and running his fingers through it greedily.

'Lovely?'

It came out part sigh, part whisper, and she brought her hand to rest on her chest, which, of course, drew his eyes back to that impressive part of her anatomy. They hungrily flicked over the hint of cleavage before he forced them back to her face, only to find that she was blushing at the compliment. A blushing Miss Bradshaw was such a uniquely charming sight that he had the sudden urge to touch the blush and feel the heat that was coming from her skin.

And to his complete consternation, the hand not holding the coffee cup did exactly that. It would not be stopped. His palm cupped her cheek and her dark eyes widened, allowing the early morning sun that crept through the windows to turn the golden flecks within her irises molten. Her skin was so soft, like velvet rather than silk, and the blatant femininity enticed him to trail the pad of his thumb over the apple of her cheek before he snatched the hand away as if he had been bitten and stuffed it behind his back. 'I trust your search for a house is coming along swiftly.'

It was better to get himself back on to an equal footing. He did not want her here. He did not want *anyone* here. Finn wanted nothing more than to be left alone with his memories of Olivia and the guilt that was his constant companion. Miss Bradshaw was one of the main reasons why he kept forgetting it.

He watched her pull back in confusion. 'My attorney will be writing to me any day now with his selections, then I shall have to visit them all.'

'Excellent. The sooner you view what is on offer, the sooner you and your aunt can leave.' And he could return to normal. And stop wanting.

'Why must you always be so disagreeable, Lord Finnegan?' Finn did not bother answering as he was already escaping through of the door.

Chapter Eight

Evie sat on the bank of the stream and swished her feet lazily in the water. Try as she might, she could not get the events of this morning out of her head. Finn's odd reaction to her new dress and hairstyle had confused her. When he had told her that she looked lovely she had believed him. For a moment, she had seen it in his eyes and the warm burst of enjoyment that had shimmered through her at the compliment had completely disarmed her. That handsome brooding man actually thought she was lovely. Her? Evie Bradshaw. It had been almost too much.

Then he had touched her face so tenderly and all logical thought disappeared from her head in a whoosh as her nerve endings positively tingled with anticipation at the smallest brush of his fingertips. Evie had held her breath nervously and gazed into his eyes hoping he would do more.

He had quickly come back to his senses, though, and had murdered the sweet moment with his usually cutting words, sending her crashing back to earth with a thud. What he had meant as a simple compliment she had misconstrued as more, like the pathetic dolt that she was. As if mere hope would suddenly render her more attractive! What a needy fool.

He had been right about one thing. She did need to find her own house sooner rather than later. Every single day that she spent with Finn, Evie found herself becoming more and more attached to him. Being soft-hearted was something Evie was used to being, but developing tender feelings for a man who was out of her reach and still hopelessly in love with his dead wife was foolish, even by her standards. It could not end well. He would continue in blissful ignorance and Evie would likely get her heart broken. If only he was more like his brother, then she would not be having this problem.

The conundrum that was the Matlock twins had her confused. As men, they looked almost identical, yet her female reaction to them was not. When Fergus had briefly touched her face at their engagement party she had wanted to swat it away like a gnat. When Finn had done the same this morning she had wanted to press her lips into his palm and kiss it. Whom was she fooling? If he had not retracted his hand with such ferociousness, Evie would have turned her face into his palm and kissed it. She had never had such a physical reaction to a man in her life.

Mind you, the closest she had ever got to intimacy with any man in her twenty-five years was a quick brush of the cheek from both Matlock twins. It was hardly a reliable gauge to assess things by. Clearly her new-found freedom was having an altogether unforeseen effect on her personality. She could not even muster the enthusiasm to paddle in the stream this afternoon because she was too busy mooning about him. Rude, surly, tortured and tender Finnegan Matlock. With a sigh, she lay back on the bank and stared at the patterns the fluffy clouds were making, and when her eyelids began to close Evie let them.

The sound of hoofbeats woke her up and she sat up with a start at exactly the same moment as Lord Finnegan crested the opposite bank on his enormous horse. By the speed of the animal and the way he was bent low in the saddle, poised, she realised that he had intended to jump the stream. Unfortunately, he and his fearsome horse were as surprised to see her as she was to see them. He barely had enough time to stop his mount from hurtling through the air and landing on her and probably crushing her to death in the process. He tugged violently on the reins and the big chestnut reared, throwing its rider from the saddle as if his big body weighed nothing at all.

Helpless, Evie watched Finn fall backwards, not on to the soft bank, but on to the gnarled, sharp remnants of what had once been a tree still embedded in the soft mud. The old wood splintered noisily when his back hit it with an ominous thud. Then he did not move. Were it not for the agonised groaning coming from his vicinity she feared that he might have been killed.

'Lord Finnegan!' Evie waded into the stream quickly to get to him, only to become entangled in her own skirts. Hands outstretched, she fell forward into the water and had to scramble the rest of the way up the bank on her knees.

He was twisted at an odd angle. One arm was thrown backwards, the other clutched his ribs. Blood oozed from a cut at the side of his head, his eyes were squeezed tightly shut. 'Lord Finnegan. Are you all right?' Evie clambered along his prone body and pressed one wet palm to his forehead.

'C-can't breathe!' His chest was rising and falling erratically. She had to calm him.

'Inhale slowly. Fill your lungs before you exhale.' Evie tried to demonstrate using her own lungs, in the hope that would be of some use.

'C-can't. Your f-fault. Get off my b-blasted chest, you s-stupid woman!'

Realising that she had, in fact, plastered herself on top of him, Evie scooted off, mortified. It was no wonder he had struggled to breathe, with her immense bulk crushing him. However, although his eyelids eventually fluttered open, his breathing still remained staccato and it was obvious he was in intense pain. 'I need to move you to flat ground.' Evie brushed away as much of the tangled wood as she could and then slipped her hand gently beneath his shoulders. As she tried to lift him up, he yelped and squeezed his eyes shut again.

'Stop!'

'But I have to move you, Lord Finnegan. There is a tree stump sticking into your back.'

'I am well aware of that! Just give me a moment…' He sucked in a pained breath and nodded, so Evie heaved again. He was much heavier than he looked and she ended up having to grip him tightly with both arms in order to get any purchase. Unfortunately, in doing so, she almost suffocated him in her bosom as she shuffled him sideways. By the time she lowered him on to the flat bank, he was quite red in the face and clearly in agony. The cut on his head was bleeding quite freely.

Evie stood and waded to the opposite bank to fetch her discarded basket, then rifled through it for her handkerchief. She dipped it into the stream, wrung it out and then crouched down beside him again to clean the open wound. Fortunately, it was a small puncture, but a deep one nevertheless. It would not require stitching, but it did need properly dressing. More worrying was the way his arms continued to hold his ribs as he panted for breath.

'Try to lie still while I go and fetch help. You need the physician, Lord Finnegan.' Evie went to stand and he gripped her wrist.

'No need. Just help me up.'

Even though she thought it was a bad idea, Evie did her best to support his weight while he struggled to sit up. After several seconds he slumped back in defeat. 'My ribs hurt like the devil!'

'They might be broken. You must lie still and I will fetch help.' Reluctantly he let go of her wrist. 'I will be quick.'

Evie did not wish to leave him lying so helpless for longer than was necessary and decided that it made more sense to run towards the house than the village. At least then she could get men, and perhaps a cart, to help to bring him home while another servant could be sent to fetch the physician. Fortunately, she saw some labourers in the fields who rushed to the house for her, freeing Evie to head back to the stream.

His big horse had returned and now stood loyally next to his master, nuzzling his big nose in Finnegan's partially upstretched hand. As she approached, the animal stared at her in accusation and let out an angry whinny that brought her up short. If he could have talked, Evie knew exactly what the ferocious beast would have said.

This is all your fault.

'It's all right, Horatio.' Finn did his best to soothe his horse, who was eyeing Miss Bradshaw with horsy disgust. 'I doubt she was actually trying to kill me.'

She edged nervously closer, her eyes never leaving the horse, looking every bit as bedraggled as Finn felt. 'I really did not mean to frighten you both. If it is any consolation, I feel terrible about it.'

'And so you should,' he managed curtly, trying to ignore the burning pain in his side and the way the damp, now muddy muslin of her new gown hugged the curve of her breasts.

The very fact that he was still acutely aware of the latter with potentially broken ribs said it all. If Finn had been paying attention, he would have seen her, but he had been thinking about her at the time and how badly he had reacted this morning, so the irony of her sudden appearance and the dire consequences was not lost on him. In truth, he had ridden past the stream at a safe distance, hoping to catch a glimpse of her, only to find her not there. Which was the only reason why he had allowed Horatio to head there in the first place. If he had seen her, he would have avoided her like the plague. When she suddenly appeared out of nowhere as if he had just conjured her, looking all gloriously rumpled with leaves in her hair, it had frightened the life out of him.

She still frightened the life out of him. 'Why, exactly, were you hiding?'

Her eyes flicked to him and then back to Horatio. 'I wasn't hiding. I fell asleep on the bank.'

'The best place you could find to fall asleep was a muddy bank?'

'I didn't intend to fall asleep there—it just sort of happened.'

'But you were laying there?'

'I was looking at the clouds.' She edged a little closer, still watching the horse like a hawk. 'I like the patterns and shapes that they make.'

Had Finn ever been so whimsical? If he had, he certainly did not remember it. 'I hope the clouds were worth it. You were damn lucky that you were not trampled to death.' Just thinking about having that on his conscience too made him angry and he lashed out. 'What the devil is the matter with you? Have you no sense at all, Miss Bradshaw?'

'I have plenty of sense, Lord Finnegan. This was just an unfortunate accident.' She bent down to retrieve her handkerchief, giving him a spectacular view down the front of her dress. For a moment he forgot his pain, then it all came back in a rush as he remembered he was supposed to be angry.

'You have no sense, madam. If you did, you would not be marrying my foolish brother!'

Instead of reacting, she calmly went to the water's edge and rinsed the cloth before returning to his side and kneeling next to him.

'You need to lie still, Lord Finnegan. Allowing your temper to get the better of you will just increase your discomfort.' She leaned closer to tend to the cut on the side of his head. Not only did that bring her cleavage back into his line of vision, it also forced him to smell her subtle perfume. Roses mixed with stream water. A heady mix that suited her perfectly and played havoc with his senses. Damp, her hairpins struggled with the weight of her hair. One fat curl hung about her face and occasionally trailed against his neck as she fussed.

'I should probably take a look at your ribs…' She blushed like a beetroot and refused to look at his face. 'Just to be sure there are no urgent wounds which need attending while we wait for the physician.'

Her fingers gently unbuttoned his waistcoat and then tugged at the tucked hem of his shirt. When she finally pulled it free of the waistband, he felt her hands brush against the skin of his abdomen and closed his eyes against the inappropriate sensations that brief, intimate touch created. Desperately, Finn tried to ignore the gentle probing around his ribcage and chest, or how good her flattened palm felt against his heart. She was so close that he could hear her breathing; her hair kept tickling his bared skin. Her womanly scent assaulted his nostrils and gave his damaged body ideas that, by rights, he should not be having now. Here. With her.

All in all, Finn was in hell. Lust and physical pain. Two uncomfortable sensations, neither of which he wanted to experience, yet did so simultaneously. He was strangely grateful for the damaged ribs. At least they led him away from temptation when his mind was struggling to come up with valid enough reasons to resist her and not grab her and pull her lush body greedily against his, and kiss her until they were both breathless.

She found a spot which hurt incredibly and he groaned again. 'Your skin is very warm here.' The flat of her palm rested against his side. 'That may indicate that it is broken. At the very least it is badly bruised. If they are broken, the physician will have to bind them. But do not worry—ribs heal quickly as long as you do nothing to jar them. Six weeks is usual. But the pain rarely lasts more than a fortnight. If it is bruising, then the discomfort will ease more quickly.' She talked as if she understood medicine and her confidence was soothing. 'Your head wound is minor. Are you feeling dizzy or odd?'

Odd! Definitely odd. He should be consumed by the pain rather than by her. 'No dizziness.' Just lust. Unwelcome, unexpected, carnal lust.

'That might change when you sit up, but I do not recommend that you try to do that yet. Let us wait for the physician fir— Eek!'

Finn jerked at her unexpected scream and

groaned in pain. 'Blast it all, what is the matter with you, woman?'

She was poised above his face on all fours, her eyes wide with fear, frozen. 'Your horse is trying to eat me!'

Finn gazed over her shoulder towards her shapely posterior and saw Horatio munching idly on the bottom of her dress. 'He's not eating you. He's chewing the flowers on your dress.'

'Why would he do that?' She was blinking furiously now, making him notice the long, dark lashes that framed her eyes. They took his mind off of his poor ribs.

'Horatio has always been partial to meadow flowers.'

'But they are not meadow flowers. They are embroidered.' Miss Bradshaw was clearly not overly familiar with horses.

'They look like meadow flowers to him. He has no idea what embroidery is.' Despite the worsening pain, Finn could see the ridiculousness of the entire situation. He was prostrate on the ground and they were discussing sewing techniques.

'Please make him stop.'

'Horatio, stop.'

'You might try it with a bit more conviction!'

'What else do you expect me to do, Miss

Bradshaw? Because of your cloud-watching, I can barely breathe and cannot move. Horatio understands less of the English language than he does embroidery.' Forgetting how much his ribs hurt, the throbbing temple and a new ache in the region of his ankle, Finn began to chuckle and then winced as fresh pain tore through him that made him reconsider the humour of the situation.

Clearly unimpressed with his lacklustre rescue, Miss Bradshaw began to tug at her skirts from her awkward position above him. The more she tugged, the harder the horse bit. In the end, she yanked it from Horatio's mouth with such force that she fell forward and Finn found his face buried in the very cleavage he had been doing his level best to avoid for the last few minutes. Fortunately, intense agony quashed the lust very effectively and he yelped.

'Oh, Lord Finnegan! I am so very sorry!' She scrambled to sit up and stared down at him in mortification. 'Usually I am a much better nursemaid, but your horse terrifies me and I am not used to treating a patient outside.' He watched her eyes lower to his bare chest and she reddened again. Nervousness made her babble. 'I am sure your men will be here any moment, Lord Finnegan, and then we can get you back home to Matlock House. I have sent someone for the physician as well, Lord Finnegan, and he should meet us directly when we return to the house. Does anywhere else hurt, Lord Finnegan?'

Too many Finnegans in one sentence. 'Call me Finn. I believe we know each other well enough now.' After all, he was practically naked from the waist up and he had been informally introduced to her cleavage.

'Then you must call me Evie. And I am so very sorry for being the cause of all this.'

Chapter Nine

Thankfully, the labourers returned quickly with a cart and reinforcements. Under Evie's supervision, four men lifted Finn on to the cart carefully and she sat next to him as it trundled its way back to the house. The meadow was not an ideal road. Every tiny pothole or bump in the ground jostled his ribs and aggravated his injury. Even though the journey was short, he was quite grey by the time they got him into the house. To save further pain, Evie had the men carry him into the drawing room where Aunt Winnie had already turned the biggest sofa into a makeshift bed. No sooner was he settled than the physician arrived.

As Evie had suspected, the doctor confirmed that Finn had broken a rib and quietly warned her to be mindful of the symptoms of internal bleeding just in case he developed them as the day wore on. The bruising was now quite extensive. A deep purple stain spread from just under his left armpit, down over his ribcage and seeped slightly across his chest. Even with that, Evie could not help noticing that it was quite an impressive chest.

Her only experience of the male form had come from tending to her aged, sick father for so many years. Finn's bore no resemblance to that whatsoever. The skin was pulled taut over muscles which her father had certainly not possessed and the dusting of dark hair across his upper torso, which narrowed like an arrowhead and disappeared beneath the waistband of his breeches, was a delightful addition her eyes kept drifting to when nobody was looking.

With her help, the doctor bandaged Finn's chest tightly. Finn began to complain towards the end, displaying more surliness than she had seen before, and Evie knew that he was not likely to be an easy invalid to deal with. Then the physician set about cutting off his boot to examine his badly swollen ankle and prodded and poked some more. He declared it not broken, but badly sprained, and as long as the patient kept his weight off it for a few days it should heal quickly.

'I cannot lie in bed for days on end!' Finn

loudly complained. 'Surely there is something else you can do?'

'Rest is the answer. For now, Lord Finnegan, I shall give you some laudanum to ease your pain and help you sleep.' The doctor reached into his bag for his bottle of medicine and Finn reacted violently the moment it came into view.

'No blasted laudanum! Get that stuff away from me!'

The doctor was used to being obeyed. 'Now, now, Lord Finnegan, I'll have none of that. Open your mouth, please. Just a few drops…' The bottle flew out of the physician's hands and smashed against the wall.

'I. Said. *No*. Laudanum!'

As he appeared intent on pulling himself off of the sofa, Evie stepped forward and laid a calming hand on his bare shoulder. 'It will help with the pain, Finn. The good doctor is only trying to help.' But she saw the blind panic in his eyes and decided to change tack before he hurt himself. 'I am sure that there are other remedies that can be used that are just as effective. Do you have a tisane, Doctor, or a recipe for a poultice that might do the trick instead?'

The doctor was affronted at being questioned and glared back at Finn angrily. 'Laudanum is the only medicine I will prescribe him.'

'Then you can take your quackery elsewhere. I have no further need of you!' Two sets of stubborn male eyes locked like gladiators about to go into combat.

'Might I suggest willow-bark tea for the pain? And I have read that turmeric has excellent healing properties for inflammation and bruising.' Evie smiled to try to ease the tension. She felt the corded muscles in Finn's bare shoulder relax a little at her idea, but the insulted doctor would have none of it.

'Old wives' medicine is no substitute for science, madam. You do your patient no service by bending to his ignorance.'

Finn's impressive muscles corded again and he made to get off the sofa and Evie wanted to punch the sanctimonious doctor for his own ignorance. His confrontational behaviour was only adding fuel to the flames. No matter what he believed, one would have thought that as a doctor he would have a better bedside manner with a frightened patient. And Finn was frightened. Of that, Evie was certain.

'If Lord Finnegan is adamant that he does not want laudanum, then he will not have it. It is his body, Doctor, and his decision to make. You will desist being discourteous to him.' She might well be a doormat in most situations, but deal-

ing with physicians and the sick was territory
that Evie was very familiar with. The sickroom
was the one place on this earth where she was
confident and, to all intents and purposes, this
drawing room was now one. Her own mother
had resisted laudanum for the majority of her
illness because she hated the way it made her
woolly-headed. The physician had not understood, but he had bent to their will eventually
and her mother was much happier for it. She shot
Finn a warning glance. 'Calm yourself, Lord
Finnegan. You have my word that no laudanum
will pass your lips unless you agree to it. There
are all manner of herbs we can substitute to ease
your pain.' Gratefully he flopped back down on
the sofa to allow Evie to fight his battle for him.

'I do not deal in witches' potions, madam!'

'Then as Lord Finnegan has stated, we have
no further use of your services, Doctor. Thank
you for your good work today. I shall let Stowers show you out.'

The physician opened his mouth to speak
and then snapped it shut again as the aged butler jumped to attention and ushered him to the
door. Before he left he issued a curt, 'Good day
to you both!', stuffed his hat back on his head
and marched away.

Evie turned to the housekeeper. 'Mrs Bowles,

would you be so kind to send someone to the apothecary in the village. There are a number of items that I will require.'

Ever efficient, Mrs Bowles produced a small notebook and pencil from her apron pocket. 'I shall make a list, Miss Bradshaw.'

'Excellent. We will need plenty of willow bark. White willow bark—that is the best kind. If they also have some turmeric, all the better, although it might be difficult to obtain so far out of London. Comfrey, horsetail and see if they have any lavender oil as well. I will also need you to send someone to scour the grounds for fresh lavender and camomile, too. There is bound to be some in the gardens. In the meadow, I saw some valerian flowers. They look like tiny cherry blossoms—but on a weed rather than on a tree. It can be either pink or white. If they are unsure, tell them to dig up as many wild flowers in those colours as they can and I shall sort through them. It is the roots that I need. Also, I wonder if you can find some ice.' The housekeeper nodded. 'Have it crushed and wrapped in a towel. The cold will ease Lord Finnegan's ribs and ankle while he awaits the medicines.'

'We have a little willow bark in the medicinal chest, Miss Bradshaw. Shall I have it brewed into a tea?'

'Splendid. It will take the edge off the pain for a little while.'

When the housekeeper left, it was only Evie, Aunt Winnie and Finn. Aunt Winnie appeared impressed at Evie's assertiveness. He looked greatly relieved, but physically drained.

'I can see already that you are going to be a troublesome patient, Finn. In case you have any ideas about refusing my medicines, let me warn you that any insubordination on your part and I will summon that rude physician again and leave you to deal with him yourself. I might also tell him to bring his bleeding cups and have the footmen strap you to your bed.'

'How do I know you are not trying to poison me?' His dark eyes stared back at her, amused. 'After all, you did try to throw me from my horse.'

'Fear not, young man. What Evie does not know about medicine is not worth knowing. She'll have you back on your feet in no time.'

Finn almost smiled at Aunt Winnie. 'If she hadn't knocked me off of my feet in the first place, I would not be in this position.'

Evie did her best not to look at his current position. Every time she did her face warmed and her pulse speeded up. Dressed in just his breeches and reclining on the sofa, the only cov-

ering on his distracting chest the pristine white
bandage that bound his ribs and looped over one
shoulder, he was quite the sight to see. Evie had
never been in the presence of such overpower-
ing…maleness. 'I shall fetch you a blanket.' And
spare her blushes.

'It's too hot for a blanket.'

'Leave him be, girl,' said Aunt Winnie with a
wink. 'He has been through an ordeal. Let him
be comfortable.'

No doubt her sudden defence of Finn's choice
to remain cool had more to do with the fact that
she was enjoying the spectacle rather than concerned about his temperature. Her aunt was incorrigible. Evie glared at her, but the old woman
simply grinned back at her from her strategically
placed seat opposite him.

Evie hurried out in search of the willow-bark
tea just to give her cheeks time to cool. Unfortunately, the efficient Mrs Bowles was already
coming towards her with the steaming cup in
her hands. She handed it briskly to Evie, leaving her no choice but to go back and view Finn
in all his prone, naked splendour once again.

'You need to drink all of this.' Evie pulled a
small table in front of him and placed the cup
in front of it. However, it soon became obvious
that he was having tremendous difficulty sitting

up. In the end, to Aunt Winnie's vast amusement, Evie had to kneel beside him and wrap her arms around his bare shoulders to support him while he drank. And because the tea was hot, it took him ages.

For more minutes than Evie was comfortable with, she held him, her hands touching his warm, smooth skin and having no idea where to put her eyes. If she glanced down, the arrow of dark hair on his abdomen drew her eyes below the waistband of his breeches to the unknown shape of what lay beneath them, if she glanced the other way she was confronted with his dark eyes, floppy dark hair and stubble-covered throat. Both views caused palpitations. If she closed her eyes, he would think her an idiot and know that he affected her, so, in desperation, Evie stared intently at the top of his head until he finally swallowed the last drop and she lowered him to the cushion. His eyes turned to hers and locked, causing her tummy to do a funny flip-flop.

'Thank you, Evie.' He wasn't curt or surly or rude and he was almost smiling.

'I shall leave you to rest for a bit.' He nodded and closed his eyes. Evie stood to leave and then glared at her aunt, who clearly intended to stay for the duration. 'Come along, Aunt.' For good measure she went to the old lady's chair and hoisted her unceremoniously out of it.

No sooner had Evie closed the door on their patient than Aunt Winnie spoke, a little too loudly for Evie's liking. 'Well, he is a fine specimen, isn't he? It's been years since I enjoyed the sight of fine, strong chest in all its glory. I don't see why you insisted on dragging me away. I could look at him for hours.'

Evie made sure she was several feet away before she answered. 'Have you no shame, Aunt? The poor man is injured.'

Winnie was unrepentant. 'I was having an adventure. We came here to have an adventure, didn't we?'

'Ogling an injured man is not an adventure. It is voyeurism.'

'Well, in that case you were being voyeuristic, too. I saw you looking at his chest when you thought nobody was looking.'

'I most certainly was not looking at his chest!' All of the outrage in the world was not going to stop the blush that bloomed violently on Evie's face and neck. Her aunt took one look at it and laughed.

'Liar. You were looking at his fine chest as much as I was. In fact, at one point you were staring at like it like a slab of the finest roast beef. Your mouth was watering. Not that I can blame you. It is quite a splendid chest and that bandage is quite dashing. Perhaps you set your sights on the wrong brother?'

'I have no interest in Fergus. You know I have no intention of marrying that wastrel.'

'Then what is to prevent you from *really* going after his brooding brother, then? Now wouldn't that be an adventure…?'

Evie rearranged her stiff body on the make-shift bed she had made out of two wingback chairs next to Finn's bed and tried to get comfortable. She had no idea what the time was, but as it was still pitch black and, as her patient was murmuring more in his sleep as the medicines wore off, she assumed it was somewhere in the small hours. Of course, nobody knew she had bedded down here. Sleeping in the same room as a man was vastly improper—but she could hardly leave him to his own devices when it was practically her fault that he was in the state that he was. Besides, from here, she could monitor his pain more effectively. Experience had taught her that it was better to keep on top of the medicines rather than let them wear off completely. It caused the patient less discomfort and ultimately that made the nursemaid's life much easier, too. Especially when the patient was as ill-tempered and troublesome as Finn was turning out to be.

He had borne the pain stoically enough—however, in doing so, he had become surlier than usual. Already, Evie knew that his pain was at its worst when his temper was at its foulest. After the initial treatment with the doctor and Mrs Bowles's strong willow-bark tea, he had rested quietly for a while. Not more than an hour later he was shouting at the servants and demanding that they remove him from the drawing room as swiftly as was possible. Evie had heard his ranting from the kitchen, where she had been brewing a sleeping draught from the valerian flowers, and had dropped what she was doing and rushed down the hallway only to find him almost upright and determined to hop from the room if he had to on his one good foot.

'What do you think you are about? Lie down immediately.'

The worried servants had gratefully parted like the Red Sea to allow her to march towards him with her hands on her hips. Even Aunt Winnie appeared cowed by his vehemence.

'I do not like this room!' His eyes had flicked briefly to the huge painting of his wife, then res-

olutely away to glare at her. 'I have work to do.
I am going to my study!'

'You will not be working, Finn. You have to
rest. Perhaps if I gave you some more willow-
bark tea you will feel better?'

'I am not drinking any more of your potions,
madam. You will slip laudanum into them!'

'I promised you that I would not.' With unreasonable invalids it was imperative to remain
calm. 'To that end I am in the process of making
a tisane out of herbs to relieve your pain and a
sleeping draught for tonight in the kitchen. Your
own loyal servants will vouch for me.'

'Unless I actually see what you put in them,
I will not take them!' His square jaw was set
stubbornly, but Evie could see the tension about
his eyes had nothing to do with his temper and
everything to do with his pain. There was also
no point in arguing with him. He was well beyond the point of reason. Already he was poised
to argue back.

'Stowers—could you organise a *chaise
longue* to be made up in the kitchen, please?
Lord Finnegan will be supervising me there.'
That stunned him. He blinked several times before he sat back on the sofa with a surly expression on his face. Evie fussed and plumped the
cushions behind his head and then sat on the

edge of the same sofa. 'As soon as your new bed is ready, I shall see to your removal from this room. I will ensure that it is done swiftly. But until I come back to fetch you, you will lie still and you will desist from taking out your temper on those unfortunate enough to be near you. While you wait, you will talk to Aunt Winnie and you will try to remember that you are a gentleman.'

'Who are you to be so bossy to me? This is *my* house.' Of course, there would be a flash of defiance.

'For the duration of your incapacity, Lord Finnegan, I am your nurse and I will not be trifled with.' He was not the only one who could have a steely glint in his eye. 'Your servants already understand that. Your life will become much easier as soon as you accept it as well.' Evie stood up and smiled down at his sulking face. 'Unless you would prefer me to summon the physician again?'

His eyes narrowed, but there was amusement swirling in those troubled depths. 'You have lied to me, Miss Evelyn Bradshaw.'

'I do not lie, Lord Finnegan.'

'I beg to differ. You told me you were a doormat. From where I am sitting, all I see is a harridan.'

In the kitchen he had been her inquisitor.

'What is that yellow powder?'

'Turmeric. It is a spice from India. It has been used in the east for centuries to reduced inflammation. I shall blend it with horsetail, which has similar properties, and add both to the willow-bark tea.' He had examined every herb, asked what it did and then watched her like a hawk as she boiled and strained her potions, bottled them and wrote labels on them. By the time she had finished, he was well aware of the fact that she had used comfrey to help mend his broken bones, willow bark for pain, lavender, camomile and valerian to relax him and help him to sleep. Evie placed them all in a basket. 'I shall have this basket transported everywhere with you, then you can be sure I am not slipping in anything untoward while you are under my care.'

Eventually, when it had all got too much for him, Finn had allowed her to give him a sleeping draught before being taken to his proper bed quite early in the evening. He had been sleeping fitfully ever since.

He moaned again and Evie saw his eyelids flutter. It was probably time that she gave him the willow-bark tea she had left to keep warm by the fire. She padded towards the metal pot and poured some into the sipping cup she had found in the kitchen. Much as the sight of the thing had offended him earlier, it proved to be the most effective way of getting him to drink while semi-reclined, and even though he would grumble and pout about it, he would drink it if Evie stood firm. Bracing herself for his stubbornness, she gently woke her patient.

Chapter Ten

Finn was having a lovely dream and he always allowed himself to have dreams. They were the only times he allowed himself to forget about the grim reality of his life. Dreams were not real, therefore enjoying one was harmless.

In this one Evie was running her fingers through his hair and stroking his cheek. *'Finn,'* she was whispering in that breathy voice that she had when she was close, *'I need you to wake up.'*

So in his dream he did as she commanded and as he had hoped she was in that proper night-gown, all buttoned up, her long hair bound in one thick plait, tied at the ends with one fat ribbon.

One tug and the ribbon undid, floated to the floor where it belonged and he let his hands linger in the ends of her hair. Silk. Just as he had imagined. At her neck was another ribbon and he knew if he tugged on it the top of that oh-so-proper nightgown would fall to the floor, too. And she would be naked underneath, exactly as he wanted. Finn let his dream self slowly wind one hand around that plait as she bent above him, gently drawing her face towards his until they were only a whisper apart. Then because he wanted to, he kissed her and she tasted exactly as he had hoped she would. Soft. Sweet. Like ripe summer strawberries just picked from the field.

At the side of a sick bed was the very last place Evie had expected her first kiss to occur, therefore when it happened it came as quite a shock. A pleasant, wholly unforeseen shock, which rendered her temporarily frozen and unable, or unwilling, to put an end to it. Even half-asleep, with broken bones and in pain, Finn was a heady mix more potent than the very best French champagne. The effects were surprisingly similar. Her legs became unsteady, her skin warmed and her body became far too languid as her wits had fainted dead away. She was hardly surprised when she found herself kissing him back. It was only when she felt his fingers working to undo the ribbon at her neck that she stopped floating on air and planted her feet unsteadily back on the ground.

Evie gently disentangled the offending hand and reluctantly prised her mouth from his. He sighed contentedly, but, as his eyes were still closed and his breathing was heavy, it was fairly safe to say that he was still asleep. Why else would he have kissed her, unless he had been dreaming about someone else? His wife probably. She had seen the intense pain wash across his features when he had glanced briefly at her portrait. His grief had been so raw and appeared so fresh it was obvious he had not come to terms with her death, nor had his love for her diminished. To weave fanciful ideas about a man still clearly besotted with the woman in the graveyard was futile. Evie knew that. Therefore, it was prudent to guard her foolish heart as best as she could and put all thought of his accidental kiss firmly out of her mind.

This time, when she tried to wake him, she tapped him on the arm rather than smoothing her palm over his cheek, because it had been that tender gesture that had caused the problem, and she stood a little awkwardly while she waited for him to come around. 'Finn, I need you to wake up. You have to take your medicine.'

His voice, when it eventually came, was gravelly, sleep-slurred and surly. 'Don't want your damn medicine, Evie. Go away.' Now she knew he was awake, but still continued to tap his arm in case he drifted off again.

'I will go away once you have had it and not before.'

After much grumbling, he stared at her murderously through one open eye. 'Then give me the blasted stuff and be gone, woman.'

Evie did just that, sliding her arm against his back to support his head and trying to ignore the warmth of his bare skin and the strange sensations that she continued to experience even though he was no longer kissing her and appeared blissfully ignorant of the fact that he had been. Once he was done, she plumped his pillow and settled him back down and his eyes closed again immediately. Within minutes all she could hear was his rhythmic breathing as Morpheus claimed him again. Only then did Evie climb back on to her makeshift bed and snuggle into the most comfortable position she could manage in such a confined space, although why she did that was a mystery. Sleep would be impossible now. Not when her lips still tingled and her body still yearned for the man who slept soundly, completely unaffected, next to her. The man who dreamed about his dead wife at night and mourned her every day.

Finn woke at dawn, his body as stiff as a board and hurting like hell. His mouth was also so dry that his tongue was sticking to the roof of it and his throat was practically burning, it was so raw. Next to his bed he spied a glass of water and the cold, clear liquid had never been so appealing as it was now. When he tried to move to reach it, pain tore through his side, leaving him feeling limp and helpless. The latter was an uncomfortable emotion to experience. Aside from the odd cold or sprain, he had never suffered a day's sickness in his life. While he could endure the pain well enough, he disliked being so dependent on others for anything. Even something as mundane as that elusive glass of water.

He turned his head to the other side to reach the bell-pull and that was when he saw her. Curled on her side, her elegant hands folded beneath her cheek, wild hair loose and tangled all about her face and shoulders, sound asleep. By the look of the rumpled blanket on the chairs she was draped across, she had been there for most of the night. The sight and the implication startled him at first, followed by the unfamiliar warmth of gratitude. Finn had been nothing but boorish to her, yet she had stood up for him with the doctor, indulged his fears about medicines, nursed him all yesterday and then given up her own comfortable bed to watch over him through the night. It had been a long time since he had experienced that sort of concern from another human being and had forgotten how pleasant a sensation being cared about could be.

Having spent more hours of his life than he cared to remember trying to sleep on a chair, Finn was loath to wake her no matter how thirsty he was. She was sound asleep now and, considering the hardness of the furniture, she had probably slept fitfully for most of the night, if at all. Besides, if he warmed his muscles up a bit, he could probably fetch his own water soon enough. To that end, he began to stretch and flex his limbs and torso from his horizontal position on the mattress and simply watched her sleep.

Evie was a puzzle. At times, painfully uncertain of herself. She had described herself to him as a doormat and, having seen the supreme effort that it took for her to be assertive, Finn believed it. Yet beneath that nervous exterior was a seam of whimsy that ran straight through her. Why else would she while away hours paddling in the stream with wild flowers in her hair? Yet she could be decisive. Her performance in front of the doctor yesterday had been magnificent and she had certainly put him in his place a time or two—which made her betrothal to his brother all the more confusing.

She claimed she wanted a new, independent life away from the stepfamily who made her miserable, yet Fergus would cause her nothing but misery. Since his disappearance over a week ago, she had not appeared to miss his presence once as far as Finn could tell—and for all he knew, maybe that was why she had chosen Fergus in the first place. Perhaps she wanted an absent husband as she had claimed she did. As a wife, Evie would certainly have a great deal more freedom than she would as an unattached woman. Was that the overriding attraction? Marriages of convenience were still remarkably commonplace, except Fergus would eat up Evie's fortune in no time and then where would she be? Impoverished independence left a lot to be desired. She did not strike him as empty-headed. Far from it, in fact. Surely there was an ulterior motive in selecting Fergus or else it made no sense. Unless she really had been ground down by her stepmother and firmly believed that that wastrel was all she could get?

Then again, even in the short time she had

been in Yorkshire, Finn had witnessed a tremendous change in her. With any luck, she would come to her senses well before she married his feckless brother. Either way, it was not Finn's business, no matter how much he felt that it ought to be. Miss Evie Bradshaw was a full-grown woman and capable of making her own decisions. Full-grown, full-bosomed and more womanly than she had a right to be. More Aphrodite than doormat. It was just a shame all of that tempting womanliness was going to be wasted on Fergus.

Gingerly, Finn propped himself up on his good side on one elbow. It smarted a bit, but nothing too awful, so he levered the rest of his body upwards with the other arm. That hurt, but he persevered. Little by little he was able to shuffle his body to sit, although the effort of it robbed him of breath and caused fine beads of sweat to gather on his forehead. He paused for a second to equilibrate, then reached out his arm to fetch the glass, only to find that his fingertips barely touched it. Clutching his bound ribs to support them, Finn lurched forward and grabbed the vessel. But the inevitable shot of pain was delayed and when it came it was merciless. The glass slipped out of his grip and shattered on the floor.

Evie sat bolt upright and blinked at him, alarmed.

'I broke a glass,' he offered lamely, feeling inordinately stupid to be so pathetically helpless. 'I wanted some water.'

'You should have woken me.' She stood then and parts of her enticing body jiggled slightly with the motion, making Finn wish that he had the power to see right through her offensively proper nightgown, then jiggled more as she shoved her feet into her slippers and made her way to the other side of the bed, wafting the sultry scent of roses in her wake. She found another glass and refilled it from the jug before handing it to him with a smile. 'How do you feel?'

'Like I have been run over by a drover's cart.' He drained the glass and held it out for more. 'Your foul-smelling witches' brew worked, however, I slept surprisingly well, all things considered.'

'Valerian root has been used for thousands of years to aid sleep, so it is hardly a witches' brew, although I believe hundreds of years ago it was also used in love potions. I have always found that surprising, especially as it smells so terrible.' She had crouched down and begun to gather together the shards of glass splintered on the floor. If he glanced her way, the jiggling was too distracting so Finn stared into his water glumly. It was a poor substitute for watching her.

'How do you know so much about herbs? Assuming that you are not a witch, that is.'

'I taught myself. When my mother fell ill, like you she also disliked the idea of laudanum because it rendered her insensible and I hated the idea of blood-letting. I never thought it ever did any good, especially as I have often read that soldiers in battle can die from loss of blood. If a lack of blood can kill you, why would there be any health benefits to withdrawing it?' She shook her dark head as she carefully piled the shards of glass neatly altogether. 'I began reading Culpeper's *Complete Herbal* and decided to try some of the plants he suggested instead. When they worked as well, if not better, in some cases, as the physician's treatments, I began experimenting. I read more books and brewed my own concoctions.'

Finn recalled how deftly she had mixed the ingredients, almost as if it were second nature. 'You must have mixed a lot of medicines.'

She lifted her head and shrugged. 'I cared for my mother for two years before her illness finally killed her. Then my father had his stroke the next year and I cared for him for another six years until he passed away in his sleep. One becomes quite adept as mixing medicines after almost a decade of experience.'

Ten years of playing nursemaid? Finn had done less than four and that had been hard enough, both physically and emotionally, and apparently she had not made her patients feel like a burden to her. This woman was practically a candidate for sainthood. 'Did you not consider hiring a proper nursemaid for either of them?'

'Not for my mother. I hated the idea of her being looked after by a stranger. She was a very private woman and caring for a sick person is such an intensely personal job. I did consider it for my father—I was older then and selfishly wanted to go out to balls and parties. However, Hyacinth felt that his needs would be better served by a member of the family and my father agreed with her.'

'She married your father—I believe she would have taken a vow to care for him in sickness as well as in health. Surely, as his wife, she should have been the one to nurse him?'

He watched her shrug again and not meet his eye. 'She could not commit to the undertaking. Not when she had two daughters to launch into society.'

'She had three daughters. All three needed

launching. Did you not have a Season or were you relegated to the role of just a nursemaid?'

She took her time answering, using the broken glass as an excuse, but as the silence stretched and he continued to wait she had no choice other than to respond. 'By the time my father had died, that ship had sailed. I was too old to be a debutante so there was no point in wasting money on a Season. All of it passed me by, and by the time I was free I was already consigned to the shelf.' The cheerful tone belied the wistful look in her pretty eyes. 'Which is why I left. I was tired of other people feeling sorry for me and bored of feeling sorry for myself.'

'As the misused wife of my brother, the people hereabouts will also feel sorry for you.'

Chapter Eleven

Evie hesitated for a moment as she considered confessing the truth. Then she remembered Finn was only tolerating her presence because he believed she would become part of the family one day. How had he put it? They were to be brother and sister—except the feelings she was developing for Finn were far from sisterly. It was sensible to maintain her charade for the time being.

'I do know Fergus is, perhaps, not the most obvious choice of husband and I am not blind to his many faults, but when a woman has been sat on the shelf as long as I have I was hugely relieved to know that anybody wanted to marry me at all.'

Now Finn appeared to be quite horrified. 'You cannot sell yourself so short like that, Evie. You are a lovely, attractive young woman who deserves to have the sort of husband she truly wants, rather than the sort she believes is all she can get. I am certain that there are many gentlemen out there who would want such a splendid wife and none of them anywhere near as troublesome as my awful brother. Unless it is his title that is important to you?'

'Of course it isn't.' It was not as if the title would ever be hers any more than Fergus would be.

'Then I am baffled as to why you would pick Fergus above all of the other men in England. He is never going to be anything close to a loving husband.' She could see concern for her swirling in his dark eyes. Brotherly concern and pity.

'Please do not feel sorry for me. When I chose Fergus, I did so with my eyes wide open. I believe that our arrangement will suit me quite well.' Evie briefly considered telling him the absolute truth about the arrangement, then decided against it. One day soon, once she had signed the deeds to her new home, she would calmly tell Finn the truth. He deserved that. She had no intention of marrying the dissolute Marquis—had *never* had any intention of marrying the dissolute Marquis—but she would not bare her hand just yet. Just in case Finn ceased feeling brotherly and tossed her out of his house for lying to him.

'I am curious,' Finn asked, gazing into her eyes as if he were seeking the absolute truth and causing her pulse to hammer because she was certain he knew she was lying. 'How can a marriage to a man that you do not love, and by your own admission has many, *many* faults, ever be the sort of arrangement that suits you?'

'Fergus is not the sort of man to want to be shackled to the country and I am not the sort of woman who would be content to live with him in town. Therefore, I shall live out my days here in Yorkshire and see as little of my husband as it is possible to see.' Saying it like that did sound a little callous, which was not exactly the impression Evie wanted to give him, but it was the truth at least. It would be safest to stick to as much of the truth as possible because she was such a dreadful liar.

'So you really are marrying Fergus so that you do not have to spend any time in his company? Now I truly am confused.'

For some inexplicable reason, Evie found herself confessing things she had never confessed to another living soul. 'My father was a selfish man. When my mother died, he was lost. In his grief, all he could think about was his own loneliness. As a fifteen-year-old girl who had just lost her mother, his despair terrified me. Instead of properly grieving, he appeared determined to replace her quickly so that he could get on with his life. He set about finding a new wife as soon as he could when he should have been still in mourning. Within a year, my stepmother Hyacinth had wheedled her way into our lives. I do not believe she ever had any true affection for my father, but she did have a great deal of affection for his fortune—and especially for what that fortune could mean to her own daughters. Because he was self-centred and vulnerable, and because Hyacinth was—is—a handsome woman and skilled at manipulation, his head was turned. He did not see Hyacinth's many faults and misguidedly believed that she held him in the same esteem as he held her.'

'What is the old saying? Marry in haste?'

'Indeed.' They shared a smile and it felt as though Finn understood. It was reassuring to know he did not appear to judge her for criticising her father. 'To begin with, it was odd, but not too difficult. My father was happier and therefore I was happy for him, and he made me promise to treat her with the same regard as I had my real mother. It did not matter that my relationship with Hyacinth was uncomfortable and I made allowances for the spiteful behaviour of her daughters because they were younger than me, because I knew it was what my father wanted. He abhorred confrontations of any sort and preferred to ignore the conflicts. But we never really became a family, if you know what I mean? There was Hyacinth and her daughters, Hyacinth and my father and then there was me. I could not shake the impression that my new stepfamily resented me in some way.'

'You felt left out—and it does not seem as if your stepmother ever had any intention of including you. You called your new sisters spiteful—that is an interesting assessment.'

Evie tried not to feel the usual discomfort or resentment that came when thinking about her 'sisters' as she clarified, 'They liked to point out my flaws, especially as they are willowy and blonde and I am neither. They never did it in front of my father—not that he was the sort of man to confront them on such behaviour.' Which had hurt a great deal. 'But they openly did it in front of Hyacinth.'

'And how did she respond?'

'Mostly she agreed with them. As time went on she became my greatest critic and her criticisms encouraged her daughters to be nastier. Apparently, even at sixteen Hyacinth could see that I would be very difficult to marry off with all of my many imperfections.' Finn's outraged expression on her behalf warmed her. 'Shortly after their hasty marriage, my father had a stroke which rendered him bedridden for the remainder of his life. From that point on, he and Hyacinth had very little to do with one another, even though he lived for another six years. She much preferred to spend her days enjoying the spoils of being a rich merchant's wife and I found myself playing nursemaid again. I try not to resent it, but I never had a Season so there was never any opportunity to meet a man who might have wanted to marry me, even if I was bound to be difficult to marry off.'

Finn shook his head angrily. 'Of course you should resent it! Hyacinth was his wife. She made a vow before God to care for your father in sickness and in health. It beggars belief that she forced you to be a nursemaid or that your selfish father condoned it. The pair of them robbed you of the life you were meant to have.'

Evie felt herself wince at the criticism of her father, even though a huge part of her wanted to agree with Finn. But doing so felt too disloyal. She had promised him to be a dutiful daughter. Even though she could not adhere to that wish with her thoughts, she had stalwartly done so with her deeds. 'I suppose it made sense I should be the one to care for him. By then I had already

garnered an extensive knowledge of medicine
and how to run a sickroom.'

'How very *convenient* for Hyacinth. A rich
husband and a dutiful stepdaughter who was
too good natured and kind to refuse to do what
was asked of her. And I will wager she made no
attempt to relieve you from the onerous task.'
Finn's hand had reached out to touch the back
of Evie's, although his eyes were stormy. He was
angry for her. 'No wonder you loathe the woman.'

Evie's own suppressed anger began to bubble. 'Hyacinth did absolutely everything in her
power to ensure that I stayed out of society during those crucial years. Having to deal with me
took her away from her own precious daughters
and she was determined to see that they made
fortuitous matches. And, of course, the cost of
their presence in the *ton* came out of my father's
purse. I believe it came as a tremendous shock
to her to discover, upon my father's passing, that
he had not left his entire fortune to her—but
to me. In fairness, I was shocked by it also. He
never had a bad word to say about the woman.
He always took her side and always insisted I
should respect her and heed her advice. After a
while I stopped fighting against her. I am certain his failure to change his will was an oversight on his part.'

'Do you really think so?'

Evie shrugged. Being endowed with such a huge amount of money had come as a great surprise and one that she had been ill prepared for. Her father had certainly given her no clue as to his intentions. Right up to the end he became upset if Evie criticised his second wife, so she always backed down until backing down had become a habit.

'By then, of course, both her daughters were out and seeking titled husbands who expected those girls to have big dowries. My stepmother is no pauper. She already had a respectable amount of money from her first husband's death—and then my father left her a very generous sum to keep her for the rest of her life, but it is not enough for Hyacinth. She was outraged. Still is outraged. Since then, I have become the main source of funding for her and her daughters' lavish life in London. I get to pay all of the bills and watch them enjoy themselves from the fringes because, to quote my stepmother, my boat had long since sailed and the money might as well be spent on something useful.'

'If you have a vast fortune Evie, why did you not leave your dreadful stepmother the moment your father died and set up your own household?'

A very good question. Especially as the house in Mayfair, technically, was Evie's household to begin with. 'I am not very good at sticking up for myself. In London, I am a forlorn spinster with nothing but a dull life of spinsterhood ahead of me. I blend into the wallpaper and allow myself to be treated like a doormat. At best, I am pitied by everyone. At worst, I am a source of malicious gossip. Marrying Fergus gave me the perfect excuse to escape my life before it really was too late.'

Finn did not look convinced. 'Does it not bother you that you are swapping an existence of being your stepfamily's doormat to become Fergus's doormat? What makes you think your life will be any better with him?'

For a start, the very long engagement Evie had planned was already turning out much better than the last ten years had ever been. She had nice dresses, paddled in the stream, went for walks. Felt freer. And that was only the start of the great adventure into life that Evie had planned for herself. She carefully carried the broken glass to the door, grateful of the excuse to escape his intelligent eyes, which saw too much and tempted the truth to spill from her lips. 'I am hopeful that it will turn out all right in the end.' Which was the truth, sort of. 'And I am in no great hurry to marry Fergus. In a few months, if things do not look more optimistic for our life together, I will call off the engagement.' Which had always been the plan in the first place, so not an altogether lie.

'I am vastly relieved to hear it.'

Chapter Twelve

Finn had a way of scrutinising her, as if he saw
right through her brave words to the wounded
creature underneath who still yearned for all
of the things which her circumstances had denied her. It made Evie want to squirm. Perhaps
if she had been prettier and not as plump then
a gentleman might have still wanted to wed her
and Evie could have had a family of her own
one day. But she had been born plain and timid.
Even in this last year, when her path had eventually crossed with single, unattached gentlemen,
she had never quite known what to say or how
to behave around them. Self-conscious and awkward, it had been easier to try to blend with the
wallpaper. The memory of the brief kiss and the
embarrassment she had for her needy response
compounded her discomfort and once again
Evie wished she was rendered invisible, only

this time from Finn. Especially as just looking at him, all rumpled from sleep and in need of a shave, made her traitorous lips tingle with desire, the stupid dolt that she was.

Fortunately, as he was behaving in his usual forthright manner and had thus far failed to mention it, it gave her hope he remained unaware of what had inadvertently transpired between them. If he suddenly remembered, and recalled the fact that she had been, briefly, quite wanton, she did not know what she would do aside from spontaneously combust from the shame. Already, she could feel her cheeks heating just thinking about it, or perhaps that was simply the effect of seeing his bare chest again. In daylight it was just as impressive, even with the bandage, and equally as distracting. Her eyes kept wandering to it and had done since the moment they had awoken and it was becoming increasingly difficult to tear them away.

Evie used the broken glass and the fact that he was now awake as an excuse to escape him. 'I shall send a maid in to clean this up while I see to the preparation of some more of my foul witches' brew.'

'I do not want to sleep,' he said adamantly, 'I will take the stuff that stops the pain, but I have work to do. No dreadful valerian root till bedtime.'

'You cannot work, Finn. You must rest and give your bones time to recover.'

'This estate does not run itself, Evie. I have no manager to do it for me. Wages need to be paid, instructions need to be given. I cannot do those things from the sick bed.' Evie merely nodded. From the stubborn set of his jaw she knew that there would be no point in arguing with him yet. When she returned, she would find a way to make him see sense, the impossible man. 'And send up Stowers. He can help me dress.'

Evie dashed to her room first and tidied herself up. Her hair was a veritable bird's nest, thanks to Finn's removal of her hair ribbon, and she could not bring herself to return to him in such a state even though she doubted he really cared about her appearance one way or another. In no time, she had washed and had pinned her heavy, wayward locks neatly to her head. She put on one of her new dresses, only partially out of futile vanity, but more because of her continued desire to cast off all remnants of her past. The new clothes gave her more confidence and now that she had been kissed by Finn, Evie definitely needed more confidence. She could hardly go about the next few days in a perpetual state of mortification, although she suspected it was a foregone conclusion.

Only when she was satisfied with her reflection did she venture downstairs to begin steeping the herbs for his tea and organising a suitable breakfast to be arranged.

By the time she headed back up the stairs with everything balanced on one tray, Evie was almost in control of herself again. Unfortunately, the sight which met her eyes the moment she re-entered his bedchamber left her unravelled afresh. Perhaps even more so.

'What do you think you are doing?'

He had hauled himself out of bed and then clearly got into difficulties. Apart from the rakish bandage, all he was wearing were his drawers. The waist had become unlaced during the night, so they hung low on his hips, showing more male flesh—smooth, golden, muscled male flesh—than Evie had seen on anyone not made of marble and on a pedestal in a museum. With the floppy dark hair, ever-present dark stubble and thunderous expression, he quite took her breath way.

'I got fed up waiting for Stowers. I decided to dress myself.' But he was leaning awkwardly against the bed post, all of his weight resting on his good arm and leg. His left ankle was still considerably swollen and it was obvious he was in great pain.

Common sense managed to drill through the fog of profound feminine admiration. 'You are a silly man! You will do yourself a mischief.' Evie deposited the tray on a chest of drawers and rushed to his aid, wrapping one arm around his waist to support him. Gratefully, he wrapped his own arm across the top of her shoulders and leaned on her. The intimacy of their positions made it almost impossible not to think about the solid feel of his almost naked body against hers, but Evie did her best to ignore it, and the strange fluttering it created, as she helped him to sit back down on the mattress.

'I have things to do,' he said more half-heartedly than he had before he had tried to move. 'I have to get dressed.'

Evie stepped away, thankful for the distance, staring resolutely at his face rather than his fine torso. 'First you will drink some willow-bark tea and you will eat something. Only then, if I feel you are in a fit state, will we discuss the possibility of you working for an hour or two.'

His dark brows came together in consternation, but he did not argue as she handed him the tea. He sniffed it dubiously before blowing on it, then, when he was satisfied it was cool enough, he gulped it down in three quick swallows while his face relayed his utter disgust at the taste. When Evie presented him with the bowl of porridge on the tray, the disgust turned to outrage.

'I am not eating this slop. Where is my bacon?'

'Mrs Bowles thought you might find porridge easier to digest.' Evie actually felt sorry for him. The stodgy bowl was not very appetising, but Mrs Bowles would not be swayed.

'I am injured not ill. I do not require nursery food.' Tentatively, he spooned some of the stuff into his mouth and pulled a face, but demolished it quickly none the less. 'Now fetch Stowers, woman, so that I can get dressed. You have delayed me long enough.'

'Don't you have a valet?'

He regarded Evie as if she was daft. 'What would be the point? I spend my days riding around my estate and my evenings working on my ledgers. Neither my workers nor my books care how my cravat is tied.' Another thing that set him apart from his brother. Fergus had travelled with a valet even though he could scarce afford to pay for him. 'But I believe that you are trying to engage me in conversation, Evie, in a pathetic attempt to stall me from going about my business. I have work to do.'

He really was proving to be the most trouble-some patient and would require constant watching for the next few days if he was going to mend swiftly. 'I will instruct the servants to set up a *chaise longue* in the drawing room. From there, you may work under my or Aunt Winnie's supervision. That way, if I believe that you are overtaxing yourself, I can take it away.'

'This is my house, madam, and I will work as and when I see fit.' The belligerent gleam was back in his eye, which Evie quite admired. Nothing cowed Finnegan Matlock for very long, not even broken bones. Unfortunately, for his own good she had to be firm or he would be laid up for weeks.

'I believe you will find that quite problematic in your current state. I have banished the servants from this room and none of them will come to help you without my express say so. A moment ago, you got yourself out of bed—however, you needed my help almost immediately to get back down again. Unless you agree to my terms, Finn, I will leave you here in this bedchamber until you are able to walk out of here unaided or I am satisfied you are well enough. And then you will get no work done and your estate will go to rack and ruin.' For good measure she folded her arms

across her chest and glared back at him with
what was hopefully an equally belligerent gleam.

'I shall dress myself.'

'Go ahead.'

His big hands pushed down on the edge of the
mattress and he used his knees to bring himself
upright. The effort this took was etched into his
stubborn face. When his arm came up to clutch
his ribs before he gingerly lowered himself back
down again, Evie knew she had won. She decided not to crow.

'Before I went to bed last night, I made you
some ointment to help heal your ribs. Seeing as
you are determined to come downstairs, I must
insist that it is applied to help ease your pain.'
He gave the briefest, curtest nod which made
Evie smile. 'I shall fetch it.'

By the time she had come back, he had removed his bandage. All of his manly chest was
now visible for her eyes to feast on and her pulse
speeded up at the sight. She thrust out the pot
of salve for him to apply it to himself. He stared
at it dully.

'Would you do it? Twisting hurts.'

Reluctantly, she sat next to him and Finn
turned his back towards her. The moment she
touched his skin he regretted it. Her touch was
gentle as she dabbed the cold ointment on to his

flesh. However, as soon as she began to rub it in, using her whole palm in sweeping, rhythmic circles Finn wanted to groan. He closed his eyes and bit down on his bottom lip, yet could not ignore the way her hands made his skin tingle or how much he wanted them to wander freely over the rest of his body.

Like a lover.

When her fingers slipped around the front, he almost sighed in bliss and realised that if he was going to get through the ordeal with his dignity intact, he needed to take his mind off of the sheer joy of being touched by this intoxicating female and on to more pressing matters.

'I am not going to stop counselling you to seriously reconsider marrying my feckless brother.'

For a moment her hand stilled, then she continued her ministrations. 'If I did that now, I would have to leave Matlock House. I can hardly remain here, an unmarried, unattached woman, alone in the home of a bachelor. And who would look after you then?' She said it teasingly, but he heard a note of panic in her voice and wondered if he might have inadvertently touched a nerve. 'Besides, at the moment I have nowhere else to go.'

'In a few weeks that might not be the case. You might have found a suitable property. Once you have set up your own household, you could still break the engagement and remain here in the north.' Because suddenly, the idea of her returning south, to London, bothered him. He wanted her close, even though he had no right to.

'You do seem very keen that I break my engagement. Do you live in hope Fergus will find someone better to marry than me?' She said it teasingly. He already knew her well enough to know she was smiling even though he couldn't see her face, just as he knew she inwardly believed she was somehow unworthy. That blasted Hyacinth had eroded her confidence to such an extent poor Evie was unaware of the fact she was selling herself short.

'I live in hope that *you* find someone better to marry, Evie. My brother has a tendency to make those around him miserable.' His voice faltered a little on the last syllable as her hand smoothed down the edge of his chest, grazing his nipple. Instantly, Finn's groin tightened and he clutched at the bedcovers just in case he needed to hide the evidence of his body's inappropriate response.

'You sound as if you speak from experience.' The mattress shifted as she sat back and he heard her close the jar of ointment with relief, although his nerve endings were desperate for her to continue exploring his body. His own hands now desperately wanted to explore hers. Finn did his best to make his voice sound normal.

'A huge wealth of experience, Evie, and none of it I would wish on my worst enemy.' And definitely not her kind and caring soul. Fergus would trample all over her and throw her kindness back in her face as he wilfully spent all of her money and dishonoured her. 'I urge you to reconsider the attachment, Evie.'

Again the mattress shifted as she stood. Briskly, she gathered the medicines and dishes together on the tray, never once looking at him. 'I shall think about your words, Finn. I promise. In the meantime, I shall fetch some clean bandages before I send Stowers in to help you dress. Once that is done, I shall have some footmen help you downstairs.'

A half an hour later and true to her word, Evie had him brought into the drawing room. Already, she had arranged for his ledgers to be brought in and they sat on the floor next to a *chaise longue* which sat facing the fireplace. Olivia's face loomed down at him, reminding him how tragically he had let her down and Finn realised that he would not be able to work as long as he could see her. How he hated this room now. It held too many memories he preferred to avoid. Unfortunately, if he wanted to work, he realised he probably needed to be somewhere more comfortable than his study, with its unforgiving, practical oak furniture, and he was damned if he would receive his foreman in his bedchamber like an invalid.

'Turn the bed towards the windows,' he said curtly to cover the knot of guilt which threatened to choke him. 'The light is better that way.'

Evie did not argue. She merely instructed the footmen to rearrange the furniture to his liking and then fussed over him, arranging cushions to support his neck and ribs, wafting those distracting puffs of crushed rose petals under his nostrils and tormenting him with the sight of her bound hair, before placing a lap tray over his legs to serve as a makeshift desk. Only then did she settle down into a nearby chair next her incorrigible aunt and picked up some embroidery.

Finn had done his best to ignore the trickle of ice down his back and worked for an hour on a ledger until Stowers interrupted them. 'I have the post, sir.'

There were two piles of letters on the tray and only half of them were for him. The other half, apparently, were for Winifred. The old lady took them gleefully and then retrieved a pair of wire spectacles from a pocket. 'At last the post has found us!' she announced to her great-niece. 'I do love my gossip.'

Evie smiled indulgently at the old woman and then glanced at Finn. 'Aunt Winnie has many friends back in town. When we came here and discovered that there was no Stanford House to speak off, she was concerned that nothing would find us.'

'Since the fire, everything of my brother's is sent to Matlock House as a matter of course. Letters, debt collectors, fiancées...'

She rolled her eyes playfully. 'Yes, yes. You are greatly inconvenienced by it all. I do not need reminding. Would your ill mood be improved by some tea?'

'If it is real tea, then perhaps. If it more of your boiled bark and roots, then it could turn very ill indeed.'

'Fear not, Finn, you are not due bark and roots for another hour. Real tea it is and I have asked the kitchen to make your favourite biscuits to go with it.'

Her thoughtfulness on his behalf was astounding. 'I would prefer bacon, but biscuits will do.' And he enjoyed sparring with her. 'I want it noted that they are a poor substitute.'

'It is duly noted. Perhaps tomorrow I can have a batch of bacon biscuits prepared. Such a thing is a little unorthodox, but if it improves your mood and aids your recovery I am all for it.' She poked out her tongue childishly and then blushed furiously at her silly gesture. The delightful pink blotches on her neck matched the delicate pink-tipped daisies embroidered on her new dress.

'If you are going for your customary walk this afternoon, I suggest that you change. Horatio is particularly fond of daisies and I will not be there to save you this time.'

'As I recall, I had to save myself. Your attempt was pitiful.'

Aunt Winnie chuckled maliciously, interrupting their private parrying. Or were they flirting? The thought of that brought a wave of fresh guilt. His dead wife's eyes were boring into his back accusingly and he was flirting with his brother's fiancée.

'Oh, Evie—you will love this. By all accounts, your stepsister Iris has got herself in a bit of bother again with a gentleman, but then she has always been a little loose in her favours. Lady Wortley says that there was some incident in an orangery which is the root of *much* fevered speculation. Especially as the gentleman she was allegedly found with is only just married. As she writes this, Hyacinth and her spawn have gone to ground. No one has seen them in society for a week.'

Evie did not appear particularly surprised by the news. 'Iris needs to behave more cautiously. She has always been too bold. Do you remember last year when she sneaked out of the Renshaw ball with that Russian Count? Hyacinth had the devil of a job covering up *that* indiscretion. In the end, she resorted to lying and claiming that I had been with the pair of them the entire time, as Iris's chaperon. As if Iris would ever willingly spend time with me? Or allow me to spoil her fun? I wish Hyacinth had given me some inkling she was going to use me as an excuse, though. We were at Mrs Frampton's at the time and I very nearly choked on my tea when she blurted it out. I am not sure I was very convincing.'

'Hyacinth has a daughter named Iris?' Finn could not help being drawn into the conversation despite the fact he should still be wallowing in guilt. Already, the snippets he heard about Hyacinth had him intrigued, yet he was staunchly on Evie's side. Hyacinth sounded dreadful. Almost a parody of a wicked stepmother. 'Hyacinth and Iris. Two floral names?'

'Three. She has another daughter called Rose.

Flowers symbolise beauty.' Evie's eyes twinkled. 'Hyacinth was so named because of her striking blue eyes as a baby. Iris inherited that particular feature from her mother.'

'And Rose?'

'Why, her pink lips, of course. They are exactly like Cupid's bow.'

Aunt Winnie grimaced. 'Those gals might be pretty, but two viler young ladies never walked God's earth. They have all the charm of their viper of a mother. What my nephew ever saw in that woman will remain a complete mystery until my dying day.' Clearly the old lady shared Evie's dislike of the family. She shuddered for effect and then picked up her next letter.

Chapter Thirteen

The next few hours passed, not only surprisingly swiftly, but pleasantly. Finn did a little work while the ladies gossiped or occupied themselves with reading or embroidery. Despite his desire to be left in peace on his own, he enjoyed their company. At luncheon, they all sat together at the dining table because Evie had organised a supportive wingback chair for him, before Aunt Winnie went off for her afternoon nap and Evie announced her intention to visit the village as she had another appointment with her new dressmaker.

She arranged for Finn to be taken back into the drawing room and gave emphatic instructions to the footmen that he remain there no matter how much he complained, but alone with no diversions he found the room too oppressive. Olivia's painting was staring at his back and the tentacles of guilt were clawing at his neck and threatened to strangle him. When it became impossible to focus anything other than the many ways he had let down his poor wife, Finn decided to escape the room himself.

To begin with, his pride refused to allow him to ask for help from the servants. He was not an invalid and he would certainly not be treated like one. And if his bossy nursemaid had anything to say about it, she could talk to him directly rather than conspiring with the servants against him. He managed to stand unaided and even got himself to the foot of the stairs without too much of an incident. However, the stairs proved to be his nemesis. The sprained ankle could not cope with his weight, which meant that he needed to rely on the bannister to support himself and hoist himself upwards. Unfortunately, as his broken rib was on the same side as his swollen foot, each step became agony. Either his ankle screamed in pain or his ribs did, until halfway up Finn could bear neither any more and he floundered.

For several minutes he simply stood there, gripping the bannister for dear life as he contemplated his options. Initially, he gave serious thought to simply shouting for help. However, such behaviour would not only leave him looking vulnerable, which was inconceivable, but it would also leave him exposed to Evie's censure. Already, she had beguiled the servants into fealty. How, in so short a time, he did not know. Yet there was no denying that her tyrannical stance since his accident had left all of his household bowing to her superior word. Finn might well pay their wages, but the moment one of them found him disobeying Evie's express orders, they would happily show their turncoat colours and report him to their new, voluptuous general and he would be hauled over the coals for insubordination. Even Stowers, usually so resolutely on Finn's side in all matters, had made it plain that he disapproved of Finn's getting out of bed in order to work when Miss Bradshaw believed such behaviour was contrary to his speedy recovery. For a woman who claimed she was actually a doormat, she could teach Genghis Khan a few things about maintaining discipline in his army.

In the end, he decided that his dogged determination and legendary stubbornness would eventually prevail. There were only fifteen steps left. Fifteen. Hardly an insurmountable number. They were just stairs. It might take him a few minutes, but as long as he tackled them one at a time, rather than as a whole, he would conquer them.

Ten agonising minutes later and he still had

thirteen to go and had quite run out of dogged determination. Even his legendary stubbornness was on the verge of waving the white flag of surrender. He was on the cusp of shouting for help when he heard her irritated voice behind him.

'I told you to stay on the *chaise longue*!'

The sound of her slippers on the stone stairs gave him mixed emotions. He could not deny there was intense relief at being saved. However, his appointed saviour was the one person in Matlock House he did not want to do the saving. He had only succeeded in giving the woman more ammunition against him.

'Go away, madam. I can manage well enough on my own!' His legendary stubbornness made one final attempt at mutiny and Finn used his weaker arm to haul himself up one more step before she came alongside him and took control.

'Put your arm across my shoulders, you silly man! Do I need to put a watch on you from now on? I leave this house for one hour and look what trouble you have got yourself into! Do you want to get better, Finn, or are you intent on making your injuries worse?'

Finn made no attempt to answer any of her questions. Answering would only condemn him, therefore silence was the best defence. Instead, he gratefully looped his good arm over her shoulder, hoping she would be able to take his weight. She wrapped her other arm about his hips to avoid his poorly ribs and braced her distracting body against his side.

Slowly, they made progress towards the landing. When they reached the top, she allowed him a few moments to catch his breath before she took him to his bedchamber and supported him as he lowered himself on to his mattress.

'You need more willow-bark tea and a soothing poultice.'

'I do not need a blasted poultice!'

Evie's hands propped themselves decisively on her distracting hips and she glared at him. 'You may have aggravated your injury with your abject stupidity, trying to mount the stairs on your own. A poultice will reduce the inflammation.'

He narrowed his eyes and scowled right back at her. She might have his servants tripping over themselves to do her bidding, but he was his own man and master of this house. 'Perhaps you have trouble understanding? I said. No. Blasted. Poultice!'

'If you refuse to listen to reason, then I shall have the physician called and he can deal with your surliness.'

Finn was going to strangle the stubborn wench. 'Stop threatening me with the blasted physician, woman!'

'Then stop behaving like an idiot and give your body chance to heal. If you keep pushing yourself while it is broken, you might cause something worse to happen. You might tear something internally and cause infection to set in. People die from broken bones, Finn. I would not see you be one of them.'

How typical that she would argue using logic. Sound, irrefutable, touching logic. And he was an idiot. The stairs had almost killed him.

'You told me that you were a doormat, Evie. I see no evidence of that.'

'In the sickroom I am invincible, Finn Matlock.' She began to smile. 'Fear not, though, everywhere else, I can assure you, I am still a doormat. My new dressmaker has bullied me into having a gown made with red trim. I look dreadful in red.'

'Your new gowns thus far have been lovely. Perhaps you should trust her judgement in that regard, seeing as she is the expert.'

'Words to live by, I believe. Now, about that poultice?'

Hoisted by his own petard, Finn made a face, but surrendered. It was nice to be cared about, after all. It gave him an odd, warm glow in the middle of his chest.

'I shall allow the blasted thing just this once, Evie, but I want it noted I am doing so under duress.'

Evie was not one to gloat when she had won, but she did allow herself a small smile as she headed back downstairs to prepare the medications. On the surface, Finn appeared a complicated and belligerent man—however, the more she got to know him, the less complicated he seemed. The bad temper, for instance, was all bluster which he used to ward off interference. Underneath it, there was a decent, honourable man. Perhaps a frightened man. Definitely a lonely one and that was apparently by choice rather than design. He was so different to Fergus in character, thank goodness, and despite the curmudgeonly exterior, Evie found she rather liked Finn. Quite a lot.

It was only as she carried her herbal preparations back up the stairs that she realised she would have to touch his bare skin again. This morning, she had barely got through the experience without become breathless. Memories of that brief sleepy kiss combined with the sight of his semi-nude body had been quite overwhelming. Her heart was already hammering against her ribs in anticipation by the time she reached the bedchamber door. If she touched his body again so soon, she would be a silly, panting puddle on the floor by the end of it. Feeling cowardly, she put down her tray and went off in search of Stowers. He could apply the poultice.

But Stowers was horrified at the suggestion. 'I do not know how to apply a poultice, Miss Bradshaw. I shall make a mess of it.'

'All you have to do is slap it on to his skin, Stowers. There is nothing intricate or complicated about the procedure.'

The old butler accompanied her reluctantly, helped Finn out of his shirt while Evie did her best to busy herself with other things to avoid looking at his chest, and then proceeded to make a complete pig's ear out of applying the poultice.

'Not like that, Stowers.' Evie tried to demonstrate how the thick mixture should be smoothed on to the skin by moving her hands in the air. Stowers mimicked her movements and made Finn yelp.

'Good grief, man. Those ribs are already broken. Do you know the meaning of the word gentle?'

'I told Miss Bradshaw that I was not confident of my abilities, sir, but she insisted I do it. I would be happy to stand down so that Miss Bradshaw can complete the task.' As he said this, he pushed too hard on Finn's side and he winced again. Because of her own cowardice, she was effectively causing him greater pain and that was hardly fair.

'Oh, I shall do it, Stowers!' She would just have to grit her teeth and think of other things instead of the delectable feel of intriguing muscle under skin. 'Fetch some clean bedlinens, if you please, as these are now quite soiled.'

Evie did her best to scoop up most of the spilled poultice from the sheets and the unnecessary areas of Finn's skin. Only then did she begin to apply it to his ribs in a thick layer while he lay on his side. She did her best to be as gentle as possible, but once or twice he was unable to hide the pained expression or the tightness around his jaw as he gritted his own teeth together. She also did her best not to think about the man beneath her fingertips.

Once all the poultice was used, Evie carefully wrapped it in gauze and then covered that with a layer of fresh, clean bandage. 'There you are,' she said with a slightly wobbly voice, 'you will need to keep it on for an hour before it can be removed.'

Gingerly, he rolled on to his back, giving her the tempting view of his flat abdomen and the dusting of dark hair that arrowed below the waistband of his trousers. 'I suppose you expect me to lie still and uncomplaining for an hour.'

'Just still,' she said, turning briskly away from the splendid sight of him. 'As I do not expect a miracle, and as I shan't be here to listen to you, you can complain all you want.'

His dark eyebrows drew together in consternation. 'I shall be horribly bored. Can you not stay and read to me or something?'

'I thought you hated company and wanted to be alone?'

'Usually, I do, however, seeing it is your fault that my ribs got broken in the first place, I would have thought you would feel duty-bound to keep me company now. You have been off gallivanting in the village for the better part of the afternoon.' His eyes were smiling even if it did not quite reach his lips.

Evie sighed and pulled up a chair close to his bed. 'Very well. What would you like me to read to you?'

'There is a huge pile of correspondence on the desk in my study. You can start by reading that.'

'You want to work?'

'Of course I want to work. Did you think I

would wish to waste time being read some silly novel, or, heaven forbid, flowery poetry? This estate does not run itself, after all.' He did smile when Evie made to fetch his letters. 'And while we are about it, you might as well fetch ink, pens and paper. Then you can write down my replies as I dictate them to you.'

'You expect me to write your correspondence.'

'Come now, Evie,' he said a little mischievously, 'I would have thought you would be grateful. I am promoting you from my nursemaid to my secretary.'

Chapter Fourteen

Finn was all right, so long as he walked around the garden slowly, slightly bent like an old man with severe rheumatism and periodically wheezing when it all became too much for him. But at least he was mobile. His ankle was mending quickly, thank goodness, so there was hardly any sign of a limp. His ribs, however, were going to take longer. Even now, they were grumbling and reminding him that they were broken.

Seeing as riding was going to be impossible for a couple of weeks, at least this gentle exercise allowed him to move from the dreaded *chaise longue*. Ten days since the injury and he had had quite enough of being treated like an invalid and remaining glued to that thing. He had also endured much longer in the drawing room than he could bear. In the last three days alone, he had accumulated more hours there than he had in three whole years and it was becoming more oppressive by the second.

It was not so bad when Evie or her aunt were with him. They provided enough of a distraction from the worst of the guilt and while he had his back to Olivia's painting he could block out the painful memories and almost forget what he had done. However, afterwards, the crushing remorse of forgetting to mourn his wife still crept in. But when he was left alone, as he had been this afternoon, those painted blue eyes bored accusingly into his back and reminded Finn of how catastrophically he had failed her when she had needed him the most.

In order to escape, he had instructed the footmen to bring the dreaded *chaise longue* into the garden to work. The sun was shining; the birds were singing, his lovely wife was still dead, but all he could think about was when Evie was coming home. Most afternoons she skipped off to the village, and no doubt paddled in the stream en route whilst singing bawdy songs, and came home smiling and smelling of sunshine and filled with local gossip she was always eager to share with him.

Once a night she still checked on him, although she had thankfully quickly abandoned sleeping beside him for the comforts of her own room, gave him more medicine which she brewed daily herself and plumped his pillows for him. Every time, she came in her nightgown and woke him gently, forcing him to watch those intriguing parts of her jiggle so they haunted his dreams for the rest of the night. In the mornings, she tortured him by rubbing her healing ointment on to his torso and then binding him in a fresh bandage, all the while cheerfully chattering about this and that and driving him to distraction with the subtle scent of crushed roses and the gentle touch of her hands.

For an hour every day she read him his letters and wrote his replies. However, when he came to sign them he would always find that his words had been tinkered with. Softened. Made polite. *Evied.* Sometimes to such an extent that on paper Finn was a much better person than he was in life. Then she insisted on sitting with him while he worked in the drawing room, sometimes with her aunt, but when Winnie went for her nap they were left all alone.

During those times, Finn tried to focus on his ledgers. Really he did. But Evie had a tendency to sing to herself as she embroidered and her breathy tavern-wench voice did funny things to his nerves, especially those in his nether regions, which distracted him further from the task at hand. Hours passed like this. Pleasant, conversation-filled hours where he forgot to grieve even though his wife was in the same room as them. When he remembered he felt awful and, like a wretch, took his anger out of Evie.

Every single day he reminded her that he would much rather be on his own, that he was only tolerating her continued presence because she was still engaged to his foul brother and that she was a huge, unwelcome inconvenience to his life. Although in truth, when she was not there he had started to miss her terribly. The house, his servants and even his mood felt lighter with Evie here. And every time he lashed out, she reacted by seeing to his immediate comfort and fetching him tea. Somehow, those simple, kind gestures made him feel even worse, which he suspected she knew. The kindness shut him up far better than a sound telling off would have.

Aside from those unfortunate moments when his behaviour lapsed, Finn now woke in the mornings with some enthusiasm for the day and even found himself smiling occasionally. More vexing was his growing suspicion that he did not really want her to leave, which would not do at all. In his heart he was still married to Olivia. He would always be married to Olivia—he owed her that much. And Evie would soon be married to Fergus. Selfish, thoughtless, feckless Fergus. Who had never suffered a moment of guilt in his entire, dissolute life and did not deserve to lick the boots of an angel like Evie, let alone marry her. Just thinking about it made his ribs ache. Or perhaps that was simply just the walking.

Gingerly, he made his way back to the *chaise longue* and lowered himself back down. What he needed to do was take his mind off of his brother's vexing fiancée and do some work. Work had been his only saviour these past three years. Work provided structure, order, and he normally had no qualms about immersing himself in it. If his ribs had not been broken, he would be immersed in it now. That would be the truth if he had not been so distracted by his voluptuous guest well before his silly accident.

Evie was very distracting and it had nothing whatsoever to do with his ribs and everything to do with her. Her kind, gentle heart. Her soothing presence. And those eyes. Those plump, ripe lips and that tantalising, womanly body. All things, by rights, he had no place thinking about, let alone yearning for. Besides, the woman trailed chaos in her wake, something Finn really did not need, and he *did* have serious estate things to do.

He was about to pick up his pen when he

heard her voice in the distance. To cover the fact that he had spent the better part of the afternoon mooning about her and procrastinating, Finn bent his head over the ledger and pretended to be working intently on a column of numbers.

'Hello, Finn! I have brought you a visitor.' Certainly words guaranteed to sour his mood, but he looked up to almost smile and then failed miserably because Evie had Charlotte Cardew in tow.

Charlotte Cardew.

Olivia's particular friend. Who had spent hours in her company during those final days. Olivia had to have confided her misery to Charlotte. The wife of the vicar who had given Olivia's cold body its final blessing, who had pocketed the empty bottle of laudanum and suicide note, then lied to his entire congregation by telling them his wife had slipped away peacefully in her sleep. Charlotte Cardew knew only too well how he had failed his wife and was possibly one of the last people he wanted to see this year, or any year for that matter.

'Good afternoon, Charlotte.' Would it be too rude if he just upped and left?

'Finn.' Charlotte was smiling warmly, coming towards him with her hands outstretched as she usually did. Once upon a time he had liked her exuberance. 'When dear Evie told me about your injuries I simply had to come and see you. How are you feeling?'

Usually dead inside, thank you for asking, riddled with guilt. Angry at the world. Bitter and twisted. 'I am well. There was no need to concern yourself and travel all this way.' He did not put down the pen so Charlotte was denied the opportunity to embrace him, exactly as Finn had intended. Her outstretched hands clasped together awkwardly.

'Of course I had to concern myself. You are my friend, Finn. I see so little of you nowadays. We have missed you in the village.'

'I am too busy to spend time in the village. This estate does not run itself.' He stood stiffly and tried to ignore Evie's chiding expression at his unfriendly behaviour. 'To that end, I shall leave you ladies to your gossip. I have work to do.' Bending to pick up the heavy ledger was a mistake, but the shooting pain was necessary to give credence to his words. He could hardly plead work and then leave it all here in the garden. 'Good day, Charlotte.' Like an old man, he strode laboriously towards the house and away from all the memories which had begun to churn and sour in his gut, to find a place to hide from the sins of his past.

* * *

Evie waited until Finn was out of earshot before apologising to her friend. 'I am so sorry. I cannot imagine what has come over him.' Finn had been particularly rude and surly, even for him, and he had made it quite plain he wanted nothing whatsoever to do with their guest.

Charlotte shrugged it off, though it was obvious that her feelings had been hurt by his unsociable reaction to her arrival. 'He has avoided me and my husband since her death. It is such a shame as we all used to be such good friends. I suppose I remind him too much of Olivia and happier times.'

That did not excuse his behaviour. Obviously, one had to make allowances for the recently bereaved, but Finn was using his wife's death to isolate himself from the world and had done for three long years, and that was not healthy. His grief had become a sickness that was eating him from inside and, while Evie had no herbs that would cure it, she could encourage him to talk and unburden himself rather than let it all fester within.

Despite her objections, she had convinced Charlotte to stay for some tea and it was only once her friend had left that she went in search of

Finn. He was not in his study and as he avoided the drawing room at all costs if Evie did not force his hand, she knew better than to hunt for him there. In the end, she finally tracked him down in the stables where he was listlessly feeding apples to Horatio and clearly feeling very sorry for himself.

'You were extremely impolite to Charlotte.' She said this calmly rather than as a chastisement, hoping he would concede the point without an argument.

He stiffened, but did not turn to face her. 'I dislike visitors; you know that, Evie.'

'Even ones that you grew up with? Who care about you?' He was silent. 'Or do you dislike only those visitors who remind you of your wife and the life you had before she died?'

'I dislike all visitors.' His voice was gruff. Belligerent. 'Even you.'

Sometimes Finn reminded her of a lion with a huge thorn in his paw. When he was in pain, he lashed out. Talking about his wife, even being reminded of his wife, apparently brought out the very worst in him.

'Tell me about her.' If Evie was going to remove the thorn which was lodged in so deeply, she had to first examine the wound. So did Finn.

'I do not want to talk about it.' Swiftly he

turned around and began to walk out of the stables. She could tell, by the stiff set of his shoulders, she had angered him. Fortunately, in his current state, it was easy to keep up with him.

'Why ever not?'

'Because it is none of your business.'

'Do you ever talk about her?' He had speeded up, which made his slight limp more pronounced. His poor ribs had to be hurting, although she suspected not as much as his heart was.

'Leave me alone, Evie!'

The sharp tone was a stark warning for her to desist or else. His eyes darted around the garden as he sought the most effective route to escape. Deciding he might be cornered in the house, he plunged across the lawn instead, hoping to be rid of her and her uncomfortable questions.

'I don't think you ever talk about her, do you? You are too busy grieving for her.' She touched his arm lightly, only to have him snatch it away as he stalked faster towards the meadow. 'Or perhaps it is not grief you are suffering. Perhaps you are angry at her? For leaving you, perhaps? Grief can be a funny emotion. It affects people in different ways. When my mother died I felt numb inside for weeks afterwards. I have often wondered if that was the best way my mind could cope with her loss. With my father it was different. When he died, my initial reaction was to feel free—of course, that was followed with a huge amount of guilt and self-loathing…' Finn stopped dead and Evie almost walked into him.

He rounded on her then, rooted to the spot with his fists clenched at his sides as he faced her. 'You know nothing of my situation! And I am tired of your bossy, unwelcome interference in my life. You cause nothing but inconvenience and chaos, Miss Bradshaw! I want you and your aunt to pack your things immediately and take yourselves off to the inn. I have had quite enough of your company.'

By the light of battle shimmering in his dark eyes, Finn wanted this fight. Attack was his chosen form of defence. Attack and then isolation. He wanted her to lose her temper so he could regain the upper hand and, in doing, maintain his self-imposed silence. Evie was determined not to give it to him, no matter what the provocation. A festering wound needed to be lanced, not left.

'If that is what you want me to do, then I shall pack my bags this afternoon. But we both know the only reason you are throwing me out is because I have been brave enough to bring up your wife in your presence, when no one else does. They are all too frightened of your reaction. You bombard them with your ill temper and force them to back down. But your reluctance to talk about Olivia is not healthy, Finn.'

'Do not speak her name!'

'Should I pretend that she did not exist? My mentioning her name will not make your pain worse. Your pain is constant, isn't it? Why, you cannot sit in your own drawing room comfortably because Olivia is there. It has not escaped my notice that you can't even look at her picture; you insisted on facing away from her when I first brought you into that room and you still sit with your back to her.'

'The light is better!' Now the gleam in his eyes resembled fear. He was no longer an angry lion, more a cornered fox in a poacher's trap who would chew off his own foot to escape rather than stay and perhaps be saved.

'No, Finn. She haunts you.' Evie risked reaching out her hand and touching him again. 'And you want her to haunt you. You have used your grief to build a wall around yourself. You hide from the world and push everyone else away. Just as you are pushing me away.'

Finn wanted to deny it and call her a liar, yet she was right. He hated he was so transparent that she had worked him out, seen through him, and pitied him for it. He tried to sound calm.

Reasonable. Even though he wanted to lash out and scream and shout his rage.

'You are wrong. I simply prefer to be on my own.'

He could tell by her expression she did not believe him, when usually his belligerence and bad temper sent even the bravest of challengers running for the hills. But not Evie. She stood firm, waiting for him to crumble as the emotions threatened to swamp him, believing his guilt and grief were another malady she could cure with her herbs. If only there was a potion that would cure his past sins? The incessant weight of it all was oppressive.

Yet a part of him wanted to beg for her help, throw himself on her mercy and make the constant gnawing guilt disappear. But of course, to do that he would have to tell her how he had failed Olivia. The moment he did, she would look at him differently. Evie would not understand how he could have been so selfish or so negligent of his patient. She had given up almost a decade to care for her loved ones. Finn had only managed a fraction of that time and had done irrevocable damage in the process. He'd pushed his poor wife to suicide. Once Evie knew the truth, she would leave him and rightly so.

'I am pushing you away because I am done

with you and all the inconvenience you cause me.' And because he wanted nothing more than to hold her and unburden himself. Absolve himself from all of the remorse which engulfed him. Smile again. Live again. Even though he had no right to do any of those things and thinking about them was disloyal to Olivia. Evie was dangerous to make him want those things again. Even for a moment. All at once Finn was vulnerable and, because the vulnerability terrified him, he panicked.

Evie saw it. She shook her head slowly and stroked his arm in sympathy.

'Talking about her terrifies you.' For a split second he almost agreed. He had not willingly heard or spoken Olivia's name since the day he had stood at her graveside. All the guilt and grief was locked inside where he could control it and, if he let it out, let it loose in the world, he did not think he was strong enough to bear it. Finn stared at his feet until he felt Evie's hand link with his. 'You are pushing me away, Finn, because I had the audacity to ask about your wife.'

He would not show her how broken he was.

'You are wrong.' He would make her leave instead. Frighten her in the same way she was frightening him and put some well-needed distance between them to allow him to continue to lick his wounds in private, away from those gold-flecked eyes that saw too much of the real him and tempted him to want what he had no right to have. 'I am pushing you away because you have the *audacity* to continue to belong to my brother.'

Without warning, Finn pulled her into his arms and fastened his mouth angrily on hers. He had hoped that she would slap his face and storm off. Only the biggest cad would behave in that way to a lady who was engaged to someone else. Except, the moment her lips touched his, all of that pent-up anger, fear and self-loathing disappeared. Because kissing Evie Bradshaw was like nothing else on earth.

Chapter Fifteen

Evie swooned against him, too shocked by the sudden turn of events and too stunned by her body's instant reaction to him to do anything other than give herself over fully to the sensory onslaught he subjected her to. To begin with it was exactly what she suspected it was meant to be. A warning shot over the bow. *Prod me and I will lash out.* But then the intensity of the kiss changed almost as quickly as it had begun. His lips gentled, his breathing became shallower and the firm grip he had on her waist eased. Instead of using the kiss to bend her to his will, Finn began to explore her mouth with his own while his hands went on a whole other journey of exploration up her ribcage, then down her back before coming to rest possessively on her bottom.

Evie could not help kissing him back or looping her arms around him to anchor him in place.

Being kissed by Finn was so marvellous, un-explainable. Necessary. Her own fingers toyed with his hair, smoothed across his broad shoulders, enjoyed the shape and texture of the muscles beneath his skin. All the while Evie was supremely conscious of the effect it was having on her own body. Tiny ripples of desire spread hotly through her limbs like fiery tendrils, making her arms and legs feel heavy even as her head became light and dizzy.

When the tip of his tongue touched the tip of hers, Evie moaned against his mouth. Far from repulsing him, the animalistic noise merely spurred him on. His mouth and hands became bolder, the open-mouthed kiss more intimate than anything Evie had ever dared imagine, yet completely welcome. Her body wanted more.

So much more.

Unfamiliar nerve endings hummed with need and, as if he knew where she ached, he used his body to soothe them. His hips pressed scandal-ously against hers until she felt the hot, insistent press of the evidence of his own desire through their clothes. Except that didn't soothe; it made her body's cravings worse.

Evie's inquisitive hands moved to his chest of their own accord. Explored. Drifted lower. His hands lazily edged further and further up her body until they found her breasts. He moaned his own appreciation as his hands were filled with the aching mounds, until his thumbs found her taut nipples beneath the thin muslin of her new gown, and then it was Evie who was moaning and writhing against him, desperate for more.

When he suddenly stepped away, holding her at arm's length, it took several moments for her brain to function normally again. When it did she was almost panting and completely stunned. A reaction Finn shared as he blinked back at her, his own breaths coming in ragged, staccato bursts.

'I'm sorry.' Evie had never heard his voice sound so strained. 'Please forgive me, Evie.' He let go of her then and ran one hand through his dark hair in agitation. 'I never meant to…'

His voice trailed off as he stared at the floor, his expression now more of mortification than desire. Already, Evie could tell he was building new walls around himself, apparently quite horrified to have kissed her. His utter disgust cut like a sharpened blade. Of course she could never hope to compare with his perfect, beautiful dead wife. The woman he still loved and probably always would. She was Invisible Evie. Plump, plain and so very dull in comparison to the stunning blonde in the painting.

'There is nothing to apologise for. I pushed you too far and you lashed out.' Evie waited for him to deny it, hoping against hope that he would contradict her and say that he had kissed her because he had wanted her. Plain and simple. But, of course, he didn't. He made it worse.

'I was trying to frighten you away. It was not supposed to turn into *that* sort of kiss.' In case she missed the point of his chastisement, he hastily did up the buttons of his waistcoat which Evie's improper, eager fingers had practically torn apart. He glanced up at her face and frowned, then quickly glanced away again as if looking at her offended him. 'You have my word it will not happen again. I have not been myself since I broke my ribs. Maybe it is time for more of your witches' brew? And perhaps sleep.'

He was pleading insanity caused by illness or insomnia. Even though he was trying to spare her feelings while he extricated himself from his mistake, the insult stung.

'Yes, indeed. Pain can make a person behave in the most peculiar of ways. We shall pretend it never happened.'

As if she could. No herbal concoction would fix Evie's shattered confidence and wounded heart. For a moment she had felt so beautiful and adored, silly, silly girl that she was. But then again, with every passing day she had begun to allow herself to become a little more attached to Finn. When you took his obvious physical attractiveness out of the equation, there was still a great deal about him that she found attractive. He was kind beneath his bluster. Commanding, yes, but there was an easygoing side to his nature which was impossible for him to disguise. He allowed her to change his abrupt letters without complaint, listened to her gossip and frequently thanked her for her thoughtfulness, even if he did so gruffly. Every morning, as Evie had rubbed her potions on to his bare skin, she had dared to wonder what it would feel like to properly touch him. Sometimes, she found herself daydreaming wistfully about it and when she slept her dreams had become scandalously vivid. It was hardly surprising that she had greedily welcomed his touch.

He, of course, instantly regretted the kiss, while she had revelled in it. Now Evie experienced a rush of shame at her wanton, needy reaction. She did not have the excuse of ill health to explain her impassioned response. She had wanted *that* sort of kiss. She still wanted *that* sort of kiss from him. Her eager body was desperate for more. More that she would have given willingly. Shamelessly. Gratefully. To know he had not felt the same urgent rush of desire was mortifying, worse, to know that he had been horrified by her obvious desire was crushing. How she managed the tremulous smile when all she really wanted to do was weep was a mystery. But she managed it and in doing held on to the last remnants of her shredded dignity in order to maintain their flimsy charade.

'There is a batch of my willow-bark tea already prepared in the kitchen. Shall I run on ahead and set it boiling?'

Finn was looking every which way but at her, a sure sign of how awkward he was feeling. He obviously wished he could undo the last few minutes of his life and eradicate the kiss which had meant the world to Evie. If he had met her gaze, she knew she would see regret in those dark eyes and perhaps disgust. She looked at her feet to defend her foolish heart.

Suddenly, staying in his company was intolerable, not when the tears were already forming. His gaze fixed on the horizon, he simply nodded, which said it all, and Evie bounded across the sunny meadow away from him, feeling like the biggest fool that ever lived. For only a fool would ever hope that a man like Finn would ever really want plain, plump, Evie Bradshaw.

Finn waited until she was out of sight before he heaved out the breath he had been holding. There were a great many things he was not proud of himself for; now he had to add kissing his brother's fiancée to the list. Kissing and groping his brother's fiancée, after throwing a huge tantrum in her presence, when she had only been trying to help him. And, God help him, he had loved every single second of it.

Her untutored, earthy response was the most natural, most humbling, most erotic thing that had ever happened to him. Everything about her aroused him: her eyes, her hair, that sinful mouth, her lush body, her intoxicating scent. Within moments, his body had been on fire and desperate to be joined with hers. Another minute of the blissful torture of her kisses and it probably would have been. He'd had every intention of dragging her with him to the ground, hoisting up her skirts and plunging inside her. It would not have mattered that they were outside in broad daylight. There would have been no finesse or slow seduction. All Finn could think about was making her his.

Which was impossible.

For so many reasons.

So he had pulled away and pretended he was overcome with pain and tiredness to cover how overcome he had truly been simply because of her, then he had seen the hurt in her eyes at his withdrawal and had almost kissed her again. He'd had to turn away to stop himself from doing just that and then forced himself not to look at the tears swimming across her wounded eyes at his crass behaviour. She was engaged to his brother, for pity's sake! She might not love Fergus, but she was still technically his until she came to her senses and called off the wedding. Yet he had kissed her and touched her in a way that no gentleman should touch a lady who was not his wife. He had ground his hungry arousal against her and filled his hands with her curves, his every thought only for her. Not Olivia. Certainly not Fergus. Just Evie and how much he desired her.

The woman who haunted his dreams and made his days brighter. Good-hearted, generous, selfless, whimsical Evie. The woman who deserved better than a man like him.

Being Evie, she had instantly forgiven him out of the goodness of her pure heart. Allowed him the excuse of pain and offered him medicines to make it better. However, they both knew that nothing would ever make it better. Finn had crossed a line, bared his hand and now everything would be awkward between them, especially if she married his feckless brother.

Unlike his feckless brother, Finn always faced up to his mistakes. Evie deserved a better apology than the pathetic excuse for the one he had just given her. A proper apology where he admitted his overwhelming physical attraction for her and explained that it was probably best if she moved out of his house with all haste, because he wanted her so badly he was highly likely to act upon his urges again. That was the only decent course of action.

There was a hollow, empty feeling in his gut as Finn turned back towards the house. Almost like grief, but tinged with the acceptance that comes when you know the thing you are about to do is the right thing to do, no matter how hard it is to actually do it. It was for the best. Yet the closer he got to home, the more miserable Finn became, until the idea of saying goodbye to Evie became a real physical pain in his heart.

Evie rushed down the hallway, feeling sick. Never had a rejection hurt as much as Finn's and Evie was quite used to rejection and being the cause of disappointment in others. What made

Finn's so dreadful was the fact that Evie had allowed him to see more of the real her than anyone had seen in years. Not so much of the invisible Evie who tried to blend into the wallpaper, but the one she had always kept locked inside. The Evie who did not suppress her humour or her opinions on a topic. Up to now, she had believed that Finn liked that aspect of her character. He certainly appeared to appreciate her wit and he constantly challenged her to be more forthright. Half of the time that he said things to vex her, she was convinced he had said them to get her to fight back. And she had. In a small way, her confidence had been growing. Now it was back to non-existent again.

She had reached the foot of the stairs when Stowers stopped her. 'You have visitors, Miss Bradshaw. Three of them. They have come with a great deal of luggage and have declared their intention to stay for a while, although what Lord Finnegan will have to say on the subject I cannot begin to imagine.' Stowers wore an expression of impending doom. 'They are sat in the drawing room with your aunt and she is most insistent that you come at once.'

Three of them.

Three words guaranteed to compound her misery and make it complete. Three visitors could only mean one thing. Hyacinth and her daughters. And the only reason that the three of them would be here, unexpected and so far away from London, would be Iris's recent scandal. Flabbergasted at this current turn of events and still blindsided by Finn's rejection, Evie sank down on to one of the stairs in an attempt to digest it all. This really was proving to be the most hideous of days.

One by one, myriad problems presented themselves. Firstly, Finn would be livid. He had made it quite plain he only tolerated the presence of Evie and Aunt Winnie out of a sense of familial duty. He would not take kindly to being invaded with more unwanted and unwelcome guests. Secondly, there was every chance that, by now, Hyacinth would know Stanford House was a complete wreck. Without a potential home to go to, it would be apparent that the wedding would be a long way off. Which meant that, thirdly, Evie would have to explain away the absence of her fiancé. Fergus's disappearance so soon after they had arrived in the north would likely put the cat firmly amongst the pigeons and give Hyacinth even more ammunition to get Evie to call off her ridiculous engagement to the blaggard and return to London. Or it might even expose the betrothal as the complete sham that it was, in which case she was right back where she started. Back in Hyacinth's clutches and control. A miserable, invisible spinster, trapped in a life that was slowly suffocating her.

Finn would tell her to send Hyacinth packing with the truth. But wanting to be rid of her horrid stepmother and telling her that Evie was determined to live her own life, as far away from them as was humanly possible, and to sever all earthly contact were two completely different things entirely. Only a brave soul would say such things to a woman like Hyacinth and Evie was not feeling particularly brave at the moment. In fact, all of the progress she had made in the last few weeks had evaporated like a puff of smoke the moment she had seen the mortification in Finn's dark eyes when he had pushed her away because she could not hold a candle to his wife.

Slowly, she became aware of Stowers staring at her in bewilderment. 'Is everything all right, Miss Bradshaw?'

Of course it wasn't. Everything was falling apart. Her carefully laid escape plan, her fledgling forays into life again, her relationship with Finn, her new-found self-confidence. 'I am perfectly fine, Stowers. Has my aunt arranged tea for our guests?'

'It was just taken in, Miss Bradshaw.'

'Excellent,' she said rather dully as she rose to her feet, 'Thank you, Stowers.'

Evie had once read a fascinating account of the life of Mary Queen of Scots and had wondered, as she reached the end of the story, how it must feel to walk towards your own execution. Now she knew. Her feet were leaden, her heart was heavy and there was a great sense of inevitability about it all. She hesitated outside the drawing-room door, took one final breath of fresh, untainted air and sailed into the room with her head held as high as she could muster before her flimsy, paper world came crashing around her ears.

'Stepmother. Rose. Iris. This is a surprise.'

The two girls sat together on one sofa, like matching bookends dressed in the first stare of fashion. As usual, they barely smiled at her. Iris wore blue, to match her eyes, while Rose, of course, wore blushing pink. Hyacinth was perched on one of the delicate chairs in the centre of the room, wearing an expensive travelling dress of forest green and an ostentatious, if somewhat tiny, hat which sprouted a plum of assorted colourful feathers from an array of mismatched birds. The tallest of the feathers shot a foot into the air. As usual, her lips were pursed but they turned in further at the sight of Evie.

'Good gracious, Evelyn, what the devil are you wearing?' She picked up her tiny quizzing glass, the one that dangled from a filigree chain and was the most irritating of Hyacinth's affectations of grandeur. 'That gown does not become you at all.'

As greetings went, it was typical from Hyacinth. Why be pleasant when you could criticise? Chisel away at her from the outset, remind her of her shortcomings, constantly undermine. Evie tried to ignore the barb even though she was squirming inside. Much as she loved her new dresses, too much of her 'magnificent' bosom was on display and, since Finn had had his hands on them, Evie was supremely aware of her bosoms.

'I think Evie looks splendid.' Aunt Winnie was shooting barely disguised daggers at her stepmother. 'Far better than in those frumpy sacks you had made for her, Hyacinth. Come sit near me, Evie. I was just telling that woman about Fergus's wonderful house.'

Fergus's wonderful house? Winnie squeezed her hand as some sort of signal, although Evie had no idea what it meant. 'Really, Aunt? What have you told her?'

The old woman was up to something. She smiled the innocent smile she wore when she was blatantly lying about something. 'Hyacinth expressed her surprise that Stanford House was so lovely. Apparently, she had been expecting dilapidation when in reality…' one bony hand swept around regally to encompass the room '…as you can plainly see, nothing could be further from the truth. Your dear fiancé clearly played down how wealthy he really is. What a fine match you have made after all.'

Evie gave her aunt a tight smile, but made sure the stark warning was explicit in her eyes. 'Oh, really?' Did the silly woman seriously think that she could hoodwink Hyacinth for long? Hyacinth was like dry rot. She crept around all of the nooks and crannies until she found weaknesses, then she mercilessly attacked those areas until they crumbled into dust. Evie was living proof of that.

'Yes, indeed,' said her aunt, undaunted, 'I was just in the middle of telling the story of how *dear* Fergus came to break his ribs the other day.'

It was getting worse and worse. 'I wonder, Aunt, if I might borrow you for a minute. Seeing as we have unexpected guests, I should welcome your counsel as I discuss tonight's menus with the cook.' Evie heaved her aunt out of her chair and practically dragged her out into the hallway. Only when the heavy door was firmly closed behind them did she hiss.

'What do you think you are doing?'

Aunt Winnie shrugged, unrepentant. 'The carriage brought them here and they are of the firm belief that this is Stanford House. As long as we can dispatch them quickly, they will not be any the wiser.'

'Aren't you rather forgetting Finn in your equation, Aunt? I dare say he will have plenty to say on the subject.'

'Nonsense!' Aunt Winnie waved it away as if it were of no consequence, when she knew full well that it was. 'Finn will play along. You'll see. The man has become rather fond of you.'

'No, he hasn't and, no, he won't. Your silly lies will make me a laughing stock. I will be hauled back to Mayfair with my tail between my legs and on a tighter leash than before.'

'You are not going back to Mayfair, Evie. I have it all worked out, my dear. Do not fret. You need to summon that layabout Fergus from York and, when he arrives, the pair of you will take Hyacinth and her brood on a tour of the north before sending her back whence she came. Once the dust has settled from Iris's latest *faux pas*, they will be only too eager to return to town.

Finn will play along till then. You mark my words, especially if it gets rid of them quicker.'

Before Evie could argue the preposterousness of the idea, Aunt Winnie was already headed back into the drawing room with a smug smile on her wrinkled face.

Chapter Sixteen

Finn took a deep breath before entering the drawing room, although instead of just Evie, there were five women staring back at him and only two of them he recognised.

'There you are, *Fergus*!' said Aunt Winnie pointedly. 'We have just been telling Hyacinth about how *you* broke your ribs and why Evie insisted that you move back into *Stanford House* while she nursed you.'

Either Aunt Winifred had lost her marbles or something else was dancing on her wily, old face. Finn's eyes darted to Evie's in question and he could see she was glowing pink with mortification, her lovely eyes quite wide and panicked. At a loss as to what he was supposed to say or do when he had expected to issue a grovelling, heartfelt apology, Finn sort of smiled and nodded in greeting while Evie rushed towards him, looking like she was about to have an imminent attack of the vapours. There was a wildness about her expression that screamed of panic. It did not instil confidence in whatever was going on.

Her expression pained, she squeezed his arm, then threaded her own through his. 'Of course, you remember Hyacinth, Iris and Rose, don't you, *Fergus*? After all, you have already met them a few times already, haven't you, *Fergus*?' Her voice was all high-pitched and squeaky and the words came out in a rush.

'Yes…of course,' he said tentatively, not wanting to call Evie or her aunt a liar in front of these strangers. Whatever was afoot here, she had his loyalty. He owed her that much. However, the hairs on the back of his neck had begun to rise along with his growing sense of foreboding. Whatever was going on here, Finn was certain he was not going to like it. He inclined his head politely towards a lady in the full throes of middle age who appeared to have all of the former inhabitants of an aviary on her head. This must be the stepmother. The horrible woman. Hyacinth.

'I trust you are well?' Although Finn already loathed her on sight. She had maligned and bullied Evie. He would not be able to get passed that irrefutable fact.

The woman stared back at him through cold, pale eyes. Her lips, he noticed, were pursed together as though she was about to blow hard on a trumpet. She disapproved of Fergus. Him?

'I must say that the country air clearly suits you. Despite your broken ribs, I have never seen you appear quite so healthy, my lord.'

'Yes, you do look healthy.' One of the younger woman shot him an admiring, predatory glance. 'Much more *vigorous* than I have ever seen you before.'

And he automatically loathed this woman, too, the hairs prickling a warning on the back of his neck as she continued to stare at him as if he were a tasty morsel of food. She was blonde and almost identical to her sister and wore blue. The other was head to toe in pink. If he were Fergus, he would know which was Iris and which Rose. Finn racked his memory for clues to their identity. Rose-pink lips like Cupid's bow, Iris for her fine eyes? It was a gamble.

'Thank you, Iris. You look well, too.' The young woman simpered at the bland compliment, her obvious vanity quite astounding. Finn smiled at the young, pink girl. 'Good afternoon,

Rose. I am delighted to see you as well, although I am surprised to see you all here. In *my* house.'

'It should hardly be a surprise that I would wish to visit my dear stepdaughter, Fergus, although I do concede it was remiss of us not to have sent word of our arrival.' Hyacinth managed a faint smile that fell off of her face almost instantly. 'But we were in such a hurry to see dear Evelyn and, as we are soon to be family, I did not think you would feel inconvenienced by our visit.' The woman did not give any indication that she cared either way. 'We only plan to stay a few days—a mere fortnight at most.'

'A fortnight?' His own voice was squeaky now, but only because he was stifling the need to shout.

'At the most,' said the over-feathered stepmother. 'Give or take a few days.'

Finn squeezed Evie's arm hard to let her know he was annoyed. A fortnight was exactly fourteen days longer than he was prepared to endure. If Evie wanted him to play Fergus, he might have been prepared to give her an hour or two out of the goodness of his shrivelled heart, but that was it. Nobody else was going to stay at his house. Ever again. Evie had already caused enough chaos in his ordered misery.

'Might I have a quick word, Evelyn?' he managed tightly as he turned to her. Finn preferred to do his strangling in private and, judging by the way his new *fiancée* stared back at him, Evie fully expected to be murdered.

'Certainly, Fi-ergus.'

Solicitously, Finn placed his hand firmly over the one she had limply looped through his, just in case she tried to make a run for it, and escorted her out of the drawing room, across the hallway and then practically pushed her into the breakfast room where he rounded on her.

'Have you taken leave of your senses?'

'Please don't wave your arms around like that, Finn. You might aggravate your poor ribs.'

'Forget my poor ribs, madam, it is the man who is aggravated. Furious, in fact.' Finn began to pace back and forth like a caged tiger in an attempt to calm himself and then gave up, throwing his palms up in frustration. 'What were you thinking?'

Evie was staring down at the floor, her teeth worrying the plump flesh of her bottom lip. The exact bottom lip that he had only recently just sampled and still wanted to taste. He tore his eyes off of it and tipped up Evie's chin with his finger, forcing her to meet his gaze.

'It really was not my idea. They were already here when I arrived back after we…' She covered her face with her hands to try to hide the ferocious blush that had stained her cheeks. The rest of her sentence came out quite muffled. 'Aunt Winnie had already concocted the lie by the time I arrived and I had no option other than to play along with it. I am so sorry, Finn. I don't know what to do. If Hyacinth finds out the truth, she will drag me back to Mayfair. I can't go back there, Finn.'

She opened her fingers enough to peek out at him and he saw tears gathering on her bottom lashes and felt his resolve to evict her unwelcome relatives waver. The very last thing he ever wanted to see was Evie upset. Not after his outrageous manhandling of her.

'Do you seriously expect me to pretend to be my feckless brother for a fortnight? I haven't seen the blighter in three years! I know nothing about Fergus's life now. I am bound to say the wrong thing and give the game away.'

'I know. But I would appreciate you trying all the same.' She dropped her hands and stared mournfully at him. 'Once she realises that Stanford House is uninhabitable and that I still have not purchased a suitable house to live in, or that

I am in no position to plan a wedding, she will force me to go back to Mayfair.'

'Force you? Don't be ridiculous, Evie! You are past the age of majority, therefore you can live where you please and this Hyacinth will have no say in the matter. Simply tell her that you intend to set up your own household in the north as soon as you are able because you refuse to live with her again. Better still, tell her you loathe her and I throw them out.'

'I cannot do that, Finn. I promised my father I would treat her with the utmost respect.'

'As she always has you?'

'I know, but...'

'Then I will tell her!'

Finn turned angrily to the door and she clutched at his sleeve. 'Please don't! Eventually, once I have my own house here, I will tell Hyacinth that I am never returning. But I cannot do it yet. Hyacinth will only leave me here as long as she believes I am actively planning my wedding. She already believes this is Stanford House and that you are Fergus. What is the harm of going along with it for a few days?'

Her bottom lip was trembling, making him feel like a brute, and he huffed out a frustrated breath. 'Your stepmother seems to be of the opinion that she will be staying here for two weeks, Evie. Two weeks is hardly a few days. I refuse to be my brother for two weeks! It is unfeasible. Unreasonable!'

'Aunt Winnie has a plan. In a strange sort of way, it might work if you make yourself scarce whenever possible and, if everything goes the way she is convinced it will, you will only be inconvenienced for a few days at most. Possibly less.' She offered him a tremulous, hopeful smile. It was his undoing.

Clearly it was not only Aunt Winnie's marbles that were lost. Common sense told Finn he would live to regret his next words, yet he said them anyway.

'What is Great-Aunt Winifred's lofty plan?' Lord save him from this vexing woman who tugged at his heartstrings and made his simple, ordered life so very complicated.

Evie pulled out one of the dining chairs and sat on it listlessly. 'We maintain this silly charade for as long as it takes to summon Fergus back here, which shouldn't be long. Once he arrives, he can take your place as himself and nobody will be any the wiser. You are identical twins, after all. Just act like the Fergus you remember and we will blame any mistakes on his constant inebriation. Once he returns, myself and Fergus will take Hyacinth and her dreadful daughters on a tour of the north and leave you in peace.'

'And I suppose your stepfamily will be thrilled to take a tour of the north?'

'No. They will hate it.' Her weak smile was tinged with some amusement. 'They are only here to escape the gossips in London and in a few weeks most of the *ton* will have left town to rusticate in their country estates for the summer. London becomes unbearably hot by the end of June and is practically deserted once Parliament goes into recess. Knowing them, they will be keen to return as soon as they deem the coast to be clear. Besides, Hyacinth detests the countryside almost as much as she detests the discomfort of staying at strange inns with common folk. If I choose the most awful inns, in the most boring places the north has to offer, it might hasten their departure south.'

'If they will hate it, how, pray tell, do you expect to convince them to accompany you in the first place?' Hearing the explanations would be entertaining, at least, even if the whole plan was doomed to fail before it began.

'I thought I would just spring it on them.'

'Spring it on them?'

'Yes, indeed. Once Fergus arrives, I will arrange carriages and provisions, et cetera, to come on a specified day in the not-too-distant future. Then I shall have them arrive here just after breakfast, and say, *Ta-da! Guess where we are all going today!* Rush them into packing their things and off we will trot.'

'*Ta-da!*' Finn laughed. He could not hold it in. Evie was nothing if not amusing.

Evie smiled. 'What do you think?'

'I think it is the most ludicrous thing I have ever heard.'

Her face fell. 'You don't think it will work.'

'Of course not! It is doomed to failure.'

'Would you at least give it a try?'

He hated the desperate glimmer of hope in her dark eyes. 'This all strikes me as a very convoluted way of going about things. I still don't understand why don't you just tell Hyacinth that she is about as welcome in your life as a dose of the pox and that you are never returning to London, no matter what she says?' Finn would even help load their trunks back on to their carriage and then wave them off cheerily.

'You don't understand, Finn. She is still my stepmother. My father would want me to obey her. He always insisted upon it. Doing otherwise feels disloyal to him.' Finn understood the power of that emotion only too well. 'And I do know Hyacinth and her daughters. Trust me, two weeks of Fergus, trees and inferior lodgings and she will leave me in peace.'

Finn remained silent, waiting for her to realise there was one huge, gaping flaw in her ridiculous plan. Unfortunately, she appeared not to notice the giant pothole in her path which was waiting to gobble her up.

'I would have thought a more pressing problem is not finding unsuitable inns, but tracking down your devoted fiancé. There can be no wedding without a groom, Evie. Hyacinth will have better grounds to drag you back to London once she realises that your devoted *real* fiancé has abandoned you here in the north and left you no idea as to his whereabouts. It could take weeks to track him down and it is highly unlikely nobody will appraise your stepmother of the truth in all of that time. We can hardly hold them prisoner.'

'Oh, I know where he is.' As soon as she said it Evie wished she could drag the words back into her mouth.

'You know where the scoundrel is?'

She winced at her mistake. 'Well, yes. He is in the Bay Horse Inn. In York.'

'When did he tell you that?'

The tell-tale pink blotches had begun to bloom on her neck so there was no point in lying.

'He informed me of his destination in the letter he left for me, just in case I needed him for anything.' Or he needed her to send him more money.

'All this time, you have known where he is?' The top of Finn's dark head appeared about to explode at this news as his temper re-ignited with terrifying speed. 'Yet you neglected to tell me?'

'Only because I thought you might throw me out on my ear while I looked for a suitable house to live in.' Which really did not sound right at all, but Evie was at her wits' end, thanks to her heated kiss with Finn and Hyacinth's unexpected arrival, and because she was nervous she had blurted out the truth without dressing it up first, to make it sound more palatable and less... selfish on her part. Although saying it out loud made it seem horrifically selfish. Evie had lied to Finn by omission to avoid being dispatched back to London. Repeatedly. She was heartily ashamed of herself.

'You are right. I would have thrown you out! Or I would have dragged him back from whatever den of iniquity he had ensconced himself in and made him take responsibility for his own problems. You and your aunt are not my responsibility and I owe my feckless brother nothing!

None of this is anything to do with me. And if you think, for one minute, that I will allow your extended family to leech off of my hospitality while I impersonate my useless twin, you are sorely mistaken.'

When he said it like that, even in temper, it sounded depressingly reasonable, but then Finn was not a doormat and Evie was. Hyacinth had a way of making her curl into an apologetic ball with no voice. The only way she had escaped in the first place was because she had sprung her hasty engagement on Hyacinth as a *fait accompli* and left within a few days. Even then, her stepmother had chipped away at her resolve mercilessly, remonstrating with her on all the multitude of ways she was not fit to be a wife to anyone, let alone a libertine of a marquis, and that her dearly departed father would be spinning in his grave to know that Evie was abandoning her stepfamily when her sisters still needed to find suitable husbands. And he had entrusted his fortune misguidedly to Evie so that she could see to launching Rose and Iris properly as he would have wanted. Had it not been for Aunt Winnie's stalwart encouragement and matching desire to live away from Hyacinth until the end of her remaining days, Evie would have caved in. Although telling Hyacinth the truth held great appeal, Evie was simply not brave enough.

Not yet at any rate. It was easier to buy a house so that there was something solid, with deep foundations, anchoring her in the north. Once she had that, Evie would write to Hyacinth and explain in no uncertain terms that she was neither marrying the odious Fergus nor returning to Hyacinth's oppressive household. In a letter, posted long in the future, Evie could be bold and brave and assertive. Because doormats did such things from a distance, if at all, and when it all was said and done, Evie was nothing but a pathetic coward. A plain, plump, old, invisible pathetic coward. Yorkshire and new dresses would not change that irrefutable fact.

Finn watched Evie's face fall at his onslaught and felt guilty, but really…three more strangers invading his private space! Was his life not miserable enough already? And all this time she had known full well where his useless brother was and had kept it hidden from him so that she could stay. And all this when he had bent over backwards to be helpful because he felt sorry for her?

Perhaps not helpful, he conceded reluctantly, he had been belligerent and surly for almost the entire duration of her stay—but he *had* let her stay out of the goodness of his shrivelled heart. Finn had been born with Fergus, had grown up knowing what his brother was capable of, knew how to deal with the wretch. Poor Evie, with her tender heart and lack of confidence had been duped and Finn had been duty-bound to step into the breach while his brother remained missing.

Except Fergus had never been missing.

Evie had known where he was the whole time. To Finn, that was tantamount to betrayal.

'I believe that you must indeed be a doormat, Evie, to allow my brother to treat you with such blatant disregard. I thought you came here with the intention of changing that?'

She stared down at her hands, drawing that kissable, plump bottom lip through her teeth again as if she were a naughty child being told off by the nanny. How could a woman be so decisive as a nursemaid, but so subservient to those who did not deserve her time? Anger churned in his gut.

'And now you are fretting about this Hyacinth, a woman you claim has made your life a misery thus far, but you are entertaining the idea of playing hostess to her and taking her on a tour of the north, rather than telling her to go away? It beggars belief.'

'In time, once she realises that I have no intention of leaving the north, I dare say she *will* leave me alone, Finn.'

'In time? Can you not hear yourself? Have you no pride, Evie?' She still refused to meet his eye.

'Hyacinth can be quite forceful...'

'I doubt she needs to be very forceful with you. The woman has just arrived and already you have surrendered! And you are willingly allowing Fergus to treat you badly. You have let him abandon you here, alone, knowing nobody, in the house of a virtual stranger and you have not even taken him to task for it. You are spineless, Evie Bradshaw!' That she had chosen to protect Fergus, remain loyal to Fergus—who had shamelessly lied to her and then abandoned her—that she had put that wastrel above Finn... well, that hurt. A great deal.

As did his broken ribs. All of the shouting had rattled them and now he was feeling the after-effects and could barely breathe, which, of course, she noticed. Instead of telling him off for his rudeness or telling him to mind his own business or packing her bags so that she could be shot of him and his moods, her only thought was for his comfort. She hurried to his side, her lovely eyes troubled, and rested her hand tenderly on his shoulder.

'Sit down, Finn. Take deep breaths. The pain will subside if you are calm. I am so sorry to have caused you all of this stress.'

It was impossible to remain angry with her when she was stroking his arm and staring at him so forlornly. If he had not been so breathless and in pain, he would have taken her into his arms and kissed her until she realised that Fergus was not the man for her. Unfortunately, powerless to do anything else for the moment, Finn sat and tried to focus on his breathing while she fussed about him, wafting the tantalising scent of crushed rose petals under his nose and reminding him of how perfect she had felt in his arms.

'That's better.' Her warm palm came up and brushed the hair out of his eyes before it smoothed down his cheek, where it remained to torment him further. 'I know you are right, Finn. Please don't be angry at me. You have been nothing but kind—in fact, you have been a godsend and I should have told you about Fergus. It was quite wrong of me not to.' Her dark eyes were limpid and sad, when they deserved to sparkle with happiness, and he was partially to blame. 'But you are right. I am still being a doormat and I will work harder at trying to change. I shall find a way to keep Hyacinth and her brood occupied and I shall fetch Fergus from York by tomorrow. I will send an express immediately. Please do not concern yourself with it all, Finn. I want you to concentrate on getting better.'

But she did not promise to put Hyacinth or his brother in their proper place, he noted, or to abandon her silly plan to fool her relatives into believing he was Fergus—and that bothered him a great deal. Evie had blossomed before his eyes since her arrival and Finn had enjoyed watching it. If ever a person deserved to live the sort of life that they wanted, it was Evie. Yet the arrival of Hyacinth apparently had the power to erase all of that hard-won short-lived independence. The way the brightness in her eyes had dimmed and her shoulders were now slumped made him feel far worse than his aching, broken ribs did. In the short term, Finn knew he would go along with the ruse. He would pretend to be Fergus because he knew that would make her happy. But he would not hold his tongue. If he had to witness Evie be bullied by Hyacinth and her simpering, pastel-wearing daughters while he waited for the return of his feckless, thoughtless brother, right now in his present mood, there really was no telling what he would do.

'I will give you three days, Evie. Three days and no more.'

Chapter Seventeen

Evie toyed with her dry toast listlessly. Finn had stalked off in a sulk and had not made an appearance at dinner either. While that served to cement Fergus's continued unsuitability as a potential groom, it made Evie miserable and guilty. Poor Finn had been dragged into all of this because of her, when he had been right. It really was nothing to do with him.

Hyacinth walked into the room, took one look at Evie and could barely hide her disgust. 'Good gracious, girl! Whoever your new dressmaker is, the woman should be shot. What was she thinking putting you in muslin? Why, that dress clings to all your unsightly bumps and lumps and exposes an excessive amount of skin. What would your father say to see you so shameless? You look like a harlot!'

'She looks lovely.' Finn's deep voice appeared

out of nowhere as he strode into the breakfast room, looking handsome in that rugged, wind-swept way he had. 'I believe you must need spectacles, Hyacinth, if you cannot see how delightful she looks.'

'There is nothing wrong with my eyesight, my lord! Although I dare say I should not be surprised that you would approve of such a scandalous neckline on a day dress.'

'Nonsense,' said Finn as he took Evie's hand and placed a light kiss on the back of it, unaware that in doing so he caused her pulse to flutter and her heart to skip a beat. 'Your own daughters' gowns have similar necklines. Evie simply fills her dresses better.'

Good gracious, not only was he actively going out of his way to annoy Hyacinth, he was also talking about Evie's bosoms. Hyacinth, understandably, nearly choked on her tea. Undeterred, Finn wandered towards the sideboard and loaded his plate with his usual mountain of food. Then he sat down next to Evie and slid several crisp slices of bacon on to her plate.

'She will burst the seams of her inappropriate dresses if you keep feeding her that. Evie has always run to fat. You need to monitor her diet, my lord. Dry toast is best at breakfast time, if you do not want an elephant for a wife.'

Finn snatched the offending toast out of Evie's hand. 'Evie is not fat.' There was a definite hint of challenge in his eyes as he stared back at her stepmother. 'And you will desist in telling her that she is.'

Had he just told Hyacinth off? How marvellous.

The older woman glared back at him agog for several moments, her lips twitching as she considered her words, but she withered under Finn's steely glare and folded them together in disapproval instead. Feeling strangely brave, Evie cut a small piece of bacon and popped it into her mouth and took a great deal of time chewing it to give her something to do in the brittle silence that now filled the room.

When neither of them appeared to want to ease the tension, Evie had to speak. 'What are your plans for the day, Fi-ergus?' It was so hard to pretend Finn was his twin. Although identical, they were nothing alike.

'I fear I shall be busy all day, *my dear*.' He was definitely laying it on a bit thick, although he managed to say such things with more sincerity than his brother and she had enjoyed the way he had kissed her hand. 'You will have to entertain your family without my help until dinner. I shall be *locked* in my study with my ledgers.'

The fact that he was taking her advice to make himself scarce should have brought her comfort, yet it didn't. He disapproved of what she was doing. That was obvious. And Evie had grown accustomed to spending her days with him. 'Perhaps I could help with your correspondence later?' A whole day without Finn now stretched before her. Without him but with Hyacinth. Every hour would feel like a month.

'No need, my dear. I am on the mend and do not need to be nursed any longer. *Enjoy* this time with your family.' There was a malicious gleam in his eye as he flicked his gaze to Hyacinth and then back again pointedly. 'I am sure you will have a splendid time without me.'

'I am not altogether sure that one can have a splendid time in the north, my lord. It lacks the vivacity of London.' Hyacinth said this with a smile. 'I am sure that you are already missing its many *entertainments*.'

Finn's fork paused in in mid-air. 'Not really. Since I met Evie, our capital and its *entertainments* have somewhat lost their appeal. I have found a new contentment in the country.'

Hyacinth's malicious laughter grated. 'Perhaps for now. In no time you will be back there, my lord. You are no stranger to the lure of temptation.'

'Would anyone like me to pour them some more tea?' It was a pathetic attempt to prevent another confrontation, but fortunately Finn took pity on her.

'Coffee, if you please, my dear. How do you like *Stanford* House, Mrs Bradshaw? I trust your accommodation met with your approval.'

'It is a charming *little* house.' As there were at least ten bedrooms upstairs, little was hardly a fitting description. 'What it *lacks* in grandeur it makes up for in character. Have you ever thought of adding to it?'

'What an interesting notion.' Finn glanced at Evie with mischief dancing a jig in his eyes. 'I have often thought I might like to build an orangery. What do you think? I hear they are the perfect location for a secret tryst.'

Evie had to cram an entire slice of bacon into her mouth to prevent the unexpected bark of laughter that almost escaped. Hyacinth's mouth hung slack for several seconds before she blinked in feigned innocence at the obvious slur.

'Indeed… I had best go and wake the girls. If you will excuse me.'

As soon as the door slammed in her wake, Evie threw her head back and laughed. 'You are a very rude man.'

'Your stepmother is an odious woman. It is easy to be rude to her. You should try it.'

The censure in his tone caused the laughter to die in her throat. 'I think it. I just cannot say it yet.'

'Spoken like a true doormat. Why, if you turn around, I dare say I shall see her dirty footprints all over your back.'

Now he was just being spiteful. Evie could be spiteful, too. 'I shall stand up to Hyacinth when you talk about your wife.'

His posture stiffened and his jaw clenched instantly. 'It is hardly the same thing, Evie.'

'Of course it is. We all have our faults. I cannot stand up to Hyacinth and you cannot even look at your wife's portrait. We are both weak and pathetic in our own way. At least I acknowledge my weakness and hope to change it. You appear content to wallow in your own self-pity and to lash out at others.'

He stood up, annoyed, and tossed his napkin on to the table. 'As I said, enjoy your day with your family, Evie. I am more than happy to make myself scarce.'

The day with Hyacinth had been interminable. The woman complained about everything, although since he had challenged her this morning, a great many of those complaints were either directly or indirectly aimed at Finn. When those barbs were actually aimed at the real Fergus, they did not sting, but when it came to criticism of Finn or his house or his staff, they hurt, which she supposed had always been Hyacinth's intention. Part of her had become immune to the insults Hyacinth constantly bombarded her with. Finn was a fresh wound she could jab at and she did so relentlessly.

The butler and housekeeper were too old and needed to be replaced, the food lacked flavour so the cook should probably go, too, the furniture was too plain and too big, the house was too small and Fergus had quite let himself go in the short time since she had seen him. He needed a haircut and a better valet. And it went without saying that he needed to learn some manners. The most sensible course of action was for Evie to call off this ridiculous engagement forthwith and come back to London, as her father would have wanted—after all, he had entrusted the care of his only daughter to Hyacinth.

Evie had listened to it all without complaint, looking forward to dinner when Finn would toss her stepmother a few of his own, well-timed, perfectly aimed arrows back, except he did not materialise for dinner. Or after. In the end, pleading a headache that was, in fact, quite genuine, Evie had excused herself and gone to bed.

It was several hours later and still sleep eluded her. It was impossible to sleep after her argument with Finn. Two days ago, they had muddled along quite well together. It was becoming familiar and comfortable and they had both liked each other's company. Since then, they had argued, kissed, argued and argued some more so that now a giant wedge had been hammered between them and he was avoiding her like the plague.

Evie probably should never have mentioned his wife. She had done so twice and on both occasions it had ended badly. Aside from the kiss, of course. Evie could not stop thinking about it. That one, brief, thrilling experience of passion would probably have to sustain her for the rest of her life and already she had squirrelled away the memory with her most precious. During several of Hyacinth's rants today, Evie had allowed herself to relive the memory, fiercely blocking out the part where he had pushed her away horrified. The way her body had hummed as his hands had touched her face, her bottom, her...

'Evie?' The door to her bedchamber cracked open and the man himself walked in boldly.

'Finn?'

'Finn…curious…were you expecting my brother? Has he been keeping your bed warm in my absence?'

The voice was slightly different, the tone mocking, colder.

'Fergus!'

He sauntered towards her bed and sat heavily on the end of it. 'You summoned me, did you not, my darling *fiancée*?'

Well, yes, she had, but her instructions had been quite specific. 'I told you to go to the inn and send word once you had arrived.' If Hyacinth or one of the girls had seen him, Evie's tenuous charade would be over.

Fergus struck a match and lit the candle on her bedside. The dim light cast menacing shadows across his face. It was odd that a face, identical to Finn's, could frighten her when his brother's was so very dear. Fergus crossed one leg over the other and tapped his chin thoughtfully, drawing out the tension of the moment for all it was worth and making her feel suddenly nervous.

'Well, that is the thing, Evie. When we made this bargain, there was no mention of me accompanying you and your family on a miserable jaunt around the north. I was merely to play the

role of your fiancé for a while. Now that the pa-
rameters of the original bargain have changed,
I am reluctant to continue without more of a financial incentive.'

'I have already given you one thousand
pounds, Fergus! Not more than a few weeks
ago. We agreed that the rest of the five thousand would be paid at quarterly intervals.'

Fergus smiled, although with half of his
face cast in darkness, it certainly did not look
friendly. 'And we also agreed that I would leave
you well alone and we would have precious little to do with one another. I would continue to
live my life, largely unaffected, while you went
about doing whatever it is escaped spinsters
do when they have run away from home. Two
weeks roaming around this godforsaken county
was never on the cards. I am already beyond
bored with York. Provincial society is so very
prudish.' He reached out his hand and traced
his index finger down her cheek. His touch was
nothing like his brother's. When Finn touched
her, her nerve-endings came alive. Fergus gave
her the shivers. 'I want another thousand now,
Evie, or I will head back to London tomorrow.'

'That's blackmail.' Although Evie already
knew he had the upper hand. By the slippery

smile that crawled across his features, so did Fergus.

'Call it what you will. Those are my terms. Take them or leave them. Perhaps my dull brother will accompany you on your little trip?' He chuckled to himself and then regarded her with complete hatred. 'One thousand pounds now, Evie, or I will wake this household and expose you for the pathetic liar you are.'

Like a startled deer, she scrambled out of bed, but before she rifled in her wardrobe for her hidden box of money, common sense returned. Evie turned to Fergus. 'Wait outside. I will bring you the money.' If he saw the four thousand pounds' worth of crisp, rolled banknotes, he would demand more.

Fergus smiled languidly and sauntered to the door and allowed himself a chuckle of triumph as he opened it. 'What a good girl you are, Evelyn Bradshaw. I knew you would see the sense of it.'

Evie promptly closed it behind him and set about gathering what he wanted. She quickly counted the money and stuffed the hardwood box back into the bottom of the wardrobe, burying it under several pairs of slippers. Only when all evidence of it was hidden from view did she open the door and thrust the wad of money at him.

'Here! Do I have your word you will accompany me on the trip?'

Fergus did not reply. Instead, he counted the notes, then folded them into a pocket. 'I shall be on my way then, dearest fiancée. Thank you for being so...co-operative.'

'You will wait at the inn, as planned?'

'Do you doubt my word?' Fergus smiled again and it made Evie's flesh crawl. 'You still owe me three thousand pounds, Evie. And after two interminable weeks in your family's company, I believe I will have earned it. Fear not. I shall await your further instructions at the inn. Like a good boy.'

'Does your brother know you are here?'

'I did not come to see my brother.'

He turned to walk away when it occurred to Evie that Finn would want to see Fergus, too. She had kept enough secrets from him and would not keep this visit quiet. 'Before you go, you must talk to Finn. You owe him an apology for foisting me upon him when you knew full well Stanford House was a wreck.'

Fergus appeared bored and examined his fingernails. 'How very dull. I cannot think what we have to say to each other.'

'This is his house. He has a right to know you have been in it. And you do owe him an apology.'

Evie watched his jaw tighten and his eyes narrow, and she realised that Fergus was perhaps not quite as casual about facing his brother as he would lead her to believe. 'I will go to Finn now and tell him you are here. Or I could call for him, but I prefer not to wake up the entire house. It will be much easier if you come with me.'

Fergus glared at her with what could only be described as raw hatred.

'If you insist.'

'I do.' Panic clutched at her chest. 'But he knows nothing of our bargain. I trust you will be discreet.' Even as she said those words it occurred to Evie that she owed Finn the truth about her engagement. She was not treating him fairly by keeping it from him. But then again, with relations so fraught between them, it was probably wise to tell him when he was in a better mood. He was already furious with her about Hyacinth, her own inability to stand up for herself and bringing up his wife when he preferred to keep his own counsel. Realising Evie had been lying to him all along, on top of all that—well, there was no telling how he might react.

As it was well after midnight and the whole

household was asleep, Evie led Fergus down the darkened hallway to his brother's bedchamber. She knocked and pushed open the door, but Finn wasn't there.

Chapter Eighteen

Finn swirled the brandy in his glass and forced himself to look at Olivia's picture. The very fact he struggled to do it for more than a few seconds probably made Evie right. Yesterday and today she had attempted to open the hornets' nest and both times he had lashed out at her for trying. He was not particularly proud of his own behaviour and he could hardly chastise her for allowing Hyacinth to bully her when he was not brave enough to stare at a painting. Like the coward he was, he turned his head away, too terrified to face the consequences of his own actions. Even without looking, Olivia's blue eyes burned into him accusingly.

Finn sucked in a deep breath. He was being ridiculous. It was only a painting. And whilst it was a particularly good likeness of Olivia, it was still only the clever brushstrokes of an artist, some paint and a canvas. Hardly anything to fear.

He took a fortifying swallow of the brandy, but was spared from facing his dead wife again by a light knock on the door. For some strange reason, he already knew the person on the other side of it was Evie. He had left things hanging badly between them for two days now. He still hadn't properly apologised for kissing her and he had been rude earlier, deliberately bating her vile stepmother and then berating Evie for not being brave enough to stick up for herself.

She had been nothing but kind to him. Perhaps he was destined to be the sort of man who treated women badly without meaning to. When the mirror was held up to his face, Finn really did not like what he saw. He had pushed Olivia into the grave and now he was bullying Evie. How, exactly, was his behaviour towards her any different to Hyacinth's?

The door opened slowly and she poked her head into the room. To torture him, he saw her hair was unbound and hung heavily over one shoulder. The proper nightdress was buttoned up to her slim neck, but his hands heated at the memory of what he had felt underneath. Full breasts, soft, enticing curves. Sweetness. Passion. Solace.

'Sorry to bother you, Finn, but your brother

is here.' The rest of the door swung open and there was Fergus.

Finn had definitely not sensed his presence, which said a great deal about the strength of their sibling bond. The sudden surge of anger said a lot more. Fergus met his gaze arrogantly, as always. If he experienced any remorse about anything, Finn had never seen any evidence of it.

'Hello, Finn. You look…exactly like me, but without the title.'

He stood as Fergus inched into the room slowly, the cocky expression on his twin's face all bravado. Fergus knew what was coming. Finn had waited three long years to tell him what he thought. It was why he had avoided coming home in so many years.

'Can you leave us, Evie?'

She nodded, although concern was etched into her lovely face. 'I shall wait down the hallway, in case you need me.' Her eyes darted nervously between the two of them for a moment before she left. The door clicked shut quietly behind her.

'No fatted calf or tearful reunion at my arrival, I see.' Fergus kept his body in line with the exit. Ready to run. Fergus was always ready to run. 'I take it you didn't miss me, dear brother.'

'It is difficult to miss something you barely

know. No, Fergus. I did not miss you. But Olivia did.'

His twin examined his fingernails. 'Olivia always was a sweet girl. I was fond of her, too.'

'Fond of her?' Finn scoffed and shook his head in disbelief. He sincerely doubted Fergus was capable of feeling anything for anyone aside from himself. Love. Remorse. Loyalty. All of those basic human emotions were anathema to him. 'I asked you to come home three years ago. Begged you, as I recall. Olivia wanted to see you and you never came. Not even for her funeral.'

'By the time I received your letter it was too late. She was dead and buried. I grieved in my own way.'

Which translated as not at all. 'You never could lie to me, Fergus. Do not try now. Three weeks before her death, just before you burnt your house down, you knew she was dying. I told you she was fading. Yet you ran away from the huge mess you caused, left me to deal with the aftermath of the fire—your remaining servants, your tenants, your many creditors, your chaos—when you knew that I had better things to do with my time.'

Fergus shrugged. 'I never did like that house. I am sorry about Olivia—but her death was hardly unexpected. She had been ill so long, what did you want me to do? Pause my own life while we waited for the inevitable to happen? She was not my wife, Finn.'

How typical of Fergus to think only of himself. If Finn's ribs had not been broken, he would have smashed his fist in his smug face. 'You denied her the chance to say goodbye to you! Despite everything, every vile, mean, selfish thing you ever did, she still adored you. She always saw the best in people, even when there was nothing there but selfishness and self-indulgence. Olivia still believed that you would revert back to the boy she grew up with. She still believed there was some good left in you.'

'You were always the good twin, Finn. Mama and Papa's favourite.'

'Are you still using that as your defence for your sorry life, Fergus? You know full well our parents were at their wits' end with you. You had every advantage. They gave you the benefit of the doubt so many times. They tried everything to turn you into a good man.'

'So that is why our father gave you half of my inheritance, Finn? I always wondered why. But now that I know it was for my own good, I feel so much better having been short-changed!'

'We were twins, Fergus, born six minutes apart. He gave me the unentailed half. And thank God he did! You would have sold it and squandered the money, just as you sold and squandered every bit of your own inheritance which was not entailed—but even those assets went to rack and ruin. The fields left barren, our parents' house burned to ash. Had he not had the foresight to entrust me with half, all of his tenants and servants would have starved to death. At least I was able to pay their pensions and employ them all! Another of your messes which I was left to clean up.'

'I never asked you to step into the breach.'

'But you knew that I would. Just as you knew that I would take care of your fiancée when you upped and abandoned her in my house!'

'Evie has pots of money. She could just as easily have rented somewhere to stay.'

'Like she easily gave you a thousand pounds before you ran away? Do you have no regard for her feelings? No affection for her at all?'

Fergus stared at him thoughtfully for a long time, then smiled as if amused by it all. 'The only regard I have for Evie Bradshaw is for her money. The woman can spare the odd thousand or ten.'

Finn lunged at his brother then, grabbing him by the lapels and slamming him back against the door.

'Evie is too good for you!'

She was more than a ready fortune. She was sweet and kind and pure of heart.

'And yet she has chosen me. Over you. Does that gall you, little brother? Was taking my inheritance not enough for you? Do you want my fiancée now as well?'

Finn let go and stalked to the opposite side of the room, annoyed with himself for feeling guilty at Fergus's perceptive barb. He did desire Evie. He had kissed her. He had a growing well of affection for her that refused to go away, no matter how much he willed it to.

'I want your fiancée to see you for what you are, Fergus. I will do everything in my power to see that she calls off your engagement before you can bleed her dry.'

'And once again rob me of money that is rightfully mine? How very predictable you are, little brother.' Fergus smoothed down the ruffled lapels of his coat, before walking to the door calmly. 'Do your worst, Finn. I really cannot muster up the enthusiasm to care.'

Evie hovered in the dark hallway anxiously. As it seemed wrong to eavesdrop, she had taken herself out of earshot, but she was desperate to know what was going on inside. Finn had not been pleased to see his brother. Animosity and fury had shimmered in his eyes and his stance had been so rigid, almost as if he were preparing to go into battle. Fergus, on the other hand, gave the impression he found the whole reconciliation frightfully dull, yet Evie had seen a flash of panic in his eyes when he had finally come face-to-face with his twin.

It had been odd seeing them both together for the very first time. Up until that point the brothers had been two separate entities to Evie, not twins. However, when she had seen them together, first the similarities and then the differences between them was so startling, it had shocked her.

Physically, the changes were slight. Fergus was a notch taller than Finn, while Finn was several inches wider across the shoulders. Fergus was leaner, in an unhealthy way, his skin duller. Dark shadows, from too many hedonistic nights, framed his eyes and hollowed his cheekbones. His dark eyes were unfathomable, almost dead and cold. Finn's swirled with emotion. They truly were the windows into his soul. Evie only had to look at them to know how he was feeling. Amused, pained, angry…guilty. And those dark eyes drew her to him, spoke to her heart and scrambled her wits.

Finn had said that he and Fergus were as different as chalk and cheese. Now she knew differently. They were fire and ice. Finn was fire; Fergus ice. One warmed her heart. The other froze it.

When the door finally opened and Fergus strode out, Evie automatically pressed her back against the wall and blended into the shadows. She had stupidly thought she might be able to control him—she who could control nothing at all in her own life. Now Fergus had the last laugh. He terrified her. As soon as their tour of the north was over and Hyacinth was gone, Evie would give him the rest of his money and swiftly terminate their bargain. She wanted nothing more to do with him. Once she had done that, she would tell Finn the truth and hope that he would still wanted to be her friend. Aside from the obvious attraction, she realised his friendship meant more to her than that of any other and it would be impossible to live here in the north knowing he hated her. But for now, she would maintain her silence and hope for the best.

Fergus headed down the hallway towards the front door. He did not turn around or seek her out. Why would he? He had got what he had come for. As soon as he was gone, Evie dashed towards the drawing room to check on Finn. She found him staring at his dead wife's portrait.

For a moment, she considered retreating and leaving him. It seemed like such an intensely personal moment, but he sensed her without having to turn around.

'Has he gone?'

'Yes. Should I have not brought him to you?'

He exhaled slowly, his eyes still riveted to the painting. 'You did the right thing, Evie. It is me who is foolish. Right up until the last second, a part of me still harboured the hope that I might get through to him, make him see reason. I wanted to hear an apology.' He laughed bitterly, without humour. 'I know now such a thought was futile. Fergus feels no remorse. I am of the belief all he is capable of feeling is linked only to his own selfish desires. Fergus thinks only of Fergus. Now I think about it, I do not believe I have ever heard him apologise for anything.'

'If he did not apologise for depositing me in your house and running away, then let me do it now in his stead. I made him bring me north. I thought he had a house here. I never would have allowed him to force me upon your hospitality.'

For the first time since she had entered the room, his eyes turned towards hers and locked.

'It never occurred to me to ask for an apology for your presence, Evie. Despite all of my grumbling, I have appreciated your company these last few weeks.'

The admission made Evie's throat tighten. Had anyone ever given her so kind a compliment?

'I can see I have shocked you.' He was almost smiling. One side of his mouth was quirked upwards. 'Fear not. I suspect I shall return to my usual curmudgeonly, ill-tempered self and be railing at you again soon enough. Right now, all my anger is directed towards my feckless brother.'

Evie came further into the room until she was almost level with him and perched on the arm of a chair. 'Why are you angry at him?'

Finn remained silent for an age, then at last his shoulders slumped and he flopped into a chair next to her. For once, he had chosen a seat that did not face away from his wife and picked up his discarded brandy glass, cradling it in his palm and staring into its amber depths as if they contained all of the answers he needed.

'As children there were always four of us. Me and Fergus, Charlotte Cardew and Olivia. We were inseparable. We did everything together. Climbed trees, made camps, ran riot. It was an idyllic way for a child to grow up. As we got older, Fergus changed and I really do not know why. He withdrew from our games, withdrew from me I suppose. He started to resent me. The only person who he still made time for was Olivia and even that was sporadic. By the time we went to university, it was obvious the breach between us was widening. Then one day Fergus disappeared from Cambridge. It was months before I saw him again and when I did he was embroiled in a crowd which ran very fast and loose. It was a pattern which became familiar. He could not settle into anything, took no responsibility for his actions, always squandered his allowance on high living. We drifted apart. After I married Olivia and moved into Matlock House, I rarely saw him. I dreaded his homecomings, as they usually signalled trouble. My parents despaired of him. They tried everything to turn him around and all to no avail. Eventually, when his debts became so large, my father cut off his allowance in an attempt to curb his spending. It only caused more resentment. Fergus believed they favoured me over him, which was never the case. I was settled and helping run the estate by then. Fergus was wild.'

'It is not uncommon for siblings to be jealous of one another.'

'Perhaps. But after my father died Fergus's irrational jealousy turned to poison. My father changed his will, you see. He did something unforgivable in my brother's eyes. He split the estate between the two of us. Equally. We both had a house, acreage, tenants. Both had the capacity to generate our own income. Since then, he has hated me, Evie.'

Finn took a sip of the brandy and closed his eyes as he swallowed. 'Yet through all that, Olivia still refused to give up on him. She wrote to him endlessly.' He stared wistfully at her portrait. 'When she was dying, she asked to see him repeatedly. He came home to Stanford House quite regularly then. It was the perfect location to hold his decadent parties. He was just across the hill and yet he never came to see her. When her health really began to decline, I went to him and pleaded for him to give her an audience. He said he would try to spare the time. That very weekend, there was the fire at Stanford House. I was roused from my bed in the middle of the night, spent hours hauling buckets of water to extinguish the blaze and what do you think Fergus did?'

Evie had a good idea. 'He left.'

Finn toasted her with his glass. 'Indeed he did. He jumped on his horse and headed to Lon-

don and left me to deal with it all. If one of the
servants had not seen him depart, he would have
allowed me to think he had been trapped in the
fire, forced me, or some other charitable fool, to
risk our lives searching for him. And that, Evie
Bradshaw, is the last time I set eyes on your dear
fiancé until tonight. She died three weeks later.
He never even sent me a letter of condolence.'

If Evie had not already worked out what a
hideous excuse for a man Fergus Matlock was,
Finn's story might have surprised her. Now it
only served to confirm her suspicions the man
had no conscience at all. To leave his brother to
deal with the tragic death of his young wife and
the fire and Stanford House was beyond callous.
But talking about such things would only serve
to expose her as a liar. And Finn was finally
talking about Olivia. Even though the intense
sadness and longing she saw in his eyes cut her
to the quick. But this was not about her, no matter how hard his words would be for her to hear.

Chapter Nineteen

'Every time I look at her picture I wonder why she is holding a butterfly.'

Finn drained the last of his glass and held it out for more. 'If I am going to talk to you about her, I am going to need more brandy and I hate to drink alone. Do you drink brandy, Evie?'

She took the glass, the tips of her fingers brushing his as she did so, causing her own fingertips to tingle with awareness. Her hands shook as she poured him more brandy from the decanter and passed it back to him, then because she needed something for them to do, she poured herself a measure and sat down in the chair to take her first tentative sip. It was strong, but not unpleasant, trickling warmly down her throat. He smiled at her reaction and then turned back to the portrait.

'Just after we were first married, we were

having a picnic in the meadow when, out of nowhere, a beautiful blue butterfly suddenly fluttered towards our blanket. Olivia held out her
palm and the thing landed on it. It stayed there
for probably ten minutes, perfectly content, before it fluttered away. They made such a pretty
picture, Olivia and that butterfly, I had a portrait
made. I didn't want anything stuffy or formal.
Olivia was neither of those things, so she sat
outside, on the blanket, wearing the same dress
she wore that day. I wanted the artist to capture
her expression of wonder.'

'You are a romantic, Finn. Who'd have thought
it?'

'Perhaps I used to be. The butterfly has always reminded of Olivia. Beautiful, delicate...
and as time went on, like all butterflies, her time
on earth was so fleeting.'

'A bittersweet portrait then, in hindsight. But
borne out of a unique and special memory which
only the pair of you shared.'

Bittersweet. An interesting turn of phrase,
yet, now that he considered it, an apt one. For
three years all Finn had seen was the delicate,
fleeting butterfly and the irony of what it sym-
bolised, not the memory of that day and how
happy the pair of them had been then. 'Olivia
had made a cake.' How had he forgotten that

detail for so long? 'She had insisted on cooking for her new husband, exactly like a proper wife should.'

'She could cook?' Evie sounded impressed.

'No, she couldn't. It was inedible. We tried breaking it up and scattering it for the birds, but even they could not bring themselves to eat it. I made her promise me she would never set foot in the kitchen again.' And Olivia had laughed and kissed him and they had rolled around on that blanket. Finn had forgotten that, too. The memory made him smile, which surprised him.

'You loved her very much.'

'I did. Olivia was easy to love. She was good-hearted and kind. She never said or did a bad thing to anyone, always saw some good in them, always believing that understanding and compassion would fix everything in the world.' Just like Evie. He took another calming sip of his brandy while he digested the thought. It was a worrying comparison—yet it had just appeared in his thoughts as if such a comparison was only natural. Clearly Finn was drawn to kind-hearted women. She was easy to love, too. Dangerously easy to love.

Where had that thought come from?

Finn buried it and conjured up his wife. Kind, gentle Olivia—Olivia would have liked Evie.

'You are smiling, Finn. Perhaps remembering is not so bad after all?'

'Not all memories are good ones. It is hard to think about her without churning up all of the bad things that happened to her.' Like the fact she had killed herself to unburden Finn of the duty of taking care of her.

Evie smiled kindly at him, as if she understood, and then gazed at Olivia's picture. 'We all have to die, Finn. It is a sad, yet irrefutable part of life and every death is a tragedy in its own way, no matter whether it comes early or late in an individual's life. Yet it is not what should define them. If every ending is predestined to be sad, which it always is, then it is the beginning and middle of their story which is the most important. Therein lies the essence of the person, the part we should remember. After my mother died, the years of her illness and how much she had suffered dominated my grief. Until I realised my mother would hate for me to dwell on those things—they trivialised her life, turned her into someone to be pitied rather than celebrated. When I delved further into my memory, recalled all of the laughter and happiness there had been, it began to outweigh the sad. I realised I carried her inside me then and those pleasant recollections sustain me.'

'Olivia fell ill within a year of our marriage, it is not that easy.'

'You grew up together, did you not? Therefore, there must be years and years' worth of joy to recall.' She made a valid point. 'What is your first memory of her? How old were you both?'

Despite his reluctance, Finn found himself answering Evie's questions. To begin with, those answers were short, giving only the briefest of details in case a particular reminiscence caught a nerve and exposed him to raw pain or crushing guilt, yet as Evie kept prompting him with more and more questions, the words came easier until they were spilling out of him. Things he had not allowed himself to remember suddenly came to the fore and demanded to be spoken. By the second glass of brandy, they were sharing stories from their past, laughing at them, and for the first time since Olivia's death he was able to speak of her without fear. In a strange way, it was cathartic.

When the first rays of dawn pushed their way through the windows of the drawing room, they both realised they probably needed to sleep. Evie uncurled herself from the armchair she was tucked up in and stretched. Beneath the soft linen of her nightgown, Finn glimpsed the womanly swells of her breasts and the surge of lust was so sudden, his throat went dry. For hours he had sat with her, talking, and she had been deliciously naked beneath that proper garment and he had failed to notice.

He noticed now. Seeing her graceful, languid movements as she arched her back and reached out her arms was like a siren call. The tousled chestnut hair in disarray hung almost to her bottom and tempted him to run his fingers through it all. When his breeches became uncomfortable, he felt the weight of Olivia's gaze again and with it came the guilt. He was thinking about another woman because he had temporarily forgotten what he had done and that brought him up short.

Evie must have seen his face fall. 'Do you ever talk to her?'

'She's dead, Evie. One cannot converse with the dead.'

'Of course you can.' Blissfully unaware of how much she tempted him, Evie threaded her arm through his as they walked towards the door, making him wish that she were not merely accompanying him up the stairs, but taking him to her bed. 'You knew Olivia so well and she you. If you tried talking to her, she would answer you.'

Finn could not help shooting her a dismissive glance, although it only made Evie smile and squeeze his arm tighter. He felt the tantalising push of one full breast briefly against his bicep and his groin ached. 'I am not being daft, Finn! Try it. You will hear her.'

'Then my descent into madness will begin. I can only imagine what the gossips in the village will say. There goes poor Finnegan Matlock. The grumpy old curmudgeon who talks to himself and hears voices in his addled head.'

'I talk to my mother all of the time.' They had reached the foot of the stairs and still she did not relinquish her grip on his arm. 'She always answers. I sometimes talk to my father, too, although those conversations are less pleasant, and if he answers, which he was always prone not to, they are usually the same so I try not to bother.'

The ridiculousness of her words made him chuckle. 'What does your father usually say to vex you so much?'

She shrugged, the motion made her breasts jiggle and he had to grip the bannister rather than act on his impulse to haul her into his arms. 'When I talk to him, it is usually to berate Hyacinth and chastise him for foisting her upon me. My father always tells me that she is his wife and that I should respect her and be a dutiful daughter.'

'Oh—Evie.' Even when her father was buried under the ground, she was still trying to see to his comfort. 'I am almost certain your father realised the error in his ways in marrying Hyacinth.'

She stared at him perplexed. 'Why ever would you think that?'

Finn allowed his hands to stroke her cheek briefly and comb itself down her glorious hair. 'Because he could have left her his entire fortune. She was his wife and that is the norm. Instead he left it all to you. He trusted you, Evie. He clearly did not trust her.'

Her eyebrows came together in thought. 'But he would never intercede on my behalf. He always sided with Hyacinth.'

'Perhaps your father was a doormat, too, then? Have you considered that? Maybe it is an inherited trait he passed on to you.' Finn could tell her mind was whirring. 'Perhaps he could never bring himself to tell Hyacinth the truth in life, so used his death to make the point? What does your mother have to say on the subject?' He could not help smiling as he said it, which rather spoiled its intended effect. Evie smiled shyly back.

'I don't know. I have never asked her. It always felt wrong to discuss his second wife with his first.'

'Then I suggest you do. I dare say she might have something to say on the subject.'

They had reached Evie's bedchamber, although Finn was loath to leave her. She looked so pretty and natural leaning against her door. She was also lingering and showing no signs of wanting to leave his company either. Even though he knew that he shouldn't, Finn took a step closer and wound his finger around one, long, curling tendril of hair. 'You deserve better than Fergus, Evie.'

She stared back at him, some mysterious emotion swirling in her dark eyes, and went to speak before she stopped herself. The tip of her tongue came out to lick her lips, drawing his eyes to them. The scent of crushed rose petals hung faintly in the heated air between them, tempting him further. The brandy, the conversation they had just shared, even the location heightened his desire to be closer to her. With every fibre of his being he wanted to kiss her, even though kissing her was wrong. He gave the lock of hair one final tug before he disengaged his fingers from it and stood back.

'Goodnight, Evie Bradshaw.'

She shrugged and smiled wistfully. 'Good morning, Finn Matlock.'

Then she turned and passed through her bedchamber door and he was sorely tempted to go in after her.

Evie practically floated into her room, closed the door and leaned against it heavily as she listened to his retreating footsteps in the hallway. She had limited experience of men, but she was fairly certain Finn had wanted to kiss her. How or why she was certain, she could not say. It was just a feeling. An odd, unexpected and delicious feeling. His eyes had focused on her lips and then darkened. He had moved so close, Evie could feel the warmth of his body through her thin nightgown and her body had positively thrummed with awareness. Perhaps if she had confessed the truth about her engagement to Fergus, he would have done. She almost told him— except she could not find the right words and his close proximity was making rational thought quite difficult. All Evie could focus on was the way her scalp tingled as he twined his fingers in her hair, then her lips tingled when he had stared at them so intently, forcing her to remember their kiss in the meadow.

Her breasts felt heavy and, shamelessly, she

cupped them with her own hands. But as they were not Finn's hands, it gave her little comfort. This was what desire must feel like. Her entire body positively oozed ripeness, like a juicy peach about to fall from the tree in summer. All Evie wanted was Finn to come along and pick her and then gobble her up.

Scandalous, shameless, wanton thoughts.

Tempting thoughts.

If she offered herself to him, would he take her? And was she brave enough to offer herself to him now? Tonight? She could explain she came with no expectations, needed no promises or declarations of affection, she just wanted to feel his hands on her body and experience the thrill of being joined with him. Intimately joined with him. It was what her body and her heart wanted.

That same heart beat rapidly in her chest and her breathing became erratic. He was just down the hallway. Probably getting undressed right at this minute. She could go to his room…

Evie huffed out a breath and laughed at her errant, muddled, passion-addled mind. She was not brave enough to do any of those things and was probably reading far too much into his friendly gestures than he had intended. A man like Finn would not want a plain, plump doormat of a

woman like Evie. You only had to see his beautiful wife's painting to see the sort of woman he
desired and, as Evie possessed none of those fine
attributes, hoping for something passionate to
kindle between her and Finn was nonsense. He
was still desperately in love with his wife. For
him, no other woman truly existed. And it went
without saying she was beyond tired, her nerves
were on edge, and therefore she was quite definitely irrational. Her feelings for Finn were best
left unrequited and it was for the best he never
knew about them. She took one decisive step towards her bed and then stopped dead.

Chapter Twenty

Her room had been ransacked. Her blankets and sheets lay strewn about the floor as if they had been ripped from the mattress in a frenzy. The drawers in the chest had been emptied out and lay discarded on top of her underthings and stockings. The wardrobe doors hung open, Evie's new dresses were spewing out of it and were scattered about the floor.

As she blinked at the carnage, Evie felt queasy. It did not take a great deal of common sense to know what had happened. She clambered across the detritus and dropped to her knees in front of the wardrobe, searching through the tangled clothes frantically even though she already knew the box she sought was gone.

Without thinking, she dashed down the hallway towards Finn's room and flung open his door without knocking. He was standing in only his breeches and turned to her, shocked, an intense, heated expression on his face, until he saw her distress and rushed towards her.

'Evie! What's wrong?'

The tears came then, because she felt like such a wretched, pathetic fool.

'Oh, Finn! I've been robbed. Fergus has stolen my money!'

The next hour flashed by in a blur. He followed Evie back to her room and saw the devastation, listened to her garbled, brief lie about why she had a box of money stuffed in her wardrobe without question. Then he took charge. Ordered her to dress and then hurried her to the stables. Finn gave her no opportunity to shy away from the idea of sitting atop his big horse. He saddled Horatio himself, climbed on and then hauled Evie on to his lap, and before she could think better of it they were galloping across the fields so fast that she could see the early morning dew spraying around the mighty chestnut's hooves and all she could do was cling on to Finn for dear life in case she fell off.

But it was all to no avail. They reached the inn only to be told that Fergus had left hours ago, in the dead of night, while Evie and Finn had still been reminiscing. And, no, they gave no indication where he was headed and nor had anyone seen which way he had gone.

With the need for haste evaporated and feeling despondent, they headed back towards Matlock House in virtual silence. What else could be done? The money was gone. Fergus was gone. Even if they went in pursuit, it was likely to be nothing more than a fool's errand. They had barely gone a quarter of mile when Finn tugged on the reins and brought his horse to a halt.

'I can't ride any more, Evie. My ribs are killing me. You take Horatio back home and I will see you there.' He went to dismount and she gripped his sleeve.

'I cannot ride alone, Finn. I'm terrified of horses.'

'Horatio is as docile as they come. He will see you home safely.'

'If you are walking back, so am I. The last time I had dealings with Horatio he tried to eat my dress.'

He did not argue. He slid gingerly to the ground and then held out his arms to help her down, too. Evie saw the wince of pain as he braced himself against her weight and felt dreadful for hurting him. Finn gave Horatio a pat on the haunches and the animal happily trotted off in the direction of the house as if he regularly went out on jaunts without his rider and therefore did not find his dismissal odd at all.

More silence stretched. Evie had never felt so pathetic and stupid in her life. All of Hyacinth's criticisms and insults paled into insignificance with the knowledge that she was indeed a silly girl. A silly, trusting, pathetic girl who was old enough, and plain enough, to know better. 'This is all my fault.'

'No, it isn't. It's Fergus's. I cannot believe that he has now sunk so low to have stolen from his own fiancée. I will pay you back the three thousand, Evie.'

As if the money was what she was worried about. Aunt Winnie's far-fetched plan was now in ruins and Evie was quietly fuming at Fergus. 'No, you won't! You have paid enough of Fergus's debts. Besides, it's only money. It was stupid of me to have put such a vast amount of money in the wardrobe in the first place. I should have left it in the bank, where it belongs.'

'But it is three thousand pounds, Evie. Nobody can afford to lose such a sum.'

Evie waved this away as the anger began to bubble, more at her own short-sighted stupidity now. She had always withheld her temper, curbed it for the sake of peace—allowing it to bloom now was liberating. Almost a decade of quiet acquiescence was determined to explode out of her and Evie was going to let it for once, but she was more furious at herself than at the Marquis of Stanford's cruel treachery.

Of course, Fergus would have listened to her rummaging for that money. He probably also knew she would go back to check on Finn, the wretch. She remembered how his calculating eyes had narrowed when she had mistaken his intrusion into her bedchamber as a clear sign for her poorly disguised affection for his brother. Now she was back to square one, with nothing between her and Mayfair except a thin veil of lies.

'I should have sent him packing the moment he tried to blackmail me!' Evie scanned the vicinity for a tree to kick. When she couldn't find one she stamped her foot churlishly. It did not help. 'I let him bully me, just as I let Hyacinth bully me. I am such an idiot!' Her pace began to quicken as her temper fermented. 'I came here to stop being a doormat, yet at every hurdle I prostrate myself on the ground, ready for the next pair of boots to trample all over me!'

'Blackmail you? What are you talking about?'

She could hear Finn coming alongside her, but by then she was too outraged to give it much thought. If she ever saw Fergus again, she would put on her sturdiest walking boots and kick him in the gentleman's area!

'We had a bargain. But could he stick to the terms? No, he could not! All he had to do was pretend to be my fiancé for twelve paltry months and then he would have his five thousand pounds, but could he wait until I had bought myself a house of my own and found the courage to tell Hyacinth I was never living with her and her vile daughters again? No! Of course he couldn't! I should have anticipated this when I made the agreement. Letting him bully me into paying him instalments allowed him to see that I was weak.'

Evie was ranting now and could not seem to stop herself. Her arms began to wave around manically as her feet tore up the ground, yet still she became more and more infuriated.

'I should have known giving him that first thousand was a mistake. I certainly never should have given him another thousand last night! Not until he'd fulfilled his side of the bargain and helped me fool Hyacinth. But then I am a doormat. A pathetic, spineless, gutless doormat. Carrying the five thousand around with me was complete stupidity. I am more furious at myself than I am at your feckless brother. What sort of a trusting fool puts five thousand pounds in a box in the wardrobe?'

The firm yank on her arm halted her progress as Finn suddenly loomed in her face. The way his dark eyes burned and his nostrils flared, he was obviously as angry as she was.

'You *paid* Fergus to *pretend* to be your fiancé!'

It had taken Finn a while to put all of the pieces in place as she ranted, but once he had worked out the gist of what she was saying, he experienced the overwhelming desire to strangle the wench.

She had the nerve to defend her actions. 'I needed a believable excuse to escape Hyacinth!'

'You could have told her the truth!' Finn gripped her by the shoulders and fought the urge to shake her until her teeth rattled. 'Instead, you have spent all of this time claiming to be engaged to my brother and living in my house!'

That appeared to register, because she blinked furiously back at him before dropping her eyes. 'I was going to tell you. I just never found the right time.'

The right time? Was she serious? 'I never would have allowed you to stay if I had known the truth!'

'Which was exactly why I didn't tell you in the first place! I thought Fergus had a house that I could live in while I found my own and you were so hostile towards me when we first met.'

'Don't you dare use that as an excuse. Whilst I will admit that I was not particularly welcoming when you first arrived, I have allowed you and your aunt to stay with me. I did the decent thing out of misplaced loyalty to my brother and the woman I believed he was betrothed to!'

He had suffered all this for nothing.

Spent hours in her company. Had his ribs broken. Endured her tender ministrations in agonised silence. Trusted her. Lusted after her. And resisted temptation after temptation right up until an hour ago. All because of misguided loyalty and his innate sense of right and wrong. Fresh molten fury obliterated all reason.

'All this time, I thought you belonged to my *brother*!'

Finn did not give her chance to answer. He was beyond caring about anything except his own outrage, however, beneath all that, fighting to be heard, was intense, selfish, unadulterated relief. He hauled her against him and pressed his mouth to hers. All of his anger, frustration and hurt fizzled and died the second she kissed him back. Her instant, passionate response lit the fuse; all Finn could do was hold on and let the fire consume them.

One second, Evie had been ranting and annoyed, the next she was standing amongst the wild flowers in the meadow, her arms and legs entwined possessively about Finn, kissing him as if she had to.

Which she did.

Resisting the temptation was impossible. She wanted this. Wanted him. And as long as he did not come to his senses, she was determined to have him right now, here in this beautiful place and to hell with the consequences.

His fingers wove into her hair and found the few hairpins she had hastily stuffed into it before they left. He plucked each out gently and pulled back to watch the heavy locks tumble around her shoulders, before he wound his hands the riotous mass again and pulled her close for another kiss. Exactly like the wanton she was beginning to suspect she might be, Evie ran her palms over the solid expanse of his chest. His waistcoat provided too much of a barrier, when she wanted desperately to feel skin, so she hurriedly undid the buttons in order to untuck his shirt and burrow them underneath it.

His smooth skin was so warm and wonderful. She could feel his heart beating rapidly under her fingertips; the erratic rise and fall of his ribcage as he fought for breath. When she slid her arms around his waist, lightly raking her nails against his back, Finn shuddered. A low rumbling groan of desire told her that he liked what she did and it emboldened her.

Evie did not mind when she felt his fingers tug at the laces at the back of her dress, allowed him to loosen the garment and drag it down her shoulders. The dress was yet another barrier that her hungry body did not want. His lips found the newly exposed skin there, driving her mad as they nipped and teased the sensitive flesh of her neck. But when the bodice of the dress exposed her shift, and he undid the ties of that, too, Evie became self-conscious. It was awkward enough trusting him with her ungainly body, even though she craved his hands on it—surely he would not lay her naked before the world?

His hands smoothed the top of her shift from her shoulders. In her rush to dress, Evie had not bothered with the hassle of a corset. The shift was the only layer between her naked skin and the air, so she pulled away, panicked.

Finn's eyes dropped to her breasts. The thin cotton barely covered her nipples and she was certain he could see them, puckered and eager through the filmy fabric.

Definitely unladylike.

Definitely wanton.

He stared and his gaze scorched her skin. It was as thrilling as it was mortifying, yet Evie could not help covering her chest with her hands. His response was to smile and tug her hips until they were flush with his. But he did not try to force her to display herself. Instead, his clever mouth nipped and nibbled the shell of her ear until she was squirming against him, her arms leaving the front of the loose garment to curl around his neck and anchor him to her.

To her complete surprise and utter shock, Finn lifted her then, as if she hardly weighed anything at all. The sudden display of male strength was impressive and made her giddy with desire. Evie loved the way his muscles bunched as he carefully lowered them both to the ground and bent over her to kiss her again. She did not notice when the front of her clothing pooled around her waist, however, it was impossible to ignore the magnificent sensations he created when his mouth wandered a lazy path down her collar bone and feasted on her taut nipple. It hardened further when the early morning breeze caught it and Finn groaned and bent his head again as if he needed to put his mouth on her again more than he needed air to breathe.

Evie arched against him, yanking the soft linen of his shirt and dragging it over his head so she could feel his skin against hers. Finn rose on his elbows long enough to remove the last of the offending article and toss it aside, then he was on her again and they were both kissing and touching one another with shameless abandon. Openly exploring all of the places both had thought about, but never dared touch.

She experienced no missish reservations when he began to lift her skirts. By then, Evie was so consumed with need and the urgency for more had blinded her. Her fingers fumbled at the falls of his breeches and they both moaned as she finally got them open and his arousal sprang free. She felt the insistent press of it against her body and acted purely on instinct. Her legs fell open, so that she cradled him near the entrance to her body and she writhed shamelessly as he slowly pushed inside, enjoying every hard inch of the intrusion. The corded muscles in his neck and arms were testament to how much effort it took to hold himself back while her body became accustomed to the size and shape of him.

The sting of pain was brief but forgettable. As soon as Finn began to move inside her, nothing else mattered but him and how glorious he was making her feel. It might have been minutes; it might have been hours. Evie lost all concept of time as her body came alive and moved with his. Every sense was heightened. She could smell the fresh, dewy grass, the wild flowers. Felt the warm caress of the sun on her face, the heat of his skin, the joy in her heart. Even the early morning birdsong was louder and sweeter than she had ever heard it.

This was right.

Not only were their bodies locked together, but Evie could feel him touching her very soul and she revelled in the warmth that came from the knowledge. She showed him how she felt with her body—giving, taking, surrendering. She had been born to love him…

And then there was only Finn and her complete and all-consuming love for him, before the world disappeared and she shattered in sheer bliss around him.

Chapter Twenty-One

Long after he had collapsed panting beside her did the world slowly come back into focus. Evie glanced to her side and saw him, eyes closed, chest rising and falling frantically as he struggled to level his breathing. His shirt was gone, but in their haste the rest of his clothing was still partially clinging on—but pushed down so that the interesting part of him could do what it had been made for.

She supposed she looked equally as silly. She was still technically wearing her gown and shift, although they had been pushed down and rucked up to form a crumpled ring about her middle, hopelessly crushed and probably stained with grass. At some point she had lost a slipper and the ridiculousness of the situation made her giggle.

Finn cracked open one eye. 'You're not supposed to find it funny.' But as he was smiling, too, Evie did not think he was particularly offended by her reaction.

'I appreciate the irony. To be deflowered amongst the wild flowers. And all before breakfast.'

He rolled on to his side and plucked a daisy out of the long grass, poked it into her hair, then picked another to join it. Satisfied with his arrangement, he bent his head and kissed her. A tender kiss which warmed her heart.

'I should say you have definitely earned your piece of dry toast this morning. Although I am certain that a deflowering warrants bacon.'

'Definitely bacon. Perhaps even sausage.' And then she glanced down his body to *that* part of him and began to giggle afresh. Her laughter was infectious and he joined in.

'You are a delightful temptation, Evie.' He trailed the tip of his index finger slowly down her cheek and over one bare breast. Then sighed. 'And I should love nothing more than to while away the day here with you. But alas, my workers will be about soon and they do like to gossip. I fear if they see you, even dressed, it will be all too apparent what has transpired here.'

Finn sat up and solicitously helped Evie to stand, then reluctantly assisted her back into the bodice of her dress. Only when she was almost respectable did he put his own clothing to rights, using the mundane task to put his tangled thoughts into some sort of order.

For the first time in years, he was not altogether sure how he was feeling. He supposed he should be riddled with guilt, although rather bizarrely he wasn't. Not yet, at least. Doubtless it would come crashing down soon enough and he would feel more wretched, if that were possible. For the moment, however, there were other feelings to consider.

The first was his self-satisfied, smug male pride. Finn had not planned any sort of seduction with Evie, any more than he had with any other woman since he had married Olivia. He had believed that part of his life to be over as he had nothing left of his heart to offer a woman. Finn had lusted after her and allowed his errant thoughts to wonder what it would be like to have her—such musings were human, after all, and difficult to suppress—but he certainly had never intended on acting on those urges. Quite how he had come to be entwined with her in the middle of the meadow, he could not say. One second he was burning with anger, the next he was consumed with passion for the lovely woman he had just, as she put it so aptly, deflowered.

Yet Evie had been no shy virgin or passive lover. She had thrown herself into their frantic, unexpected lovemaking with the same lusty enthusiasm as she did every other pleasure she enjoyed. And she *had* enjoyed it. Of that, he was certain and it had nothing to do with his own inflated opinions of his sexual prowess and everything to do with the way she had responded to his touch. It had been Evie who had torn Finn's clothes off and she had eagerly touched and kissed every part of his body she could manage as they had writhed on the floor. Thinking about the wonderful, earthy little sounds she made as he pleasured her threatened to make him hard all over again. He recalled his first impressions of Evie had been entirely physical. He had thought then that she had a body made for sin. Just now, she had confirmed it. Evie in the throes of passion was one of the most splendid experiences Finn could ever remember.

In fact, Finn could not bring himself to be sorry for compromising her. He had purposefully made her his. He should not have done. It had been a wholly selfish and ill-conceived act, yet the ramifications of it would now irrefutably change both of their lives for ever. It went without saying, they would have to marry. Evie might already be with child—something which

should terrify him, yet did not. The prospect
was not completely unwelcome. The idea of her
swelling with his offspring held a great deal of
appeal. Even if there was no babe, he had ruined
her and as a gentleman he was duty-bound to
do the right thing. However, Finn did not seem
to feel trapped by that, a part of him actually
welcomed it—almost as if he had intended to
marry her all along and just needed the push to
do the deed. The excuse to be with her.

If that was the case, perhaps he should feel
guilty at trapping Evie? Yet he found himself
strangely comforted at the idea of having her as
his wife. Despite her assertions she wanted her
independence and her own household, she was
too generous in nature and too nurturing to live
out her days as a spinster. Finn might not be the
husband she had hoped for in her girlish dreams,
but he was a vast improvement on Fergus. The
relief he experienced to know Evie would not be
subjected to a life of sheer misery with his twin
almost made up for his own selfishness in wanting to have her for himself. There was also no
denying Evie made his days brighter and eased
the constant ache he held in his heart. Already,
in the short time she had invaded his lonely life,
he could not envisage ever having to say goodbye to her. If she left, it would break his heart,

an ironic turn of phrase when he had long believed his heart to be nothing but a dried husk in his chest.

However, at the moment it did not feel quite so dead. Which led Finn to consider the other emotion which was rearing its head, the overwhelming and heart-stopping tenderness he was currently consumed with. As they strolled back to the house, Finn indulged his need to hold her hand and found himself smiling at the constant stream of chatter, about everything and nothing, that was so Evie. It was hard to explain exactly what that tenderness was borne out of, although it had nothing to do with lust or attraction. Finn felt those things for Evie. He always had. But this new feeling was different. Gratitude, relief, a sense of camaraderie, a need to be near her, talk to her and touch her, a sense of wonder at the way she moved or spoke or reacted. All of those things were swirling around in the mix—but there was something more worrying, a familiar forgotten sensation of rightness, of completeness, and the certainty that he would do whatever it took to make this wonderful, vexing, kind-hearted angel happy.

For ever.

His heart began to knock against his ribs in panic. The last time he had experienced such a powerful emotion had been for Olivia and then he had had no qualms about calling it love.

Good grief!

Finn experienced a moment of complete, stunned light-headedness. Was he in love with Evie? Even as he pondered it and tried to talk himself out of it, he acknowledged it was the truth. He was confident enough of his feelings to drop to his knees propose to her here and now. His realisation might indeed be sudden, but those unique features, which all bound together created love, had been gradually creeping up on him since she had arrived without him seeing it. When they were all put together and bit by bit they had worked their heady magic, the terrifying end result had been a foregone conclusion. It explained why he had found their joining so emotionally satisfying as well as physically. It had been the last piece of the puzzle. It had awoken his shrivelled dead heart and given it something Finn had long abandoned, even before Olivia died.

Hope.

'Are you all right, Finn?' Evie was regarding him with amusement. 'You look like you have seen a ghost.'

He laughed and dismissed it with some silly comment, ignoring the difficult lump in his throat and tightness in his chest. He might not have seen a ghost, but he certainly needed to talk to one and explain himself. Here he was, contemplating marriage and love and children rashly again, while Olivia lay in the ground because of him. What if he failed Evie, too? He had hardly made a success of his first attempt of being a good husband and, like Olivia, Evie was such a kind and caring soul while he was such a bad-tempered, surly individual. Poor Evie had suffered years of turmoil with her unreasonable stepmother and now he was planning on condemning her to a lifetime of his moods and churlish comments, when in his heart he knew she deserved better.

Hastily, he grabbed Evie's hand and sneaked her into the house and up the back stairs as quickly as he could. He kissed her at her bedchamber door, because he selfishly could not help himself, and then explained he had important things to do and probably would not see her till after breakfast. Then he went to his own room, washed and changed, and headed out again where he could be alone with his thoughts, this new dilemma that had presented itself and the guilt which now felt heavier than ever.

Evie seriously contemplated going to bed. Not only had she not slept all night, but, thanks to

Finn, her body was now deliciously languid and relaxed. She had had no idea physical intimacy could create such a glorious sense of well-being. However, as soon as she entered her bedchamber and saw the evidence of the chaos Fergus had made of her things, Evie knew she would not sleep until it was all put to rights. Once the room was tidied and the tantalising aroma of freshly cooked bacon wafted around the house, she was starving.

To make her morning even more perfect, there was no sign of Hyacinth in the breakfast room so Evie guiltlessly piled her plate with everything that tempted her and sat down to eat in blissful peace. Unfortunately, it soon turned sour as Hyacinth sailed in.

'Good gracious, Evelyn. Are you really going to eat all of that food?'

Evie ignored the barb. She was not going to let Hyacinth spoil her good mood. 'Good morning, Stepmother. I trust you are well.'

Hyacinth sat in the chair next to Evie and sniffed. 'Not really, Evie. I am not at all well. This dreadful places bores me stiff. There is nothing whatsoever to do.'

'Well, you could walk in the parkland. It's very beautiful at this time of year and—'

'Oh, pish! One only walks in a park to be

seen, Evelyn. As far as I can tell, the only society hereabouts are farm labourers and sheep.'

'The exercise and fresh air are very—' Her words were cut off by her stepmother's impatient groan.

'Rose and Iris are desperate to go shopping. How far away is the nearest village?'

'At least ten miles.' Evie could feel the blotches bloom on her neck at the hasty lie, but really, until she told them the truth, her stepfamily could not go to the village.

'We could take the carriage then. It would at least give us something to do.'

Now would be the perfect time to tell the truth and be done with the sham. 'It is Tuesday. Nothing happens in the village on a Tuesday. Friday is market day. All the *best* people in the area only visit the village on market days.' Which gave Evie a few more days to pluck up the courage to say what she had wanted to say for years and was still putting off like a coward.

As she had hoped, this titbit gave the social-climbing woman pause. 'Really? Well, I suppose it would not do to go on the wrong day. Are there many *good* people in the local area?'

By 'good people' Hyacinth always meant the titled or the excessively wealthy, preferably with eligible and marriageable sons.

'You would have to ask Fi-ergus. I have not really been introduced to local society yet.'

'But you have been here weeks, you silly girl! I suggest you get *Fi-ergus* to do his duty and put you amongst the correct circles at once. I shall take him to task if he ever decides to grace us with his presence.'

It had been a stupid mistake on two counts. Firstly, Evie's consistent inability to call Finn Fergus made it sound as if she had some strange jaw-affecting palsy which only served to increase her nervousness at the lie. And, of course, it only perpetuated the ridiculous charade Aunt Winnie had talked her into. Finn would be livid to find out she was still hiding behind the lie rather than telling the truth. It was quite pathetic to continue with it in view of Fergus's disappearance and the pertinent fact his brother had made it quite plain he had no intention of playing along with it. Common sense told her she needed to simply tell the truth and get it over with. She was prolonging the inevitable. Evie gazed longingly at her breakfast. Not only was it going cold, but Hyacinth had ruined the taste of it. She pushed the plate away and hardened her heart. Hyacinth had provided her with a perfect opportunity to end her career as a doormat.

'Actually, I have been meaning to talk to you about Fergus—'

The door to the breakfast room slammed open and a furious Rose stalked in. 'For the second morning in a row, I have had my beauty sleep interrupted by all the horrid birds outside. I hate the countryside. Don't you have a gamekeeper here or something, Evie? I want him to shoot the lot of them. It is barely half past eight, for pity's sake.'

Her mother nodded in sympathy. 'Those birds are a nuisance, Rose. We do not have to listen to all of that uproar in Mayfair in the mornings.'

'I want to go home, Mother. I hate it here. I do not see why I need to be here when it is Iris who—'

Hyacinth's forced, tinkling laugh brought her daughter up short. Clearly they both wanted to keep Iris's scandal a secret from Evie. 'Where is you dear sister?'

Rose pouted and sat down with a huff. 'Iris can sleep through anything. Her beauty sleep will not be disturbed.'

'I like the dawn chorus,' said Evie, hoping to diffuse the tension, 'I find it soothing.' It had been quite lovely this morning while she and Finn had been enjoying intimacies in the meadow. She doubted she would ever hear bird-song again without thinking about it.

'Well, it is not as if you need any beauty sleep, do you, Evie?' Rose scowled. 'Pour me some tea, will you—and be quick about it. I have a headache.'

Like a servant, Evie dutifully went to the side-board and began to prepare the drink, all the while castigating herself for allowing herself to be treated like a doormat. She had just added the sugar when Hyacinth piped up again. 'There must be a gamekeeper on an estate of this size. I shall speak to Fergus and demand he has those birds shot. Where is Fergus?'

Evie almost dropped the cup at the outrageous request. 'He left earlier. I believe he had estate business.'

Now that she thought about it, Finn had been in an awful hurry to leave her. He had even skipped breakfast, the one meal of the day he never missed. Perhaps he had regretted what they had done, just as he had the kiss a few days before? It was certainly something to consider and made her feel quite uneasy.

Her stepmother's lips began to purse, their default position when she encountered anything which displeased her. 'Estate business! Really, Evelyn, how can you be so naive? Fergus has never done a day's work in his life. He disappears from dawn to dusk, and, knowing his reputation, I think he is probably up to all manner of unsavoury mischief. This marriage to Fergus is foolishness, Evelyn, can you not see you are making a dreadful mistake? Your father, God rest his soul, would want you to call it off.'

'But I love him.' It had been her stock response to all of Hyacinth's objections since Evie had sprung the engagement on her and bolted. For once, the lie did not make her neck bloom in blotches because it was not a lie any longer. She loved Finn with all of her heart. 'My place is here, in the north, with him.' Well, she hoped it was—unless Finn did regret what they had done, which didn't bear thinking about because then she would have to leave.

'But he doesn't love you, Evelyn. He certainly does not respect you. All he wants is your fortune. Everyone can see it except you!'

Evie shrugged and sipped her tea. It didn't matter if Finn loved her or not. She had enough for both of them, yet after last night and this morning, she had been hopeful he was fond of her at least. For someone who had been so desperately alone for so very long, Evie could be content with fond. It was considerably more than she had ever expected from any man and

Finn had said he appreciated her company. Unprompted, too. With him she was not invisible and he was challenging her to be braver. Already, Evie was not frightened of asserting herself with Finn. He did listen to her and he allowed her to finish her sentences. If only she could summon up the same courage against Hyacinth. She really needed to tell her the truth. 'Actually, Stepmother—'

'You mark my words, Evelyn: you will be doomed to a life of misery with that man. Once he has control of *our* money, he will return to London without you and continue his libertine ways. He will spend our money and sell your father's house. We will all be destitute within a year. You are a means to an end, Evelyn.' Hadn't she always been? 'A man like Stanford needs a more boisterous wife. Your plain face and lack of charm will bore him to tears in a fortnight.'

Finn had been most enthusiastic about her 'charms'. The thought made Evie stifle a grin. How magnificent would it be to appraise Hyacinth of that wonderful truth? He had called her a delightful temptation and his eyes had darkened with passion. Real passion. She doubted men could pretend such things, what with the physical evidence being so gloriously obvious.

'Come home, Evelyn. If you have your heart

set on marrying, I will help you to find a more suitable husband. Perhaps I should have done so sooner, although I had thought you were content as you were. Now I see you are not, then I am sure I can find you a nice, suitable gentleman. A man who does not put stock in age or beauty or appearances.' That comment wounded as it always did. As it was always meant to. 'I beg you to reconsider. If not for me or your devoted sisters—do it for your father. It is what he would have wanted.'

It was always the same. If Hyacinth's criticisms did not hit their mark, she resorted to using her father's wishes as a weapon, knowing Evie would buckle under the weight of the guilt. It was funny. Usually those words pricked at her conscience and brought her up short. Since Finn had suggested her father had also been a doormat, and might have left his fortune to Evie as his one and only act of defiance, Evie finally saw it as the divisive tool it was.

'My father would want me to be happy. Being with Fi-ergus makes me happy.' She wanted to stamp her feet for being so spineless. Why could she not tell the truth?

His name is Finn! And he is nothing like his odious brother. He is kind and loyal and quite the most wonderful man I have ever met—and

I love him. And he is still in love with his beau-
tiful, dead wife so my love for him is futile. Pa-
thetic. Just as I am.

'Please stop saying all those awful things
about him.'

Hyacinth's lips disappeared in a grim, flat
line at such open defiance. 'Your father knew
the only man who would ever take interest in
such a plain and plump creature as you would be
a fortune-hunter! I promised him I would protect you from such men, Evelyn! But you always
were such a silly girl.' Hyacinth stood, clearly
affronted by Evie's blatant insubordination, to
issue her parting salvo. 'Take a look at yourself
in the mirror, Evelyn. A good, long, hard look
and ask yourself what it is he sees in you. Aside
from the money, Evelyn, I can assure you, there
really is nothing.'

Chapter Twenty-Two

It was late morning when Finn found himself at his wife's grave. After hours of painful soul-searching, he had decided two things. Firstly, he had to tell Evie the truth about Olivia's death. She had the right to know exactly what sort of man she was marrying, even if that meant she might ultimately decide he wasn't worth the effort once she knew what he had done. And secondly, he needed to tell Olivia he had had the audacity to fall in love with another woman despite his chronic failure as a husband to her. He was not particularly looking forward to either conversation.

He stared down at the well-tended plot, feeling quite ridiculous to even be contemplating talking to a dead woman—but if Evie was convinced she would answer him, he was prepared to give it a go. Evie had displayed an annoying tendency to get things right so far.

'Hello, Olivia. I hope you are...' His voice trailed off on a sigh. What platitudes did one offer the dead? *I hope you are well* was hardly appropriate and as he could not think of something more suitable, he got straight to the point. 'The thing is, I have met a woman. I thought she was engaged to Fergus, but it turns out she isn't and I probably have to marry her.'

That made it sound as if his hand was being forced, which of course it wasn't. Evie had made no demands so far and, knowing Evie, he thought she probably wouldn't.

'Actually, Olivia, selfishly, I want to marry her. What do you think of that?'

Not so much as a faint breeze could be heard in the silent churchyard. No birds were singing. No noise wafted from the village beyond. Nothing. Only stony, unforgiving silence.

'I know I let you down. You have no idea how much I have regretted my actions on that last morning. I should have stayed with you and talked you out of it. I should have convinced you that you were not a burden to me. I let my temper get the better of me and stormed off and I live with the guilt every day. Please do not think me marrying another will mean I will forget. I shall continue to carry it with me every day. I deserve to.'

Finn paused again to wait for some sort of sign from the heavens. There was still nothing.

'I should like your blessing, Olivia. I know that is a great deal to ask after I failed you, but...' Should he tell his wife he loved Evie or would that be cruel? He had pledged his undying love to Olivia on the day they had married and he had still made her feel like a burden to him in the end, even though he had tried to hide his frustrations from her. Poorly, as it turned out.

'I think you would like Evie. She is a kind and generous soul. She brings happiness with her wherever she goes. A bit like the sunshine... and...it was her stupid idea that I talk to you. She has silly ideas like that. As if the dead can hear us? As if you can hear me? As if you would want to?'

If he had come here seeking answers, he was going home empty-handed. Olivia was not speaking to him. Perhaps that was because she was still angry at him for letting her down or, more likely, as he had always suspected, the dead could not converse with the living.

Because they were dead.

Finn could not help feeling irritated at Evie for putting such nonsense into his mind in the first place. He was about to walk away in utter disgust at himself when he heard a voice which made him stop in his tracks.

'Hello, Finn. Are you feeling better now?'

He turned and came face-to-face with Charlotte Cardew.

'Yes, thank you, Charlotte.' Now he felt queasy as well as remorseful and stupid. How much had Charlotte heard of his pathetic, guilt-ridden monologue? Charlotte, who knew too much and who he had recently been horrifically short towards. Finn might not be able to hear the dead, but he apparently had no problem channelling Evie.

He could hear her quiet, disappointed remonstrance in his head. *Charlotte cares for you, Finn. Your rudeness hurt her feelings.*

He gritted his teeth and tried to smile. 'Hello, Charlotte. I trust you are well.'

She smiled in return and stared down at Olivia's grave. 'I come here to talk to her sometimes, too. Olivia always was very good at listening to my troubles.'

'Does she ever answer you?' He had meant it to sound dismissive, but it came out more desperately curious instead. He instantly blamed Evie and her reinstatement of his social conscience.

'Oh, yes! In her own way she always answers.

I find it a great comfort, especially when I am in a temper. Olivia always had a matter-of-fact way about her when I was angry.' As she had with Finn. 'Do you remember how she never shouted when she wanted to get her own way? She would reply oh-so-calmly and make you feel like a fool for raising your voice.'

The painful memory of their last conversation jarred through Finn's mind.

'Stop telling me that you want to die, Olivia. I do not want to hear it.' He had been pacing around her bed, refusing to listen to her words.

'Oh, Finn,' she had replied, so very calmly, *'my life has become a burden. It is not fair on me and it is not fair on you.'*

He should have realised he needed to stay then. Olivia was always at her most determined when she had been calm. The pain the memory brought must have showed in his expression because Charlotte slipped her arm through his.

'Come and have some tea, Finn, and let us remember her properly.'

Too choked to do anything other than nod, he allowed her to lead him up the narrow path to the vicarage. He regretted the decision the moment she pushed open the front door and called to her husband. 'Edward! Look who I have brought to visit with us. It is Finn!' Now he was confronted with both Cardews and had no idea exactly what he was supposed to say.

'Perhaps this is not the right time…'

Charlotte gripped his arm and practically dragged him in the door. 'It's been three years, Finn. We are your friends. Do not shut us out.'

Edward Cardew appeared in the homely kitchen and held out his hand to shake Finn's. Not taking it would be churlish, although why Edward would want to shake his hand when he knew what he had pushed Olivia into, Finn did not understand.

'Finn—it has been an age.' He pumped his hand enthusiastically and then ushered him inside, while Charlotte issued orders to a maid to see to tea and bring it into the parlour. The two of them together were like a whirlwind. They picked him up and forced him to follow, whether he wanted to or not. Before he could argue, Finn found himself seated on the sofa with a cup balanced on his knee, Charlotte anchoring him in place with her linked arm, and Edward sat opposite, smiling benevolently.

'I came to call on you a few times, Finn.' Edward had called incessantly that first year and, every time, Finn had instructed Stowers to claim he was not at home because he had feared what the clergyman might say.

'I am sorry—I…' Clearly, today, all attempts at eloquent speech were doomed to allude him.

'No apology is necessary, Finn. I understood you were grieving your wife. Everyone knew how much you loved her.'

'So much that I pushed her to kill herself, Edward?' Finn shook his head and stared at his hands. 'We all know what happened that day. Please let us not pretend differently.'

The ensuing prolonged silence forced Finn to look up. Instead of censure, he saw blatant shock on both of their faces. Charlotte was the first to speak.

'How exactly did you push her into taking her life, Finn?'

'I made her feel like a burden. Do not try to deny it. She had become convinced her illness was not fair on me.'

The husband and wife exchanged one of those meaningful glances that only husbands and wives shared. 'I spent many hours with Olivia in her last week, Finn, and I can assure you she never believed you thought her a burden.'

Edward Cardew sat back in his chair and regarded Finn thoughtfully.

'She was tired of the burden of life. We discussed that a great deal. She was tired of the pain and all the effort it took to keep going.

But she also worried about you. She made me promise I would look after you when she was gone, but, alas, I fear I failed her in that task. I hoped you would eventually feel able to continue our friendship and I am delighted to see you finally here.'

'You were there, Edward!' Finn was beginning to feel annoyed at their determination to brush over what happened. 'You saw the laudanum bottle and the letter. You took them both! You know she blamed me.'

'Blamed you? Of course she didn't, and as for the bottle and the letter, I prefer to think about Olivia's death as what it was—an inevitable tragedy. Do you seriously think it was the laudanum that killed her?'

'Of course it was. The bottle was full before I left and drained when I returned!'

Charlotte placed her hand on top of his. 'We are not denying she hastened the process, Finn—but she was going to die with or without it.'

'Not then she wasn't—'

Charlotte interrupted angrily. 'Stop this, Finn! You are so busy blaming yourself for what happened that day, I believe you have lost sight of the truth.'

Her husband shot her an exasperated look and

continued in a calmer vein. 'Her illness was advancing rapidly, Finn. In those last few months, it had progressed from her legs to other parts of her body. She was losing vision in her eyes, she had already lost much of the use of her left arm. She had what? Perhaps another few months to live—but she dreaded those months, Finn. Olivia hated the idea of being completely helpless. Of being completely paralysed and locked in the dark. She knew there was no hope. We all knew there was no hope. That is why she said goodbye to everyone in the weeks leading up to her death.'

'She tried to say goodbye to you, too, Finn,' Charlotte added, stroking his hand, 'except you would not hear of it.'

'I didn't want her to kill herself!'

'And she did not want her last days on earth to be left to the mercy of her disease, powerless and filled with pain. The decision she took was hers to make.'

Finn glared at the vicar. 'Suicide is a crime against God, Edward. You hid it to spare her reputation. Do not deny that.'

'I hid it because I did not believe I, or anyone else, had the right to judge her. Only God can judge our actions, Finn—and I did not believe, and still do not believe, he would have judged Olivia harshly for doing what she did. She is at peace now. And I am content with that knowledge.'

'She was not at peace. We argued that morning.' The Cardews did not know that pertinent detail. 'She told me she felt living was unfair on me. I stormed off and when I returned she had done the unthinkable. You saw the note, Edward. You saw she blamed me!'

Edward stood and walked to the bookcase. He located a slim volume, opened it and removed a piece of paper. 'Here is the letter, Finn. I see no blame in it.' He held it out and Finn recoiled. He had not known it still existed.

'I do not want to look at that again. I am well aware of what it says. The words will be seared into my brain for ever. *I hope you are happy, my darling.* Happy you have succeeded in killing me.'

'You are choosing to read a particular meaning into them, Finn.' Edward placed the offending letter open on to Finn's lap and removed the cup. 'And one I do not believe was ever there. I read it quite differently and so does Charlotte. We see it as Olivia's dearest wish. She loved you and wanted only your happiness. She would hate to see you torturing yourself like this when all she wanted was for you to have a happy future, even though she could not be in that future with you.'

They were in all earnest—yet Finn knew they were quite wrong. 'She could have been in it.'

Charlotte sighed and regarded him with pity. 'No, Finn. She couldn't. Her death was imminent.'

Finn could feel his tenuous grip on his temper slipping. 'I do not believe that, Charlotte. She still had good days and bad days. On that particular morning, she had full use of her right arm and some movement in her left, when only the day before she had been unable to move either. Her condition was improving… Perhaps in time the damage would have reversed. It is not as if any of the physicians knew what was wrong— nobody could emphatically say the condition was permanent.' Olivia had been able to sit up in bed that morning, he remembered. She had been able to feed herself her breakfast and they had talked for hours, reminiscing and laughing. She had run her fingers through his hair.

Touched his face.

Then her eyes had clouded.

'It is time to say goodbye, Finn.'

She had said goodbye to him twice before already and both times he had refused to listen. He had put his foot down and denied her further opportunity to discuss it. Both times she had smiled sadly when he had returned, when the dust had settled, and the topic had been ignored again for a week or two. Except the last time; when the goodbye had been real and his harsh words had been the final ones she had heard from him. Emotion clogged his throat and threatened to overwhelm him.

Charlotte rested her hand on his shoulder, smoothing slow circles across his muscles which offered him no comfort. 'The good days were few and far between and becoming less frequent. She acted then because she knew it might be her last opportunity to leave on her terms, Finn, before she was completely incapacitated and helpless. The very idea of that horrified her. Olivia decided to hasten her departure because she was tired of the effort of staying alive. Even for you. And you are the only reason she held on as long as she did. Would you rather she had lingered? In agony or insensible from the laudanum? She did not deserve that sort of ending, Finn. Instead she took the bold decision to leave you whilst she was still in a position to control her own destiny.'

Finn grabbed the letter as he stood and walked angrily to the door with it clutched in his hand. Coming here had been a huge mistake, but not quite for the reasons Finn had always believed. He had expected their blame or condemnation, not this. 'I could have taken care of her for however long it took. At least she would have still been here.'

'But ask yourself this, Finn.' Edward Cardew's soft voice followed him out. 'Whose sake were you keeping her here for? Olivia's or yours?'

Chapter Twenty-Three

'Where is Fergus?' Aunt Winnie asked for the fifth time in as many minutes. 'Our luncheon will be burned to a crisp if we continue to wait for him to arrive.'

Evie pretended she was not worried. 'I am certain he will be home soon, as he did not eat breakfast. We shall continue to wait for him a bit longer. It is barely one o'clock. He has obviously been waylaid by some pressing estate matter.'

Although now she seriously suspected he was avoiding her. Nobody had seen hide nor hair of him since he had kissed her goodbye this morning. Then, she had been infused with the heady aftermath of their lovemaking and hopelessly thought he had been, too. Now, she was becoming increasingly worried that he regretted it.

Hyacinth was not helping. Her personal criticism of Evie had been almost constant all morning, gradually eroding her new-found confidence and making her feel ugly again. That and her continued requests for more money because she was practically destitute, thanks to her father's careless oversight, and reduced to begging for scraps at Evie's table. Until, inevitably, Fergus gambled away the table as well and they were all doomed to spend eternity in the workhouse. Together. Evie's personal idea of hell.

'I am becoming increasingly of the opinion your fiancé wants little or nothing to do with you, Evelyn.'

Hyacinth shared a pointed look with her two daughters, indicating the three of them had obviously been discussing it at great length behind her back.

'I dare say I have never seen a man so less enamoured of his betrothed in all of my life. He has not favoured us with his presence for more than five minutes since our arrival, which is beyond disrespectful. Nor, if you will forgive me for pointing it out, has he spent any time with you. No doubt he is off gallivanting with some mistress somewhere, his plain, plump fiancée already a distant memory. I tell you, you are out of sight, out of mind, Evelyn. That can be the only explanation. It is beyond me why you are so insistent you will marry him. As I keep say-

ing, the only thing he finds of interest in you is
the fortune your father *meant* to leave to me. If
only the silly man hadn't died before he could
complete the formalities.'

The way Hyacinth told it, her father's death
was merely a huge inconvenience to her.

It was all making Evie's head ache. Finn's
sudden disappearance was also making her heart
ache. After what they had done, why wasn't he
here? If he had been, then perhaps she would finally find the courage to say all that she wanted
to say to their uninvited guests. Every single
minute in their company was pure torture.

'I must say, I did think it quite scandalous to
find out you were both living under the same
roof when we first arrived, Evie.' Iris was wearing her malicious I-am-so-innocent face. The
one she wore when she was about to deliver
a crushing set down designed to make everyone else laugh at Evie's expense. Evie wanted to
punch it, push her thumbs into Iris's eye sockets
and tell her to shut up. Instead she stared down
at her hands and waited to be bludgeoned. The
way she always did. Finn was right, if she could
spin her head around to look at her own back,
Evie would probably see hundreds of footprints
wiped carelessly all over it.

'I was convinced that something improper

had occurred,' continued Iris with a tinkling laugh, 'but I needn't have worried when nothing could be further from the truth. Why, I doubt he has even kissed you, has he? Poor Evie.'

'And you would know all about kissing, wouldn't you, Iris?' None of her stepfamily acknowledged Aunt Winnie's barb, so Evie glanced at her gratefully, wishing she had been brave enough to have said it.

'Actually, he has kissed her.' Finn strode into the room, looking all windswept and delectable, making Evie sag with relief. 'And he has done so repeatedly.' To prove the point, he walked right towards her, picked up her hand and placed a lingering kiss on the back of it. Being unaccustomed to public displays of affection, and suddenly very aware of all of the other places on her person where those lips had recently been, Evie blushed like a beetroot.

'Hello, Fi-ergus,' she managed awkwardly and then blushed some more when Finn raised a questioning eyebrow at the fact she was still pathetically trying to maintain her silly ruse. Within moments, the tell-tale nervous blotches were blooming all over her neck. He would be disappointed she had still not told Hyacinth the truth. Evie was beyond disappointed she still apparently lacked the ability. Hyacinth had been driving her mad all day.

'We had despaired of your presence, my lord.' Hyacinth picked up her quizzing glass and stared at Finn. 'I must say your attention to your wardrobe has diminished quite shockingly since you arrived in the north. Is that the best jacket you could wear when everyone else has made the effort?' Her eyes flicked to Evie and her lips pursed. 'Well, most of us have made the effort.'

Hyacinth had been most scathing of Evie's choice of gown today, comparing her figure to a sack full of writhing puppies about to be drowned.

Finn gave Hyacinth a look that could freeze water, then tossed Evie one which made her blood heat. 'You look ravishing today, Evie. I can only remember one time when you were lovelier.' She offered Finn a shy smile of thanks which evaporated the moment she saw his eyes. Regardless of what he really thought of the dress, he was referring to this morning, she was certain, and was looking at her as if he wouldn't mind ravishing her thoroughly again. Right this minute. It did wonders for her confidence.

Momentarily.

'Do I look ravishing, my lord?' Iris purred, as she prowled towards him. She appeared to have been poured into the peach silk she was wearing and the neckline left little to the imagination. If Iris's dress was ever to be likened to a sack of puppies about to be drowned, there were a couple of eager puppies on the verge of escaping the sack. Evie experienced the sting of jealousy as Finn's gaze slowly raked her gorgeous stepsister up and down, his eyes stopping for far longer than was necessary on her cleavage.

'You, madam, look like you have just *been* ravished.' His gaze wandered lazily back to Evie's and froze. 'Might I borrow you for a minute, Evie?' he said pointedly and she felt her shoulders drop with shame.

'Of course.'

He led her out of the drawing room and into another, then promptly closed the door. 'Fergus?'

She was beginning to squirm under the intensity of his gaze. 'I know, I'm sorry.'

'Why am I still pretending to be my feckless, thieving wretch of a brother?'

'I have been trying to tell her the truth.' She had started the sentence a few times, at any rate, but had happily let it trail off the very moment she had been interrupted. 'I am just waiting for the opportune moment.'

His dark brows came together in consternation. 'When will that be? At this rate, another ten years of your life will have been wasted. What happened to the foot-stamping firebrand from this morning who was tired of being a doormat?'

Evie looked at the floor and Finn began to pace, one hand dragging through his hair, in agitation. When she did not immediately answer he stopped pacing and went to her.

'After everything that has happened since last night... I had hoped you would put an end to all of this stupidity.' His hand came up and cradled her cheek tenderly. 'I always thought it was an idiotic plan in the first place. The longer you drag it on, the more you run the risk of exposure, Evie. Tell them the truth.'

'I will—perhaps after luncheon. Everyone has been waiting for you. They are all starving.'

The fact she could not meet his eyes was telling. Yet seeing her so submissive angered Finn.

'For days you have been pushing me to face my fears and talk about Olivia. I did. Because I knew you wanted me to. I want you to tell Hyacinth and her noxious daughters the truth, Evie. I want them gone. You and I have important things to discuss. We need to talk about what happened between this morning and what we are going to do about it. I have things I need to say. Personal things. I do not feel comfortable doing that while they are still here.' Especially if at the end of them, Evie spurned him.

She nodded, but her eyes still did not rise to meet his. 'I know. But I need time to prepare myself, Finn. Let us get through luncheon and then I promise you I will tell them.'

She was procrastinating. Avoiding the inevitable. And Finn knew how terrified she was to act in a manner that had always been anathema to her, especially as she was still riddled with misguided guilt on account of her father's damning words. Evie's quiet acquiesce was like his storming off. A refusal to face up to the truth and a defence mechanism. Perhaps Evie needed pushing, just as Finn had?

'All right. I shall play Fergus until the meal is finished. After that, either you tell Hyacinth to pack her trunks and leave, or I will.'

Evie's lovely, gold-flecked eyes finally locked on his and she nodded, then walked heavily back towards the dining room like a condemned man about to be hanged.

Finn felt cruel. Yet pretending to be Fergus, pretending that wastrel was still engaged to Evie after all the dreadful things he had done to her, even for the duration of a small meal, angered him. Evie was his now—at least he desperately wanted her to be his—and saying otherwise made the bile rise in his throat.

And Hyacinth had already directed one of her pithy insults at Evie. He had seen the hurt flit across her expression and had had to bite his tongue to stop himself from roaring at her stepmother in return. Realistically, it would be a miracle if he could keep his mouth shut if she spoke to her like that again. He gritted his teeth and followed Evie back into the vipers' pit and pasted a smile on his face, although he already suspected the meal was doomed from the outset.

The first few minutes were relatively painless. The conversation was stilted and awkward and Finn did not try to make it less so. He welcomed the awkwardness if it spurred Evie to be assertive. He grunted responses and focused on his food. Unfortunately, Iris Bradshaw had planted herself in the chair directly opposite him and seemed determined to engage him in conversation.

'I suppose you miss the entertainments of town quite keenly, my lord.'

'Not really.'

'Oh, come now, we both know you enjoy the Season, don't we?'

'Do we?'

'Why, yes—surely you recall the many *conver-*

sations we have had in some of the…ballrooms we have been in together?' Her meaning was quite explicit. A deaf man with no eyes could work out what she was alluding to. Fergus and Iris knew each other, perhaps a little too well.

'Nothing immediately springs to mind.'

Iris simpered and giggled like a practised courtesan. '*Really*, my lord? Yet you are still just as outrageous with your compliments. The one you gave me when you arrived was so very *typical* of you.' Had he complimented her? He couldn't recall it. He gave the silly girl a quizzical look and she gave him a well-practised knowing smile and licked her lips suggestively.

Was Iris flirting with him? Here? In front of Evie?

'You said I looked as if I had been *ravished*.' One of her fingers trailed down her neck and lingered at the top of her shamelessly displayed cleavage—and then Finn knew Iris was doing her best to humiliate Evie. She was flirting. Openly, insultingly flirting to make her stepsister feel small and insignificant by emphasising her charms. Which were, as charms went, nowhere near as tempting as Evie's. Two could play at that game.

'Indeed I did. I have never seen a gown so unsuitable for a family luncheon. I meant no compliment when I stated you appeared to have been ravished, dear Iris. But from what Aunt Winnie has told me about your character, I dare say if the cap fits…?' His gaze wandered lazily back to Evie's and he winked, making sure her toxic stepsister saw it before he turned back to his plate and idly cut his meat. 'I am surprised your mother allows you to be seen in public dressed like that. You are a scandal waiting to happen. Or perhaps the scandal has happened?'

Iris's eyes widened at the insult while Hyacinth's jaw almost dropped to the floor. Aunt Winnie cackled with delight. Finn was deliberately bating them. He couldn't help it. Even by his own standards, he was being shockingly rude. He hoped such behaviour would galvanise Evie to stand up for herself. But like a true doormat, she was nowhere near ready.

'Who would like some ham?' She was wielding the carving fork and knife so cheerfully, one might have thought no harsh words had been exchanged at all.

Hyacinth was vibrating with outrage, her icy glare remained rooted on him. 'How dare you insult my daughter like that?'

Finn shrugged and offered her a cheery smile. 'I dare, madam, because it is the truth. Even here, in remote and desolate Yorkshire, we have heard about Iris's recent indiscretion in the orangery. That is why you are here, is it not? You are not here to spend time with "dear Evelyn" at all. Admit it. Be honest for once. You are waiting out the scandal, hoping it will go away like the other one with the...?' He clicked his fingers impatiently.

'The Russian Count?' Aunt Winnie offered helpfully, enjoying the opportunity to fan the flames further, so he grinned at her in encouragement.

'The very one, Winifred. Thank you.'

Hyacinth stood, incensed. 'I came here to visit my dear stepdaughter and to try to talk her out of her travesty of a betrothal to you— the most shocking, debauched and scandalous libertine of the *ton*! I have your measure, sir, I assure you.'

'And I have yours.' He was actually beginning to enjoy himself. If only Evie would join in. 'You are a manipulative, conniving, spiteful...'

Evie panicked and grabbed his arm. 'Look— your food is getting cold.' Perhaps she could still salvage the situation and put off the inevitable until later. Or preferably tomorrow. Or the next day. Or the next. *Arrgh!* She was beginning to disgust herself with her pitiful attempts at pouring oil on troubled waters.

Hyacinth bristled for a moment, then turned on Evie. 'If he continues to be so outrageous, Evelyn, I must warn you he will not be welcome in my house in Mayfair. Tell him to stop immediately. Stand up for your family, Evelyn. Your lack of backbone astounds me.' Which was ironic, as it disgusted Evie, too. And if she wasn't mistaken, she could feel her dear mother's ardent disapproval from the heavens. Just to be sure, Evie stared up at the ceiling before Finn's words cut through her self-pity.

'As I understand it, the Mayfair house belongs to Evie, not you. And once I marry her, it will belong to me. Think about that, Hyacinth, before you insult her again. Evie has a soft heart. The most shocking, scandalous and debauched libertine of the *ton* has none.'

Hyacinth was practically foaming at the mouth. She turned towards Evie and pointed her waving finger at her. 'Are you going to stand by and allow him to threaten me with *my* home, Evelyn? Surely you will not countenance his making me and your devoted sisters homeless? Your father, God rest his soul, promised me that house. If you have any regard for him whatsoever, you will abandon your foolish desire to marry this…this…foul creature.'

'Why? So you can spend her money instead,

Mrs Bradshaw?' Finn decided to stand, too, and was looming over Hyacinth, making no attempt to temper the roiling hatred contorting his face. He did look magnificent. Decisive. Nothing like a doormat, like her father.

Evie had the overwhelming urge to cover her ears with her hands and run screaming from the room. 'Just stop it!' She turned and gave Finn a pleading look, only to have him fold his arms and glare back at her. The wretch was trying to force her hand.

And he was right to do so.

Listen to him, Evie. Your father was a door-mat. He needed a strong woman to guide him. That is why he picked me!

Her mother's voice in her head was exasper-ated; Evie remembered she had been a strong woman and her father had been a better man for it. Hyacinth was also a strong woman—but selfish. Self-absorbed. Cold.

'Your fiancé is a beast, Evie. A money-grabbing, whoring, gambling beast.'

It was well past time this pathetic charade came to an end. Evie took a deep breath and faced her stepmother. 'The thing is…er…um…'

'Oh, spit it out, you silly girl!'

'She is not a silly girl!' Finn's temper had snapped. His eyes had hardened and his nos-

trils had flared, and she loved him all the more
for his loyalty towards her, yet it was not his responsibility to fight Evie's battles. It was hers.

'The thing is, Hyacinth...'

'Tell him what is what, Evie!'

'Stop interrupting her sentences, you vile,
malicious hag!'

A strange, surreal sort of calm settled over
her. She rested her hand on his sleeve. 'I shall
deal with this.'

For several seconds Finn stared deeply into
her eyes, seeking the truth in them, no doubt,
because he always knew when she was lying.
He nodded curtly and sat back down. The very
fact he believed Evie *could* deal with it gave
her strength. She turned back towards Hyacinth
proudly and inhaled deeply.

'I am not marrying Fergus. I never was. I
made it all up and paid him to go along with it
because I wanted to escape you.'

Evie released the breath in a whoosh and
smiled at Finn. He grinned back encouragingly
and winked at her. In her head, her mother was
cheering.

'You had to pay him?' Iris exchanged a malicious look with her younger sister. 'I do not recall having to pay for your attentions, Fergus.
As I recall, you gave them all freely. Even at

your own engagement party, you still begged me for a kiss.'

If Evie had one iota of affection for Fergus, she might have been wounded by this announcement. Instead, it made her smile.

'He is not Fergus. This is Finn.'

'Finn?' Iris tilted her head to scrutinise him and was rewarded with a sour glare which could have curdled butter. Finn really was unbelievably, gloriously, outrageously rude at times and she loved him for that, too.

'Yes—Finn—Fergus's twin brother. When Fergus left me in the lurch, Finn stepped into the breach.' Bless him. He might well have disagreed with it and he certainly did so with a great deal of resentment, but he had done it. For free. For her. In a life so desperately short of romance, it had been the grandest romantic gesture Evie had ever received.

'Finn?' Hyacinth swept him with a thoroughly disgusted gaze and then did the same to Evie. 'I am not sure I have any idea what the devil is going on here.'

'I lied, Stepmother. I was too pathetic and lily-livered to tell you I was leaving home. I came to the north to buy my own house, as far away from you and your daughters as was humanly possible.' An errant bubble of laughter

escaped her mouth and Evie momentarily covered it with her hands, until she saw Finn's look
of encouragement, and decided to hell with it.
'The truth is… I *loathe* the lot of you.'

Finn looked proud. Aunt Winnie was beside
herself with joy and just kept grinning. Evie
began to giggle. The truth was addictive. And
so wonderfully liberating.

'You are mean, embittered and greedy and
have never been anything that even remotely
resembles a mother to me. You criticise and undermine me. Constantly interrupt me, and most
of the time you ignore me and make me feel invisible. Irrelevant. All you are, Hyacinth, is a
leech—and I was the poor victim who allowed
you to leech off me and was too frightened and
too polite to stop you because I wanted to carry
out my father's wishes. He wanted me to be a
dutiful daughter to you—what a joke! Well, I am
all done with it!' It was like being drunk and the
pent-up words just kept on coming. 'I want you
to pack up your things and leave.'

'Leave!' Hyacinth made a strange choking
sound. 'Leave!' Her lips drained of all colour as
they pressed together so tightly they resembled
a cat's bottom. 'Your father, God rest his soul…'

Evie stood and smashed her hand down on
the table with such force the dishes rattled. 'My

father was a doormat! He let you walk all over him, which was his choice, but he let you trample all over me in the process. Every year, your behaviour became worse and worse, and he never had the courage to tell you off!'

'Your father adored me—why, he entrusted his only daughter into my care—he…'

'Then why did he leave all his money, his house, all his worldly goods to me?'

Hyacinth's lips were so pursed they were turning blue and one of her eyes was twitching. It was wonderful. Feeling giddy and almost drunk, Evie stalked towards her and prodded her finger into the woman's chest as Hyacinth had done to her on so many occasions.

'Has it ever occurred to you that perhaps his will was his parting message to both of us, *dear* Stepmother? He could have left you everything, Hyacinth—but he didn't. He left it to me for a reason. I am only sorry it has taken me so many years to realise it.'

Chapter Twenty-Four

'Stowers!' Finn bellowed into the hallway. 'Have some maids pack the Bradshaws' trunks for them and send word to the stables to have their carriage brought around immediately.'

After that, everything happened in a bit of a blur. Finn took charge of the ensuing chaos and commotion, protecting Evie from the worst of it and chivvying their unwanted guests upstairs to supervise their own packing, lest he instruct his loyal servants to scoop it all up and deposit all of their things in the road for the beggars to help themselves to.

To begin with her stepfamily were furious. Then the fury turned to shock, and now they were merely silent in their outrage. Within the hour Evie was standing next to him on the gravel drive as her horrid stepmother and vile step-sisters climbed into their conveyance without so much as a backwards glance, their noses in the air, but clearly subdued. They were obviously terrified Evie might follow through on Finn's threat to evict them from the Mayfair town house, which meant for once the final word had gone to her.

And then they were gone.

Evie was astounded, yet euphoric.

'I did it.'

'Yes, you did.'

'You forced my hand.'

'You forced me to face my fears, Evie—I simply returned the favour. After everything you have done for me in the last few weeks, it was the least I could do.'

'I feel very proud of myself.'

'So you should.'

'Who would have thought that a plain and plump doormat like me could be so forceful?' She shook her head in wonder as they reached the front door.

'Oh, for pity's sake!' Finn growled and grabbed her hand and began to march her down the hallway at such a speed that by the time they got to the stairs, she was laughing.

'Where are you taking me?'

But Finn did not turn around. Instead, he took the stairs two at a time and forced Evie to practically sprint to catch up with him. 'Hyacinth is a demon. And like all demons, she must be exorcised. We are going to do what is necessary to get rid of her once and for all.'

Whatever he was planning, there was no denying his determination to do it. Evie's feet had never moved so fast. When they got to Evie's bedchamber he opened the door and then reversed their positions so that his hands were on her shoulders as he gently pushed her inside. 'I am tired of you putting yourself down because that woman has filled your head with rubbish.'

They came to a stop in front of the long mirror in the corner of the room and his eyes met hers in the reflection. 'I want you to see what I see. You are neither plain nor plump, Evie Bradshaw.' His hands slid down her arms possessively, before they snaked around her waist. 'I love your body.' His warm breath whispered against her ear, setting her nerve endings tingling. 'I love the way it curves.'

Evie watched his eyes darken in the mirror as his palms moved over her ribs and cupped her breasts. 'When I first saw you, I thought you had a body made for sin. Now that I have sampled it, I can assure you, I can think of nothing else.'

Her breathing became ragged when she

watched one of his hands massage her aching breast through her clothing while she felt the other begin to loosen the ties of her dress. In no time it was hanging loose. Finn slowly pushed it from her shoulders, his eyes never once leaving hers, until it pooled around her feet and she stood in her shift. Then, with deliberate slowness, he released her bound hair from its pins and nuzzled her neck with his lips.

There was something scandalous, and thrilling, in watching him intentionally seduce her. Evie could feel the tension in his body behind her, the press of his hardness into her bottom—but his eyes were hypnotic. They swirled with need and passion as he began to peel away the barrier of her shift, exposing first her bare breasts and then all of her to both of their gazes.

'Look at you.' His voice was gruff and laced with need. 'You are beautiful, Evie. I ache from wanting you.' His hands began their exploration of her skin by smoothing along her sides. 'Have you any idea how much you tortured me when you nursed me back to health, Evie? Every morning I had to feel your hands on me and every single morning I wanted you.'

When the pads of his thumbs finally grazed her puckered nipples she moaned. Finn's eyes darkened and he smiled. 'Now I am going to torture you, Evie, by worshipping this magnificent, womanly body while you watch me do it.'

One flattened hand began its sedate, thrilling descent down her abdomen. Her heart began to hammer as his fingers found their way into her dark curls and she arched when one of them found its way to her core and stood powerless in his arms as he caressed her in lazy, insistent circles.

'I see nothing plain or plump. All I see is beauty.' When her legs began to buckle, he took one of her hands in his free one and pressed it against his groin.

'Feel what you do to me, Evie. I am yours. Heart and soul.'

Evie almost collapsed against his chest. 'Finn…' It felt so good. 'Please…'

'You are not a doormat any longer, my darling. Tell me what you want.' His own breathing was fast and shallow and his dark eyes burned. 'Demand it.'

'I want you naked.'

He turned her in his arms and kissed her hungrily, while she slid the jacket from his shoulders. He helped her untuck his shirt, then yanked it swiftly over his head, waiting impatiently as Evie undid his falls with trembling fingers. He stepped out of his breeches and kicked them away, and stood before her in all his naked, aroused glory. Her eyes devoured him and she licked her lips nervously. His body was primed for her. Her eyes dropped to his arousal, yet Finn stood firm, waiting for her to make the next move.

'Don't be coy, Evie. I am yours. Command me.'

Bravely she reached out her hand and wrapped it possessively around the part of him her body yearned for. 'I want you inside me, Finn. Make me yours.'

He did not make her ask twice, he grabbed her and kissed her deeply. They tumbled on to the bed, panting. Both eager to do what nature had made their bodies for. He pressed his hips between her quivering legs and then stared down at her so longingly, it humbled her.

'I love you, Evie.'

At first, she did not want to believe it. They were just words, empty ones said in the heat of passion. But then she looked into his dark eyes and saw the truth of them written plainly there, and finally knew what it meant to be beautiful. He loved her.

Not her fortune.

Just her.

Tears stung her eyes as her heart burst with joy.

'And I love you, too, Finn.'

She brushed her mouth over his tenderly, pouring everything she felt inside into it and he slipped inside her with a low moan that she swallowed in a kiss. Despite all of the pent-up passion and the need to find completion, he made love to her slowly. So slowly, and so thoroughly, that she thought she would die from the pleasure. When it finally came, it dazzled her and she clung to him as the universe exploded around them. Then she held him tight and vowed never, ever to let go.

Chapter Twenty-Five

'I have a question to ask you, but before I do I need to tell you something.'

Finn climbed out of bed and padded to where his jacket had been discarded hours earlier. He handed Evie the damning piece of paper and then lit a candle so that she could read it properly. She scanned the seven words and gazed back at him in question.

'What is this?'

Finn sat down on the edge of the mattress. Climbing back into bed with her, when there were so many things still left unsaid, did not feel right. 'It is Olivia's suicide note.'

She sat bolt upright, her lovely eyes troubled. 'Suicide note? Charlotte told me she passed away peacefully in her sleep.'

There was no pretty way to dress it up. 'The Reverend Cardew took away the evidence and told everyone she died peacefully—but it is not the case. I drove her to kill herself, Evie.'

She looked rightly horrified, so he stood to give her some space and stared at the full moon through the open window rather than see more of her disgust.

'Oliva kept saying she felt like a huge burden to me. For weeks she talked about ending her life and I ignored it, preferring to lose my temper rather than put precautions in place to prevent it. One morning, after another argument, she drank an entire bottle of laudanum and said her final words to me in a letter.'

Evie read them again aloud. 'I hope you are happy, my darling?'

Somehow, hearing her say them made them even worse. His voice faltered slightly and he cleared his throat gruffly to try to cover it. 'Seven damning words, which effectively convey my selfishness and lack of care as a husband, and serve as a daily reminder of how I had failed her. There was nothing peaceful about my wife's death, Evie. She wanted to die because of the way I made her feel.' He turned to her briefly and shrugged despondently. 'The guilt eats away at me.'

'Why did Reverend Cardew disguise the truth?'

'At the time, he said we owed it to Olivia to respect her wishes, which I happened to agree with, and that only God has the right to judge.'

'And what has he said since?'

'I avoided talking to him until yesterday… Him and Charlotte. I thought they would hate me.'

'But they didn't.' He sensed her as she came to stand behind him and desperately wanted to hold her. But he deserved none of her comfort, so stared out of the window bleakly instead.

'No. They said Olivia chose to end her life because the burden of her illness was so terrible and she feared a slow, painful death. They believed her final words were meant as a gift because she wanted me to go on and have good life.'

She was silent. 'And the awful thing is, Evie, I desperately want to believe them. I am so tired of feeling guilty all of the time. Does that make me selfish?'

Evie rested her head on his back and wrapped her arms around his waist. 'Tell me everything that happened, Finn.'

So he did. He left nothing out. Every symptom, every diagnosis, every failed treatment. Even the events of that dreadful morning. If he was going to ask Evie to marry him, and if he was going to be a better husband to her than he had been to Olivia, he did not want there to be any secrets between them. She would have to enter into any union, understanding the sort of man she had chosen, or she could walk away. She deserved the right to decide.

Evie listened to everything without a word, yet he felt her comfort in the warmth of her arms and hoped she could find it in her enormous, generous heart to forgive him. He finished by confessing his failed attempt to talk to Olivia in the graveyard that morning.

'Did she answer?' How typical of Evie. Only she had enough heart to believe such rubbish.

'No. She did not. I did not hear a single voice from above.'

'Sometimes the answer does not come with words, Finn. Sometimes, they send us a sign, or perhaps just a feeling. She didn't show her anger at you either, so perhaps that is its own sign in its way. From everything you have said, and everything I have been told from Charlotte, I think Olivia loved you very much and you loved her. You said she tried to say goodbye to your before?'

'Yes. Twice. I stormed off then as well.'

He felt her smile against his back. 'Oh, Finn. I doubt she cared about that. You do have a bit of a temper. It is impossible to reason with you when you refuse to listen. I am sure she was quite used to it, much as I am becoming, and completely ignored it, just as I do. But you are a good man, Finn. Like Charlotte and her husband, I cannot believe you are responsible for your wife's death. Nor can I imagine she would have ever wanted you to think it. Your guilt is misplaced.'

'But I *was* frustrated by her illness, Evie. She saw that.'

'Of course you were. Illness is frustrating. Especially when you can do nothing about it. I know that, Finn. I have lived through it twice and both times I was angry at my inability to fix it. But you were frustrated at the illness, Finn, not her. It sounds as if Olivia accepted the futility of it all before you did.'

'I still did not want her dead.'

'And she stayed with you as long as she could stand the pain. It must have been soul-destroying to be confined to a bed for such a long time, dependent. You barely managed a few days when you first broke your ribs.'

Finn had felt trapped and at the mercy of the world. He had hated being reliant on others. Had Olivia experienced those same emotions? He had never considered the possibility. 'They were just broken ribs.'

'And thank goodness it was nothing worse. Do you think you would have made a better patient if it had been something worse than broken ribs?'

Whatever had laid him up would have made no difference. He would have been a nightmare regardless. A bad-tempered, curmudgeonly, nightmare. He would not have dealt with illness with the same good grace and accepting calm Olivia had. For years.

'You have an annoying tendency towards logic, Evie.'

She took his hand and led him back to bed, then curled up in his arms. 'There is a chance this guilt you cling on to is your own fear of letting her go, Finn. When the truth is, she will always be with you. She is a part of you, just as my parents are a part of me. Remember the good times fondly. And be happy, Finn. That is what Olivia wanted. That is how I read her letter.'

Finn mulled all night and gave up trying to sleep at dawn. Evie was practically unconscious, curled up on her side as she had been the night she had slept beside his sick bed, her beautiful, thick chestnut hair spread over the pillow, completely at peace. He eased himself off the bed cautiously to let her sleep and tiptoed out of the room. Finn was going to make one final attempt at talking to Olivia, then he would try and let the guilt go. It was ridiculous and he held out little hope it would bring him any closure, but if he wanted a happy future—and he did want a happy future with Evie by his side—he had to lay the ghosts of his past to rest and move on with his life.

Because his ribs did not hurt, and because he was tired of walking everywhere, he saddled Horatio and took him on a slow meander towards the churchyard, via the stream. Any ride with Horatio usually involved a brief stop there. When he got to his wife's grave, Finn sat down on the grass next to it and lay down the posy of wild flowers he had picked on the way, then stared at the ground, feeling daft.

'Good morning, Olivia. I suppose you will be surprised to hear me again so soon, especially after we have not talked to each other in three years, but I owe you the courtesy of explaining. A few days ago I told you a little bit about Evie. Well, today, I am going to ask her to marry me. I am hoping she says yes because…the thing is… I love her. I never planned on falling in love with her. Left to my own devices, I probably would never have met her, but fate thrust her upon me and ever since then, despite all the chaos and upheaval she has caused me, I have become quite attached to her.

'If she accepts my proposal, she will be living in your old house. I hope you don't mind, but I will also have to move your painting. I will put it somewhere else. I shan't stuff it in the attic. It will still hang in the house. I just don't think it is a good idea to have you watching me every minute of the day—I am sure Evie will keep me in line well enough, so I hardly need the pair of you reminding me what an unreasonable fool I can be. I will not forget you, my darling. I still love you as much as I ever did. I will always love you. I just did not realise I had room in my heart for someone else, too. That came as a bit of a surprise, I don't mind telling you. Up until a few days ago, I thought my heart had died with you. Evie has made it beat again and, now that it is, it yearns for all of the things we had once dreamed of together. If she will have me, then she deserves children and laughter and a home filled with love. And I intend to give it to her.'

Finn scanned the churchyard, the sky and his own heart for any sign of Olivia's answer and, when he did not find one, he stood.

'It's time to say goodbye, Olivia. I hope you can forgive me, but it is time for me to move on.'

He was too shaken to go straight home. Instead, he took Horatio around the estate, checking on the crops and the sheep, his tenants and his workers.

It was almost two hours later when they finally turned towards the house. True to form, the old chestnut took the route past the stream.

Her earthy, tavern wench voice travelled on the breeze, calling him like a siren's song. She was singing something about a lusty sailor and his true love. As Horatio climbed the bank, Finn was not surprised to find her ankle deep in the water, splashing her feet around contentedly. She was wearing a new dress. Another one with embroidered flowers climbing up the ivory skirt, only this time they were poppies. They grew almost to her hip. The neckline and sleeves were trimmed with crimson ribbon.

As she had her back to him, Finn indulged himself and watched her fondly for a moment, until she sensed him and turned around. Her beaming smile warmed his heart.

'You lied to me, Evie.'

Her nose got tiny creases in it when she was perplexed, he realised.

'I did? What about?'

'You told me you looked dreadful in red when, in fact, you look quite beautiful.'

She blushed prettily. 'This dress only has dashes of red, so it is allowed. And after yesterday, I was feeling bold. When I woke up this morning, you were gone. That's the second time you have missed breakfast in a row. I missed you.'

'I was wide awake and you were sound asleep. After all of the excitement yesterday, and after I repeatedly woke you up in the night to have my wicked way with you, I thought you would appreciate the rest.'

She smiled. A secret smile that told him she had not minded him waking her up in the least.

'I came to find you. I told the kitchen to delay breakfast. I thought we should have it together. To celebrate my retirement as a doormat.'

'But you got waylaid by the lure of the stream?'

'I haven't been here since Hyacinth's arrival, I decided I deserved it.' She began to wade towards him, smiling.

Out of nowhere, two delicate, blue butterflies fluttered towards him and danced around his head. Then they dipped and soared and floated towards Evie. The first one settled on her shoulder. The second landed on her waist.

'Look, Finn,' she said, giggling with delight,

'they think the embroidered flowers on my skirt are real! Just like Horatio!'

But Finn knew differently.

It was sign.

And perhaps, now that he considered it properly, it all had been. Evie's unexpected arrival, the chaos she brought to his miserable, ordered, lonely life. His broken ribs, her healing hands, Fergus's treachery. Hideous Hyacinth and her vile, spoiled daughters. Aunt Winnie's preposterous plan of action. Perhaps it was all part of some grand, chaotic celestial design. There had been so many things forcing him to be in Evie's company, pushing them together, that perhaps there *had* been messages from his beloved wife after all. There had been too many times that fate had noisily intervened, giving signs they were meant to be together, and he had simply been too determined to wallow in his own private hell, too stubborn—as was his way—that he had ignored it all.

Emotion tightened his chest and he stared up at the sky and smiled at Olivia. It was only then that he heard her voice, clear as day and filled with love.

Goodbye, Finn. I hope you are happy, my darling.

For the first time in three years he was. Deliriously so. The guilt lifted instantly, and seemed to flutter away with the butterflies. When they disappeared into the trees and out of sight, he slid off his horse and waded into the water towards his future. Evie held up her hands to stay him, her lovely brown eyes dancing with amusement.

'Finn! What about your boots?'

'To hell with my boots.' And to guilt and to misery and to loneliness. Finn was done with all of it. He grabbed her about the waist and spun her around in his arms, soaking them both. Laughing.

'Marry me, Evie.'

'Are you sure? Please don't feel you have to propose because of…well, you know…' He absolutely loved the way she blushed, so grinned afresh because he knew precisely what she was blushing about. 'All I am saying is I don't want you thinking you have to marry me.'

'Of course I have to marry you. I love you, you irritating, inconvenient, intoxicating woman. I cannot wait another day to spend eternity with you.' He kissed her then. A searing, branding kiss that left her in no doubt as to his feelings. 'Say yes.'

'Yes! Of course yes. Aunt Winnie will be thrilled. She always said I should go after you.'

'Aunt Winnie is a sensible woman—most of

the time—besides, that baby in your belly is going to need its father. It's bound to be trouble.'

Her hands automatically went to her stomach and he saw the yearning in her eyes as she denied it. 'There is no baby there, Finn, yet—it is far too soon to tell.'

But he saw those two butterflies again, in his peripheral vision, and knew that his suspicion was right. There was a baby there. It was Olivia's parting, mischievous gift of chaos, just in case he wavered and allowed guilt to stand in his way of his life again. One final, irrefutable thing to bind him and Evie together in case he forgot to be happy, as his wife had wanted.

As if he ever could. Not with Evie by his side. Finn never expected twins, though. Those two identical, brown-eyed, vexing, adorable daughters caught him completely by surprise.

* * * * *

If you enjoyed this story, you won't want to miss these other great reads from Virginia Heath

THAT DESPICABLE ROGUE
HER ENEMY AT THE ALTAR
THE DISCERNING GENTLEMAN'S GUIDE

MILLS & BOON®

HISTORICAL

AWAKEN THE ROMANCE OF THE PAST

A sneak peek at next month's titles...

In stores from 23rd February 2017:

- **Surrender to the Marquess** – Louise Allen
- **Heiress on the Run** – Laura Martin
- **Convenient Proposal to the Lady** – Julia Justiss
- **Waltzing with the Earl** – Catherine Tinley
- **At the Warrior's Mercy** – Denise Lynn
- **His Mail-Order Bride** – Tatiana March

MILLS & BOON®

EXCLUSIVE EXTRACT

When Lady Sara Herriard's husband dies,
she decides it's time for her to live as she pleases.
She won't change for anyone—and certainly
not the infuriating Marquess of Cannock!

Read on for a sneak preview of
SURRENDER TO THE MARQUESS

The hoofbeats behind her were getting closer, much closer. She risked a backwards glance and realised that the only danger to her just at that moment was the Marquess himself. He looked as though he wanted to throttle her.

Sara twisted back round, wishing she was riding astride and not wearing this so-fashionable habit with its trailing skirts and broadcloth that slid on the saddle. As she thought about sliding a buzzard flapped up out of the long grass, a rabbit in its talons. The mare jinked, stiff-legged, swerved back and Sara lost her stirrup, lost her balance and went over Twilight's shoulder down to meet the turf with a thud.

Instinctively she rolled, tucking herself up into a ball as her great-uncle the Rajah's *syce* had taught her. The clifftop was almost as hard as the sun-baked Indian plain, she thought as she tumbled, arms around her head, braced for the hooves of Lucian's horse.

There was the sound of furious, inventive, swearing,

then she came to a stop, untrampled, and lifted her head warily in time to see Lucian dismount from a rearing horse in a muscular, controlled slide.

'Sara!'

He was by her side and she closed her eyes strategically to postpone his anger and in sheer self-preservation. He had looked like a god just then and she could put no reliance on her own self-control. 'Mmm?' she managed.

'Are you hurt?'

Yes, was the honest answer. Her left shoulder hurt, her right wrist stung and her pride as a horsewoman was severely dented. 'No,' she said and opened her eyes.

'Excellent,' Lucian growled. 'Because I fully intend wringing your neck.'

'Why?' Indignant, Sara moved too quickly, found several other things that hurt and was hauled into an upright sitting position. 'Ow! What are you doing?'

'Checking.' His hands worked along her collarbone, wriggled her fingers and prodded her ribs. 'Move your feet. Let me see your eyes, your ears. What day of the week is it?'

'Thursday.'

'Correct.' Then he kissed her.

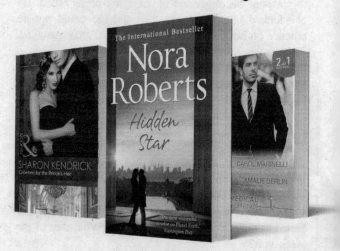

Join Britain's BIGGEST Romance Book Club

50% OFF your first parcel

- **EXCLUSIVE** offers every month
- **FREE** delivery direct to your door
- **NEVER MISS** a title
- **EARN** Bonus Book points

Call Customer Services
0844 844 1358*
or visit
millsandboon.co.uk/subscriptions

* This call will cost you 7 pence per minute plus your phone company's price per minute access charge.

B3